TERROR at
5280'

Cover design: The Rïpröck

Layout: Henry Snider

"Deep Veins" was originally published in *Georgetown Haunts and Mysteries* by Hex Publishers

"Taste" was originally published in *Once Bitten ~ Never Die* by Wicked East Press

ISBN - 978-1-7341917-0-7

ACKNOWLEDGMENTS

From the bottom of our black hearts, the Denver Horror Collective Editorial Team would like to thank/blame the following individuals and businesses for making *Terror at 5280'* possible.

Henry Snider
Joshua Viola
Bookbar
Crestone Law Group
IndyInk
Lighthouse Writers Workshop
Yaya's Euro Bistro

CONTENTS

i	PREFACE
iii	FOREWORD – *John Palisano*
1	THE DEPTHS – *Matthew Lyons*
19	LAFFING SAL – *Lindsay King-Miller*
33	THIS WAS ALWAYS GOING TO HAPPEN – *Stephen Graham Jones*
39	ELECTRIC STALKER – *Rebecca S.W. Bates*
57	GAZE WITH UNDIMMED EYES AND THE WORLD DROPS DEAD – *Carina Bissett*
69	GRAVE MISTAKE – *Joshua Viola & Carter Wilson*
85	THERE IS SOMETHING UP THERE – *Joy Yehle*
103	SCRAPE – *Gary Robbe*
121	THE COPPER DOOR KARMA JAR – *Cindra Spencer*
127	BLOCK 12 – *Thomas C. Mavroudis*
145	A PLACE FOR CADY – *Melinda Bezdek*
157	TASTE – *Henry Snider*
177	CHRONIC COLD – *Josh Schlossberg*
191	THE DEAD SPOT – *Angela Sylvaine*
201	THE GHOSTS OF CHEESMAN PARK – *Grace Horton*
203	OLD GOLDEN ROAD – *Jay Seate*
215	IF I SHALL WAKE – *Desi D*
231	THE BLUE LADY – *Sean Murphy*
243	MOUNTAIN LOVERS – *Bobby Crew*
251	LEFT BEHIND – *P.L. McMillan*
265	DEEP VEINS – *Travis Heermann*
283	THAT TIME MAGGIE GHOSTED ME – *Jeanrus Wilkes*
307	LAST WORDS: CANNIBAL KINGS AND QUEENS – *Larry Berry*

PREFACE

An urgent message for anyone thinking about relocating to—or even visiting—Denver or any of Colorado's Front Range Rocky Mountain communities: TURN BACK NOW!

Chances are you've heard rumors of cloudless skies, world-class recreation, and legal cannabis all under the wholesome label of "Colorful Colorado." Unfortunately, the only colorful things in this arid wasteland are the lies they're telling you to lure you in. That, and the blood.

Here are a few things the tourism websites haven't told you about: The vicious creatures stalking the mountains. The brain-eating disease epidemic. The defiled burial grounds upon which our children play. Sound like paradise to you?

For years, those of us unlucky enough to be stranded in this mile-high hellscape have watched the carnage unfold, standing idly by as limb, life, and soul are lost. After seeing things our eyes can never unsee, some of us vowed that—even if there's no hope for us—we have a duty to warn others.

Calling ourselves Denver Horror Collective, we

recruited twenty-three resident writers to share true accounts of the foul and shocking goings-on in the Centennial State, all disguised as a harmless horror "fiction" anthology to fool those who would silence us.

To lend credence to the ruse, we went so far as to enlist horror master Stephen Graham Jones and bestselling thriller author Carter Wilson, among other insanely talented local scribes.

So, it's with dread in our hearts that we present you with *Terror at 5280'*. Reader, beware.

Our deepest sympathies,
Denver Horror Collective Editorial Team

Josh Schlossberg, Gary Robbe, Mindy Bezdek, Bobby Crew, Desi D, Lisa Mavroudis, Thomas C. Mavroudis, and Jeamus Wilkes

FOREWORD
John Palisano

Colorado is magic. From the top of Pikes Peak all the way deep down inside the Cave of the Winds, its varied and remarkable geography is as inspiring and fertile a place for the imagination as anywhere. Generations of creative people have nourished on its offerings and blossomed timeless works. Let's not forget that creativity is not limited to fine arts, either.

The first time I knew Colorado had something special to offer had to have been that famous U2 video of "Sunday Bloody Sunday" from Red Rocks Amphitheater back in 1983. I'd seen many concerts and videos, but never one that seemed to have been filmed on another world. The spirit and sentiment in that song and performance reached not only myself, but people around the world.

Of course, Colorado's amazing landscape has inspired countless musicians as well. "Rocky Mountain High," indeed. John Denver's song and ethereal voice captures the imagination in a way only a song born in Colorado can do.

A rich literary world has existed in Colorado as

far back as we have records. Beat poet and writer Jack Kerouac spent many a day and night here, and some of his most famous writings have major acts played out in the area. Most notably, a good part of *On The Road*—his most famous work—takes place in Colorado. Could its style of a continuous scroll have been inspired by Colfax Street in Denver, the longest street in the country?

In the 1960s and 1970s, Aspen resident Hunter S. Thompson invented gonzo journalism and his timeless book, *Fear and Loathing in Las Vegas* cemented the style. And it's not a secret the 1970s and 1980s saw a boom in horror fiction and cinema that continues to thrive to this day.

That's where Denver Horror Collective has built bridges to history, to the here and now, and to the future. With so many highly regarded examples of new literary practitioners and champions in the area, it's hard not to be inspired. And hard not to feel there is a catalyst somewhere deep inside the soil and rocks, something mystical and special to the area that gives such a fertile environment from which so much creativity grows.

Much must also be said about the vast and epic support system Colorado has for writers and lovers of the written word. Populated by many independent bookstores, the state also has an amazingly robust library and education system that truly makes sure the best minds of Colorado are not only grown, nourished, and brought to potential, but that they are supported outside in the real world, as well.

Within these pages we have many storytellers lending their voices to you for a short time. Let's lower the lights, get comfortable, and let the readings begin. May I present to you Denver Horror Collective's *Terror at 5280'*. See you on the other side.

John Palisano
President, Horror Writers Association
Bram Stoker Award®-winning author

THE DEPTHS
Matthew Lyons

They build it at the edge of the known world, underneath the blown-open sky where the mountains meet the plains, out where nobody goes unless they don't want to be found. The Facility.

To its designers it's *efficient*, to its financiers in the government it's *a modern marvel*, to them that dig it into the earth, *a curse*. They bury dozens of their own before the work is through, body after body left to rot in the soil, poured over with concrete and officially forgotten in pursuit of whatever horrible thing they're going to do with this place. By the time it's done, no one even knows how far down it goes, only that the black hole at its heart has a bad habit of swallowing any unwary thing that wanders too close.

For years—decades—they work in the shadows, crafting weapons and wonders while, all over the world, humanity churns and grinds and blasts itself to bloody hell, armed to the teeth with the nightmares and atomic horrors shipped straight from the Facility. Under their eye, the earth blackens and curls like paper tossed to flame, powerless to resist its own destruction. They revel in the annihilation; they worship it like some forgotten elder god. Burrowed away, miles underneath the rocky flats, they watch on screens as the world is remade according to their design.

But then, one ordinary day, it ends. As everything does. A letter, a man from Washington, a detachment of marines—the method matters less than the result. The doors are shut, the bulldozers come, they erase as much of the Facility as they possibly can—but they don't erase it all. They can't. They couldn't possibly. There are too many ghosts buried there. So, they do the next best thing: They sell and sod the land. They build matching tan clapboard homes over it. They give it a new name, something fancy, scribbled hastily over the top of the old one.

As if that would ever be enough.

Travis is playing in the dark when he finds it. He's been down here plenty of times since he found the old manhole in the woods, but never this deep before. Stuck in a new neighborhood in a new state with a month left of summer vacation, it isn't like he has anything better to do but explore, anyway. At least he brought a flashlight this time.

He swings the white beam around the big empty room like a sword, lunging and parrying against imaginary foes until the light twists and falls on the small door in the corner of the room. Was that always there? Travis traces its drab, battered edges with the flashlight as he steps in close, laying his empty palm flat against it. The metal is gritty and rough and warm to the touch, as if someone had been here only moments before, pressing against it, leaving their body heat behind in the steel for him to find.

He pushes against the door, swinging it wide under the slightest pressure. The frame is small, but the darkness that throbs beyond it is enormous, swallowing his light whole. Travis has to track the beam along the ground at his feet to see where he's going, but even that's only so helpful. He isn't sure when he stepped through into that hungering gloom, or why his legs aren't stopping when he tells them to. As if he were a minecart on a rail, following its track deeper and deeper down still.

The rail takes him back and forth, crisscrossing his own path again and again through derelict labs and conference rooms, wending through whatever this place used to be until he finally gets to where he's going: a small chamber tucked away far, far down, fixed between two hallways, perfectly unremarkable but for the thing sitting in the cracked glass case at the center of the emptiness.

Black and silver, coiled and knotted, it stands alone, absorbing the light from Travis' flashlight as he holds it stead on its ridged surface. *Silver and coal.* The words bubble up to the surface of his brain like gas pockets loosed from the ocean floor. That's what the thing—this icon— looks like to him. Twin veins of silver and coal braided together in an agonizing, impossible configuration and left to collect dust in the dark.

A thread of sweat darts down Travis' spine between his narrow, bony shoulders, dragging a glimmer of cold along in its wake. It's hot in this little room, and when he wipes a sheet of sweat from his forehead, for a second, he could swear his palm comes away slick with blood. The sound of his breathing is so loud in here, pulsing in half-time against the rattle of his heartbeat. Behind the cracked glass, the icon's curls seem to shift and dance under the weight of the light.

From further in, Travis hears a grinding noise, distant and indistinct; so brief and swamped in echoes that it could be anything. Rats in the tunnels, a wall collapsing on a lower level, anything. Travis tells himself it could be anything. When he hears it again, he bites back a scream and throws the case open, gathering the icon in clumsy hands, then bolts from the room as fast as his legs will carry him.

He isn't sure why he did it. Holding it close to his chest as he runs, he can't shake the feeling he's made a terrible mistake, but it's too late to take it back now. He jams his legs like stakes into the earth as he sprints back through the scrubby woods at the edge of their new subdivision, and pretends he can't feel the curious, dead eyes that follow him all the way home.

He goes in through the back door so no one will see him or ask any questions about the twisted thing in his hands. He takes the stairs two at a time, planting his sneakered feet at their outside edges so he won't creak the wood. He shuts his bedroom door tight and buries the icon at the bottom of his hamper because he doesn't have anywhere better to hide it.

For the rest of the night he holes up in his room, ignoring calls for dinner and everything else, and when he finally sleeps, his dreams are infected with filth and dread and burst sores that spread like waking eyes.

The next morning, Travis wakes to the sound of someone outside spamming their doorbell like the sky is falling. Underneath the covers, he rolls over and listens to his family rouse themselves from their beds. Dad's already grumbling and cursing while Mom tries to shush him down across the hall. Next door, Travis can hear his sister rustling around, doing something or other, maybe hiding the scuffed old bible Mom and Dad still don't know she brought home from camp last summer.

At first, Travis doesn't know what could be so important that whoever it is would wake the whole house up this early, but then he remembers the thing in his closet, piled under the layers of dirty T-shirts and tighty-whities. A second later, he's on his feet, digging through his laundry in a mad plunge, throwing clothes aside while beyond his bedroom door, the doorbell still hammers against the house's fractured silence. Dad's feet are heavy against the hardwood, and icon in hand, Travis listens to him thunder down the stairs, throw the front door open, and demand

"*What?!*"

There's a pause that stretches out into the distance, all the way past the suburb-obscured horizon before snapping back when a soft, calm voice Travis doesn't recognize asks, "Where is it?"

"Where is *what*?" Dad's doing the gruff grownup thing, dropping his voice half an octave to underscore who's in charge here. Travis has heard him do it a ton of times before.

Keeping low, Travis pulls his door open halfway and duckwalks out into the hall to watch from behind the banister. He thinks he can do it without being seen, but of course, he's wrong. The man at the front door is old, bald and bespectacled; Travis has seen him around the neighborhood before. From the doorway between the front porch and the foyer, the old man zeroes in on him, and the twisted thing cradled in his arms like a baby. The old man makes a trilling noise in the meat of his throat and raises a finger gun in Travis' direction, straight past Dad's head.

"Him," the stranger says, voice suddenly shaking with tension. "*That.*"

Dad turns to look, confused. "That? That's my son," he says. "You don't talk to him."

"Where'd you get it?" the stranger demands. "Where'd you find it? Did you take it? Did you steal it?"

"My son doesn't steal. You must be mistaken," Dad says, rolling his bare shoulders as wide as they'll go.

"Ask him then. Ask him about it."

At the top of the stairs, Travis presses the icon tighter against his chest. Dad turns to look at him, his expression turning slack.

"Trav, what is that?" he asks. "Bring that down here."

But Travis shakes his head. "No, Dad."

"*Filth!*"

Behind Dad, the stranger—Travis thinks he might live next door?—snarls and darts forward, faster than he'd have thought an old guy like him could move. Travis flinches, but Dad blocks the guy like a linebacker, rocking him back on his heels before sticking a hairy-knuckled finger in his face.

"Hey, back up," Dad barks. "This is my house. You can't come into my house like that."

"Make him give it over," says the stranger.

"No."

The stranger doesn't say anything else; he doesn't need to. His eyes go flat and waxy, and his shoulders bunch up around his ears, and Travis knows he's going to charge again half a second before it happens. Dad must see it too because he's ready for him. He drops his shoulder and crashes into the old guy full-force, but this time it's not enough. The two men spill backwards into the foyer in a bent knot of joints and limbs, braying like warring animals. Mom's shrieks shatter what little is left of the morning's peace while Dad hammers the old man with bone-white fists, ducking away from his withered, mottled claws as they lash out for his eyes.

"Craig, stop it," Mom shrieks. "Craig, please don't, he's just an old man!" But Dad doesn't hear her. He rolls on top of the stranger and starts pummeling him, staining the floor underneath them with arcs of spatter-red. "*Craig!*"

Travis starts for the stairs but comes up short, held back by a small, slender hand closing around the crook of his elbow. Emily. He didn't even hear her come out of her room. Underneath her tangle of red hair, her eyes burn bright with psychotic intensity, but she's not looking at him. No, she's locked onto the icon, all of her attention drawn narrow to the thing in his arms. Her mouth hangs open on one side like she's having a stroke. Downstairs, Dad is still beating on the stranger; the sounds metronomic against the silence.

"Let go," Travis tells his sister, pulling free from her cold grasp. "Emmy, *let go.*" She follows him with her hands, tracing the place he used to be like a blind girl searching for a face. Not once do her eyes leave the icon.

In the middle of the foyer, the stranger is still trying to fight back, but it's clear he's on the losing side. Dad's too big, too strong, too young and too angry for the old man to keep pace. Travis bounds down the stairs and goes to his mother, latching onto her tight as he can, and watches as her tearful eyes jump from his own to the icon.

"Travis...? What... is that...?"

A big, meaty hand falls between Travis and his mother, ripping the icon from his grasp—he barely has a chance to twist in place to look before Dad brings it down on the stranger's bloodied face like a hammer.

Crunch.

The old man's flailing arms jolt like their power's been cut, then float lazily to the ground, coming to rest in the tidal mess spreading out from underneath his body. That should be it. It should be done now, except Dad isn't done. He belts the stranger in the skull three more times—*crunch, crunch, crunch*—opening a deep white-

and-red gash from his hairline to his teeth.

The house is quiet again. The air in here tastes like warm pennies. Standing there, feeling them all spiraling inward as if hurtling toward a gravity well, Travis wants to scream but finds himself unable. Panting, still curled on top of the fallen old man, soaked in blood, Dad looks around at his family, hands curled tight around the icon, eyes wide and awful.

"Help me get him into the back," he gasps.

Travis and Dad dig a hole big enough to fit what's left of the stranger in the middle of the backyard where the crabgrass is almost too thick to mow, while Mom and Emily stand beside the new grave, watching over the body. Dad says he was their next-door neighbor. It takes them all morning and most of the afternoon to get it done, but they get it done, burying him between the spider's web of power lines and sprinkler lines set deep in the soil. Carefully they cover him over, and by the time they head back inside, the sun has already burned itself to sour orange, dipping below the foothills at their backs.

In the living room, Dad, still filthy with blood and sweat and dirt, crosses over to the fireplace and sets the icon in the center of the mantel, straightening it back and forth with grubby fingers until it sits *just so*.

"There. All better now," Dad says.

Travis stands with the three of them, watching the icon with silent regard until his feet start to hurt. When he heads up to his room to try and sleep, he tells his family goodnight, but he isn't sure that they hear him. Hours later, when he wakes up to go pee, the other bedroom doors are wide open, and the lights downstairs are still on. Travis finishes his business quickly and retreats to his room, locking the door behind him before diving back under the covers. He watches the knob from between the soft folds until his eyelids are too heavy to hold open anymore.

Sunlight creeps into his room like a plague, warming him from the toes up until he finally surfaces from the cruelty of his dreams, gasping and sputtering like a failed drowning. Knotted in sweat-drenched sheets, Travis lays still and listens to the house around him, same as he did yesterday, and the day before that, and the day before that. The house is still and quiet, but the quiet's wrong somehow, a jigsaw puzzle that fits together perfectly with the picture all garbled.

Rising silently, Travis pads across the floor to bend back the beige aluminum blinds: Up and down both sides of the street, the neighbors are out on their front lawns, dead still, heads all turned toward his house. If they see Travis standing there in the window looking back out at them, they give no indication. Underneath their empty gazes and the warmth of the sun, his skin starts to itch something terrible; with bitten-raw fingernails, he scratches until it comes away in damp flakes.

Downstairs, things are so much worse than they were last night. Dad's eyes are wide and bright-red wild as he walks circles into the kitchen floor; Travis can see that he hasn't showered or slept at all. On the couch, Mom's sitting corpse-still, her skin wan and bloodless, bony stick-fingers playing at the fabric of her pants, pulling holes in the stitching. The skin of her legs is pale to match the rest of her and mottled with marks and scratches.

Then there's Emily. Travis's big sister is still where she was last night, square in the middle of the living room, turned toward the mantel and the icon. But where last night she was standing, now she's kneeling, hands clasped together, eyes downcast. From the way her lips are moving, he thinks she might be praying.

Dad sees him first and nearly drags him down off the last three stairs, pulling him over to the big bay window that looks out the front of the house. With one rust-smeared hand, he yanks the curtains to one side, slapping the dark room with blinding light as he jabs a finger out at the rest of the neighborhood.

"Did you see them out there? Did you see?" Dad's voice is a hoarse ruin like he's been up all night shouting himself raw. Travis doesn't have to look to know what he's talking about.

"Yes, Dad. I saw."

"They don't think that I see them out there, but I do. *We* do."

Travis turns to look at his Dad—the old man's breath is hot and stale and stinking, yesterday's five o'clock shadow already grown into a coarse, patchy beard, all black shot through with sickly gray.

"They're all like him," Dad says. "Bastards. All bastards."

Travis' wrist throbs sharply. "Dad, you're hurting me. Dad, that *hurts...*"

But his Dad doesn't hear him, his maniac's gaze still trained out the glass, leering at the neighbors. Travis wrenches his arm loose from his father's iron grasp, rubbing the aching joint while Dad mutters to himself.

"See if we won't... come and see if we won't," he chatters, grinding his molars together like mortar and pestle. Travis backs away from him slowly, hands out to his sides as if to keep balance. None of them see him leave, slipping out the back door and across the chopped-up sod in his bare feet, tracking up arcs of Saturday morning dew in the seconds before he's up and over the fence.

The house next door is big with dark windows, and when Travis tries the back door, he finds it unlocked, so he lets himself in. The house is a mirror image of his own, the rooms and hallways identical if reversed; he explores the quiet mirror world silently, leaving little, wet footprints in his wake. The air in here is hot and smoky and smells like desiccated old things.

Travis ghosts from room to room, examining the differences, trying on the fittings of a life that isn't his. The hallway coat closet is overflowing with shoes. There's a coat tree where the floor lamp should be. All the mail poking through the slot is addressed to *Carl Noonan*. Everything's wrong in here, but Travis knows back home it's worse, so he makes himself a sandwich, turns on the TV to one of the channels Mom and Dad don't let him watch, and cranks the volume. The walls rattle with the noise, and he doesn't exactly understand the fleshy things he's seeing on the screen, but he knows he's getting away with something, and that's what matters.

From the big, cigarette-burned sofa, he can see out the side window into the living room next door, and the fireplace, and the mantel, and the awful, twisted thing that sits upon it. Emily's still praying on the floor, and every few seconds, Dad stalks past the window, pacing like a caged bear. He doesn't know where Mom went, but if he had to guess, probably not far—she didn't seem like she'd be moving much before he left.

Rolling to his feet, Travis walks across the sticky green leather to snap the curtains shut, dousing the room in darkness but for the anemic flickering from the television. When the credits on the skin flick finally roll, he hops off the couch and stretches, luxuriating in the crackle that ladders up his spine as it pops.

Upstairs, he rifles through the dressers and the closets, spilling their contents across the hardwood in messy, multicolored piles. Behind the sound of the TV blaring downstairs, Travis can hear shouting outside. Probably next door. He sings songs to himself until the sound fades into the background and he can explore undisturbed.

He finds a shoebox of yellowing old photos in the attic, a glass case filled with tiny decorative spoons in an unused room. He finds the tatters of a marriage license and a pistol wedged far underneath the mattress in the master bedroom. He can't figure out how to get the cylinder open to see if the gun is loaded and he doesn't really know how guns work anyway, so he leaves it in the middle of Mr. Noonan's bed, heavy and black and cruelly indifferent.

In the spare bedroom at the back of the house, there's a window that overlooks Noonan's back yard, and if he stands just right, Travis can see the spot next door where he and Dad dumped Noonan's body. When he looks at it for too long, he gets a bad twinge behind his belly button and has to leave the room.

Down in the kitchen, he pulls all the flatware and knives from the drawers and pins them deep into the plaster walls. He smashes the glasses and mugs from the cabinets, he kicks holes beside electrical outlets and tells himself that it's fun. He stays inside Noonan's house, making a mess until the sunset claws through the windows and stains the chaos and rubble a deep umber and Travis knows he has to go home. He has to see.

He leaves the mess where it is and the back door hanging wide open. It doesn't matter. It's not like anyone lives here anymore.

There's a crowd of people Travis doesn't recognize out on the front long, maybe fifty or sixty of them, clustered around the front door with bloodshot eyes and bared teeth. Ducking back, so none of them spot him, he circles around to head in through the back. Inside, Dad's sitting cross-legged on the kitchen floor, shirtless and bleeding from deep gashes dragged through the meat of his chest, thumbing brass shells into the breech of a rifle.

"You been gone," Dad says, his voice like grave dirt. "Been away all day." Click-click. He sinks another round into the gun.

"I guess so. Sorry."

Click-click. "Did they see you? Them out there?"

"I don't think so."

"Good." Click-click. "They're not smart, but there's a lot of them. All they need now is a reason."

"They didn't see me, Dad."

"I already said *Good*."

"Dad, I—"

His father whips out a hand, nearly slapping Travis in the chest before twisting his fist in Travis' T-shirt, pulling him close. One of his eyes has gone dull and milky and drifts off to the side as Travis watches it.

"It showed me the truth," he snarls. "It opened up its heart when no one else was looking, and it showed me *goddamned everything. It chose me.* Not them. Never them."

"Okay..."

"I love you, you know." The stink coming off his father is so foul that Travis can nearly see the stink lines bending the air around him. "I love you more than anything."

"I know, Dad. I love you, too."

If Dad clocks the lie, he doesn't give any sign. He just unclamps from Travis' shirt, sending his son stumbling on his heels as he goes back to loading the gun.

"Go check on your mom and sister."

"I will."

"*Now.*"

"Okay."

As if it's the most normal thing in the world, he leaves Dad sitting there with his gun, muttering to himself. In the living room, Emily's still on the floor, caked in her own filth, still kneeling, still praying. The skin on her face and arms has broken out into glossy, swollen boils that pulse and weep yellow fluid in time with the tiny movements of her lips. When Travis gets close, he strains against the silence of the room to hear her prayer:

"Among us, among us, among us," she chants. Her voice is sloppy and wet and comes out half-garbled, as if the sores blanketing her skin have bubbled through to her throat, too. "*Amongusamongusamongusamongus—*"

WHAM.

Across the house, Travis hears someone outside hammer a fist against the front door.

"*You unlock this door right fucking now!*" they scream. "*We have a right, don't act like we don't! It's not yours! IT'S NOT YOURS!!*"

Nobody opens the door. Nobody moves. The only sounds in the house are Emily praying (*amongusamongusamongus*) and the oily mechanical *click-click* of Dad loading the rifle.

Outside, whoever it is, punches the door again and again and again and doesn't let up. They're going to knock it down, and Travis realizes, *If I stay down here, I'm going to die. They're going to come through, and they're going to take it and I'm going to die.*

—WHAM WHAM WHAM WHAM WHAM—

Travis bolts for the stairs, dashing for his bedroom past his sister, past the icon, past the shaking front door and the messy rust-stain on the floor. He almost makes it, too—he barely touches the hardwood as he flies across it, scrambling madly for his bedroom. *I can block the door. I can hide. It's not me they want. I'm just in the way. I'll be fine if I can just—*

CRACK.

Something hits him in the back of the head, and

he feels his legs go out from under him, but he doesn't feel it when he hits the ground. He doesn't hear it when the neighbors finally kick down the front door, or the gunshots, or when his family starts to die. He doesn't hear or feel anything else for a long time.

Then, hours later, his eyes open.

The house is filled with blood. That's one of the two things Travis notices when he comes back to the world. The house is filled with blood, and the silence is back, worse than before.

Rising painfully from the floor, he looks over the banister down to the foyer and the tattered bodies piled there, dashed with murky red. He wonders how many of them Dad was able to tag before they finally brought him down. Seems like it was probably a lot. Probably turned on themselves after they finally did him in.

Standing above what's left of the fray, Travis' mind flashes to his last memory before the blackness took him down, and he raises a hand to gently probe the back of his skull: The hair there is sticky and plastered over what feels like a hell of a bludgeon mark. The wound itself lights up with electric fire when he pushes his fingertips into it. Recoiling, his nails come away streaked with grimy, clotted blood—he sucks them clean and wipes them dry on the bottom of his shirt. At the other end of the hall, the bathroom door hangs half open like a seizure eye and from where he's standing, he can see a thin, pale arm floating in a bath of crimson. A stained tack hammer lies on the floor beside the tub. Sorry, Mom.

Limping down the stairs, Travis steps over and in between bodies, nearly ankle-deep in gore as he looks for any sign of Dad or Emily, finding none. They could be anywhere in this mess; they could be any of these parts. He picks through what he can, digging through the loose meat where he can get a hand in, but there's too much. Sorting everything out now would take him weeks, longer. They're in here or they're not. It doesn't matter to him as much as it used to.

On the mantel above the fireplace, the icon is gone, a black circle burned into the surface of the wood where it stood and a trail of bloody footprints pressed into the floor, leading through the house to where the back door hangs ajar. Travis follows the tracks out into the sunlight, out to where they shine wet and black in the bright green grass, past the fence and the houses, out to where the greenbelt meets the scrubby young pines and the foothills.

Of course.

He laces his shoes tight and stops by Noonan's for the revolver from atop the big bed, clutching it in both hands because it's too heavy for him to carry in one. He takes his time chasing the tracks out into the trees, going slow, listening to the chittering and chirping from the branches overhead, stepping lightly, staying shy from the light.

The tunnel down into the far, winding dark is exactly as it was the first day Travis found it—little more than a rusted old manhole set in the earth with a heavy hatch wheel in the center. If it wasn't for the gory handprints smeared all across it, he could almost convince himself that nobody—or nothing—else but him has been out here. He kicks at the bloody footprints beside the manhole until they disappear into the dust, then kneels and sets the gun down so he can heave the hatch open again.

The darkness underneath is warm and foul and absolute, and if he has to go down there again, he's going to lose his mind like the rest of them. But he can't go back. Nothing to go back to, now. Nowhere else to go but down, into the shadows, just to see how deep they go. It's down there somewhere—the truth, the icon, the rotting hole in the heart of the world.

Travis picks up the pistol and takes one last look at the sun, then he climbs down and never comes back.

> *Matthew Lyons is the author of dozens of short stories, appearing in Best American Short Stories 2018, Black Dandy, and Kzine, among others. His work has been nominated for Best Small Fictions, Best of the Net and more. A Colorado native, he's probably taller than you, not that it's a competition or anything. You can find him online at matthewlyonsauthor.com and on twitter at @cannibalghosts.*

LAFFING SAL
Lindsay King-Miller

A spider crawled across Sal's tongue as the three girls came down the stairs. Haloed in the glow of a flashlight, the first two were giggling, standing very close to each other but not quite making contact. That interested Sal, the way they wanted to touch but were a little afraid to. The third girl hung back, watching them and listening to their conversation without speaking, and that interested Sal too.

"Are we allowed to be down here?" one of the girls, the shorter one, asked. She had big brown eyes and generous curves—her bosom nearly rivaled Sal's own.

"No," said the taller girl, and they both laughed, high-pitched and nervous. The third girl didn't laugh. She stood at a distance from the other two and Sal couldn't tell how her height compared to theirs.

"I mean, these tunnels are like a hundred years old, and stuff just gets left down here. You could turn this place into a museum, I bet, but right now it's a total fire hazard."

The spider reached the back of Sal's throat and found

nowhere to go, so it turned around and made its way back toward her teeth. She wished she could snap her jaws shut on it and feel it crunch. She wished for a great many things. That was all she had to do, down here in the dark.

"Hey Billie, what's that?" the short girl said, pointing straight at Sal.

The girls came closer. The pane of glass Sal looked through was smeary, its corners choked with cobwebs, but still, Sal could clearly see the mix of fascination and revulsion in their faces.

The spider crawled over her lower lip. With a little shriek, the two girls jumped back. Behind them, the third girl didn't flinch.

"That's Laffing Sal," Billie said. "She's been down here for, like, fifty years."

"She's creepy as *fuck*," I said, staring at the human-sized doll. She would have been scary in daylight. Down here in the dark, giant shadows distorting her face, she was gruesome. I loved her on sight.

Billie grinned. "I bet she was even creepier when she was plugged in. She used to, like, move, and do this recorded laugh thing outside the fun house." Billie has only worked at the amusement park for three summers, but some of the older guys have been there for decades, and they like to tell stories. Then Billie passes the stories on to me. It's her weird way of flirting, which I appreciate.

The figure—Sal—was large and rounded, her big breasts maternal, not sexy. There was something almost welcoming to her apple-cheeked smile, but the cracks in her graying paint gave away the brittleness to what should have been soft.

"Where's the fun house?" I asked.

"They took it down years ago," Billie said, "but you can see it in old pictures of the park. They made, like, hundreds of these things at the turn of the century and put them in theme parks all over the place. Some of them are in real museums and shit."

I faked a shiver and stepped closer to Billie. Down here in the maintenance tunnels, it wasn't actually cold, not in the middle of an August afternoon. The labyrinth of abandoned park paraphernalia—cast-off pieces of rides, warped decorations, faded rolls of unused tickets—was thick with greasy dust. I was sweating, but I still wanted Billie to put her arms around me.

And she was about to. She tucked a lock of hair behind her ear and leaned toward me.

Then her eyes opened wide and she screamed.

Sal wished she could still laugh. She wasn't a good judge of time, but it had probably been years since anyone had used these tunnels for amorous purposes. This would be more entertainment than Sal had had in forever.

As the taller girl moved in for the kiss, Sal's gaze flickered to the third girl. Neither of them had so much as looked at her the whole time they were down here, but she was staring at them with something that looked like hatred. *She* was cold, Sal suddenly realized, the only cold thing in the stifling heat of the tunnels.

Who was she? Why was she following them?

Sal knew about fear. Fear had brought her to life. Electricity had animated her but fear was what gave her depth, allowed her to know herself. The more people were frightened by her, the more real she became, the layers of their dread accumulating over years and decades until she was *something*, not quite human but far more than a doll.

The third girl was the same. Sal could see it now. A feeling so dreadful it had to take human form.

She raised her hands, fingers curled, and any possibility she might be a real live girl disappeared. As she reached for the tall girl, her arms *stretched* to twice, then three times their normal length. Her fingers gnarled into corkscrews of shadow. Sal couldn't stand to look at her face.

She clawed with her phantom hands at the tall girl's eyes.

"Fuck! Fuck!" Billie dropped the flashlight and stumbled backward, waving her hands in front of her face like she was trying to knock something away. If there was something there, I couldn't see it. The flashlight rolled on the floor, a drunken searchlight sweeping our ankles.

"Billie?"

"Oh, Jesus. My eyes! Linnea, where are you?" She started to cry, which was almost worse than the screaming. Billie wasn't a crier.

"Is there something in your eyes?" Was she having a seizure? A panic attack? If I ran for help, people would find out we'd been in the tunnels and Billie might get fired. But if I didn't—

Billie sobbed, pressing the palms of her hands against her eyes. "Fuck. I'm bleeding," she wailed.

I wanted to run, but I moved closer to her instead, putting a hand on her shoulder. Her head whipped around in surprise and I realized she hadn't seen me approach. She still didn't see me. I gripped her wrists and looked at her hands.

"There's no blood," I said, trying to sound soothing. "You're OK. Did you get something in your contacts?"

She shoved my hands away. "You bitch," she hissed. "You ruin everything. Leave me alone."

I stepped back just in time. Billie groaned and hunched forward, clutching her stomach. Then, with a hideous noise, she vomited. What came out of her mouth looked black in the darkness of the tunnel.

Billie braced her hands on her knees and vomited again. This time, it spewed across the space between us, splattering my feet, my flip-flops no protection. The flashlight on the floor shone a halo onto the vile puddle. There were *pieces* in it, pieces the size of marbles that looked like clots of blood.

I looked down. One of the bloody chunks had landed square on the top of my right foot. It looked slick and felt horribly warm.

Then it wriggled.

Billie retched a third time. I screamed, and the flashlight went out.

Things rustled and shifted inside of Sal. The spider wasn't the only creature making a home within her crumbling shell or between her rusted gears. Usually, vermin hid when humans were near, but some instinct now told them the two girls were no threat. Insects and small animals smelled something new, something hot and freshly rotting amid the stale stink of the maintenance tunnel, and went to gorge themselves.

The tall girl was still crying and vomiting, and the short girl was making little breathless screams. Sal watched the third girl approach them slowly, pensively. The background roar from above ground, the rattling and clanking of roller coasters, grew louder and louder. It turned sharp and bright, piercing like a scream, and the girls covered their ears and wailed. Sal realized the spirit, or whatever she was, was amplifying the noise.

With her vision and hearing disabled, the shorter girl was trying to grope her way back the way she'd come, trying to get out of the tunnel.

A broken carousel horse with a splintered hole where one eye should have been lay against one wall. As Sal watched, the third girl reached out an inhumanly long arm and stroked its head. The horse struggled to its feet. The brass pole through its belly dragged on the ground with a shuddering shriek as the newly animated thing limped toward the two terrified girls.

It was so dark, the kind of dark my eyes couldn't adjust to. The sounds of the park above us were so close it felt like they were piercing my skull, but I couldn't follow them back to safety. Billie had brought us through a door marked "Employees Only," through a zig-zag of hallways, and down a flight of stairs—I'd be able to *see* the stairs if I had light, but I didn't.

The hot, noisy space smelled like blood and bile. I gritted my teeth and knelt, feeling on the ground for the flashlight. My hand sloshed through a puddle of whatever Billie had thrown up. It was warm and viscous, and I clenched my jaw tight, trying to suppress my own gag reflex. The flashlight was close, I was sure.

"Linnea?" Billie had stopped throwing up. Her voice sounded sticky and wet, like she was crying.

"I'm here," I said.

"I'm sorry," she said pathetically. "I got sick." I heard her breathing, slow and heavy.

My hand hit something, and I almost crowed in victory. But no, this was something that gave when I touched it, something fibrous. Something that tangled around my fingers—oh God. It was a clump of hair, like you'd pull out of a shower drain. Wet and heavy with vomit and blood, it clung to my hand as I tried to shake it off. I screamed.

I felt a bump against my shoulder. "Billie!" It came out half a sob, and I reached to grab her, to hold her tight, to stand together against whatever was happening to us.

But it wasn't Billie. My hand touched something that felt like wood, hard and grainy, but supple like flesh. I pulled away, but it bumped against me again. What I'd thought was Billie was right in front of me now. Something exhaling hot into my face, smelling like a hundred years of dust and decay.

Whatever it was, it snorted.

Sal didn't need light to see by. She thought about laughing again as the two girls scrabbled past each other in the dark, barely missing each other again and again, increasingly desperate. When the carousel horse huffed in the short girl's face, she scuttled backwards on her hands, crablike.

The laugh she'd let out if she could, thought Sal. The guffaw. She'd pour it out of her until her whole body shook, her head bouncing on its springs, hands flailing in the air like she was begging the world to stop being so hilarious until she could catch her breath. She could feel it, all the laughter building up inside her throughout these years, ready to explode. She wanted it so badly.

Sal focused on the girls, on their fear. The third girl didn't interest her so much anymore. She wasn't funny, except that she wanted to make the other girls afraid, and *that* was funny. Fear was Sal's blood. Fear gave her life.

Gathering all the terror in the room toward herself, Sal pushed with her mind as hard as she could. And it started to work. Metal creaked and groaned under her old-fashioned dress, and her head tilted forward. A low "Haaaa" wheezed out of her.

That was when the third girl finally looked around and realized Sal was there, and her face went stark white with hatred.

The laughter was the worst part.

Every day the girl worked at the park, operating The Whip in the hot sun, she felt sicker and sicker. The motion and noise of the rides, the crowds, the smells—it was nauseating, all of it. She spent her shifts swallowing bile and pulling her uniform polo shirt down over the growing bump she was sure everyone could see. She had never sweat so much in her life, and her head throbbed constantly.

But the worst of it all was the goddamn cackling fat lady, right outside the fun house, where she had to listen to her all day. Racked with mirth while the girl swam in misery. It felt more and more like the thing was laughing at *her*.

There were options for girls who got in trouble. She'd heard about them in whispers, rumors, in the girl's bathroom at school. But school was out and she didn't have the kind of friends that got together over the summer, the kind of friends you come to with problems. And the longer she waited, the bigger the thing grew.

The boy worked at the other end of the park, at the go-kart track. The girl used to walk over there during her breaks with a big cup of Coke. She didn't do that anymore.

One day she got to the park early, just at opening time, and raced to the roller coaster before there were any lines. As the chains began to clack and drag the cars up the first hill, her eyes fell on the sign at the entrance. "Do Not Ride If You Have Back Or Neck Problems, Heart Problems, Or Are Pregnant."

Her heart kept rising as the rest of her plummeted down and around curves. That was it. That was the answer.

She rode the roller coaster three times, not clutching the safety bar as she usually did, but letting her small body bounce around with the motion of the wooden coaster. The seatbelt pulled taut against her too-round belly, and her hips and shoulders slammed against the sides of the car. As she climbed off the ride the last time, a cramp twisted her guts, she staggered and clutched the rail. *It's working.*

But she had to make sure.

So she rode The Round-up, pinned against the wall by centrifugal force and tilting wildly through the air. And The Wild Chipmunk, rattling around hairpin turns until she was dizzy. And The Hammer, hanging upside down at the high point of the arc with her whole weight suspended from her lap bar. And if she screamed, well, she wasn't the only one screaming.

Wherever she went in the park, she could hear the animatronic dummy outside the Fun House, its voice carrying farther than the smell of popcorn or the carousel's music. Laffing Sal, mocking her, giggling every time her stomach lurched and she choked down bile.

When she climbed off The Hammer, she ran for the bathroom behind The Hall of Mirrors. Sitting on the toilet, biting into the side of her hand to keep from screaming, she sobbed without sound as she bled out the thing growing inside of her.

The pain was so much worse than she had imagined.

And as her fear and pain and rage coalesced into something so thick with bitterness she could almost touch it, the girl still heard Sal laughing.

Billie was still crying, and sounded far away. The thing in front of me, whatever it was, sighed. I took a step back and heard it step forward, a heavier sound than my own footstep—hooves?

Where was the fucking flashlight? I struggled to my feet.

"Linnea, where are you?" Billie whimpered.

"I'm here," I said. I hear her shuffling, uncertain which way to go. My own voice sounded like it was coming from a long way away. This tunnel distorted sounds, made it impossible to tell where anything was.

I needed light. The flashlight was a lost cause. I felt for my phone, but it must have fallen out of my pocket. "Billie, do you have your phone?"

"I think," she said, then, "Yeah!" Her voice suddenly sounded clearer.

"Can you turn on the flashlight?"

"Yes, just let me—" There was the sound of her fumbling, and then an instant's bright light. Not a flashlight, but a camera flash. For a splinter of a second, I saw what was in front of me. I saw its teeth.

"Jesus!" I jumped backward and bumped into something solid. I screamed again, but this time it was Billie. She wrapped her arm around my shoulders, and despite the dark and the noise and the smell, for a moment I felt safe. Tall girlfriends are amazing.

She kept her arm around me as, finally finding her

phone with her other hand and opening the flashlight app. I held my breath as she aimed it into the tunnel ahead of us.

There was nothing there.

"Maybe we just—" Billie started to say, and then I realized I couldn't breathe.

The two girls made her furious. Look how they adored each other, in their awkward, flinching way. Look how they tried to find reasons to touch. She remembered that feeling. The adolescent shivers of hope, of discovery, the way the boy's fingertips seemed to pull all the blood to the surface of her skin, leaving her flushed and dizzy with bliss.

The girls were idiots. That feeling was a lie. It was poisoned bait. Love only led young girls to suffering. She knew.

In the dark, they had found each other, had grasped each other's hands while she was still alone, still screaming without making a sound. They would leave together, hand in hand, if she let them.

Her fingers were steel cables. She wrapped them around the smaller girl's throat.

The phantom, that half-sentient thing born of fury and grief, tightened its grip on the dark-haired girl and lifted her into the air by the throat. The girl's face went red, her jaw working furiously, trying and failing to gulp air.

"Linnea!" shouted the tall girl. "Oh, what the fuck?!" She couldn't see the phantom, Sal remembered; she just saw the other girl strangling, hanged by nothingness, dying.

Just beyond Linnea's dangling feet, the phone's light illuminated the stairs the girls had come down, but Billie didn't move. She just stood there, staring in terror, holding up the phone, shining the light into Linnea's bulging eyes.

Fear. It was everywhere. Sal felt it, drank it, bathed in it. They all had so much of it, these three girls, so much delicious fear, and it coursed through her, sparking wires that had been still and dark for decades.

Gears groaned. Wood creaked. And Sal began to laugh.

I saw Billie's face, yellowish pale in the light from her phone, but I couldn't see what had me by the neck. Swirls of black and red clouded my vision, and there was a ringing sound in my ears, almost like someone laughing. I kicked my legs wildly but didn't touch anything. My eyesight got dimmer. The laughter got louder.

It wasn't just the ringing in my ears—it really was laughter. Billie? No, she hadn't moved, her mouth still gaping with terror and confusion. The voice was too far away to belong to whatever was choking me, though the steel grip around my throat seemed to falter, loosening just enough that I was able to take a tiny sip of air.

The laughter was coming from the glass case, from that grotesque mannequin. It rocked back and forth, its head bouncing with barely contained hilarity. It waved its hand through the air. And it bellowed, it brayed, it convulsed with laughter.

Laffing Sal glowed with her own horrible light, every painted freckle clearly visible in the tunnel's darkness. She howled, gasping for breath, her laughter shuddering through the air like thunder. I felt the vibrations not just in my ears but in my whole body. And with every peal, the grip on my throat loosened.

As though retreating from the force of the laughter, the thing holding me seemed to shrink, folding inward on itself. It grew more solid and weaker at the same time, and I watched it take shape, coagulating into a sort of bloody fog and then into a body.

She was just a girl. She didn't look any older than me.

She was still holding me up by the throat, but now she was smaller and the toes of my high tops scraped the ground. I gathered all the strength I had left and kicked, hard, my heels slamming into her stomach. She dropped me and doubled over. Billie was there almost before I hit the ground, helping me to my feet. I clung to her, the wind knocked out of me, my lungs in spasm.

The laughter went on and on. I looked up at the figure in the glass case. A moment ago it had been life-sized, but now it seemed larger, ten or twelve feet tall—which didn't make sense because I was sure Billie could touch the roof of the tunnel standing on tiptoe. There was no way this enormous dummy could fit in such a small space, yet here it was, looming over us, laughing and laughing and laughing.

And the girl who had tried to choke me—she had fallen to her knees. Her long hair hung in her face. Her shoulders shook, and I realized she was crying.

Despite everything, my heart twisted. She looked so helpless.

I reached for her.

She raised her head and looked at me, her mouth a bleeding wound, too big for her face. "Run," she screamed, loud enough to hear her over the deafening laughter.

Billie yanked on my arm, and we ran.

The laughter followed us as our feet pounded up the

stairs. It rushed with us down the dim hallway, tight on our heels around corners, and it burst with us out the door into the sunshine. It didn't fade. It kept going, that terrible sound, nerve-jangling, throat-scraping, louder and louder and louder until I finally realized that the only person laughing now was me.

Lindsay King-Miller grew up in Denver and still lives here today. Her fiction has been published in the anthologies The Fiends in the Furrows (Nosetouch Press, 2018) and Dark Rainbow (Riverdale Avenue Books, 2018) and in the fall issue of Speculative City.

THIS WAS ALWAYS GOING TO HAPPEN

Stephen Graham Jones

There's no traffic out this far, so the only real danger when the tire on your trusty Accord blows is that you might panic, wrench the wheel over, plummet a few hundred feet down. You don't.

Instead you slow, ease over to the shoulder, then scooch a little closer to the guardrail—as close as you can get, since there's a blind turn up ahead that Porsches with ski racks can come whipping around. If they have to overcorrect from that hairpin situation, it might point them right where you're sitting. No thank you, mountain gods.

Really, you consider it lucky that that rear tire went when it did. Ten, twenty seconds later and you'd be changing it in the cool shade of those giant red rocks, and every car coming down the mountain would only be seeing you at the last possible instant.

But then ...luck? Real luck would have been the tire not blowing at all.

Anyway, you call Marcy because that's the safe thing to do, but of course, cell service being spotty all up and down this road, you can't get through. The faster you swap the flat for the donut in the trunk, the faster you can tell her about all this in person, you figure. It's not like you haven't changed a tire before.

So.

Five minutes later the back of the Accord's hiked up on the scissor jack. You're just cranking on the first lug when a slow crunch turns you around.

It's a cyclist in full-bib tights, bright white with orange and yellow stripes and accents, one of those helmets made to reduce wind drag, his legs hairless because smooth skin slips through the air that much faster. He's doing that balancing-on-the-pedals thing they all do, like the ground's lava, and if they just make it two more seconds they'll be safe.

His mirrored sunglasses are nearly ski goggles.

"What is it?" he asks, more chipper than anybody should be after the climb he just has to have made.

"Flat," you tell him, kind of obviously.

He pauses, like rolling through response options, then says, "You got it, then?"

"Old hand at this," you say, the lug wrench loose by your thigh.

"Well, if you need anything," he says, and nods bye or good luck or ...it's hard to tell, actually.

He pedals off, continuing his classic ride or Sunday afternoon burn or whatever it is he's crazy enough to be out here doing. More power to him.

You're rolling the spare around from the trunk when a flash up at the jumble of red rocks catches your attention.

It's the cyclist, coming back, whipping in and out of the yellow stripes on the faded asphalt.

He pulls to a soundless stop, feet down in the lava this time, and works what he's found down off his shoulder, along his arm.

A cast-off air filter, its accordion paper packed with seed heads and dirt.

"Thought this might help," he says, and sets it by the flat tire.

You consider it, come up to the cyclist again, consider him all over again. Is this what counts for humor at eight thousand feet?

"O-*kay*," you say.

He throws a jaunty salute your way, flashes a perfectly symmetrical grin, his leathery cheeks crinkling up from it, and pedals easily away. This time you watch him until he disappears around the red rocks.

You don't get it. Not even one little bit. In an *effort* to, you inspect the air filter, but it doesn't hold any answers, was completely content with its life in the ditch before being hand-delivered back to you.

Marcy is going to love hearing about this one.

You're on your stomach, your arm shoved as far under the Accord as it can go after a gotten-away lug nut, when you realize you're not alone. Again.

You roll to the side, see two high-dollar road bike wheels, tires that are weighed in grams.

"Found this," the cyclist says, grinning wide and eager.

It's a two-gallon gas can, its plastic body faded from a season in the sun.

"I have a *flat*," you can't help but reiterate, watching his mirrored lenses for a sign of—of anything, please. Any sort of clue.

"Just thought you might need it," the cyclist says, and sets it down on the shoulder of the road like the most delicate vase, the most sacred artifact.

"Thank you?" you say.

He nods sagely, almost reverentially, and hauls his bike around, pedals uphill.

You study the road behind you this time. There's no one to witness this, whatever it is. You're alone out here. With this crazy person.

You edge over to the gas can, toe it over onto its side. It's empty, light, probably brittle. After checking the road both ways, you step out into it, take a running start, and kick the gas can with everything you've got. It sails over the guardrails, hangs like a cartoon for a moment, then drops.

You've got to get off this mountain.

You spin the three lug nuts you *do* have onto the studs and walk around to the other side of the Accord, the long fall past the guardrail taking your breath away a bit. Don't look, you tell yourself, while completely looking. Your prayer was that the lost lug nut had rolled this far, that it would be there waiting for you.

Nope.

With your luck, it's probably dead center under the car—right under the muffler, which wants nothing else in the world but to sizzle into the skin of your forearm.

You *could* tighten down the three lug nuts you didn't fumble away and roll the Accord back, expose their missing brother. But what if one of the studs, carrying its weight plus a third, snaps off? And then you're stuck up here?

No, better a burn on your forearm than having to walk down for enough bars to call for help.

When you come around the car to get that lug nut, damn the consequences, the cyclist is playing his balancing game again, turning the front wheel of his bike this way and that way, pedaling forward degree by degree.

He looks up like he's surprised to see you.

"Oh, hey," he says, "found this, thought—"

It's a bezel. Thin, aluminum, all twisted up and dull. In a former life it probably framed a taillight. In its current life, it's just trash.

"Um," you say, "yeah."

"Got to look out for each other up here, right?" he says—or, recites?

"Thank you," you say, sort of chilled even though it's hot. He shrugs like it's nothing, like pleased with himself—that's it: It's like he's a dog, isn't it? And dogs don't understand flats, or cars. They just know to bring you stuff. It means they get petted.

He nods, accepting your verbal pat, checks the road both ways, and hauls his bike around, stands on the pedals to make this climb a third time.

Marcy is going to *flip* for this.

And you really need that fourth lug.

You lie down, reinvigorated, can *see* the dull glint of the lug nut now, can...*just* touch it with the leading top of your middle finger, and then, your eyes pressed tight now so your fingers can feel better—a thing happens.

The cool lug nut is placed on the back of your straining hand, and then held there until your forearm figures out how to rotate in that tight space, let your palm accept this gift.

Except.

You reel your arm in, open your eyes, have to look.

It's the cyclist, shimmied under the car from the passenger side, the muffler smoking against his cheek but not messing with his grin one iota, his mirrored lenses absolutely unreadable.

You jerk back, dropping the lug nut, and roll fast away, stand.

"What *are* you, even?" you bellow, having to back up to try to keep a line on him under the car, which is when a horn blows and tires scream, and you realize you're standing in the middle of the road.

At least for about a hundredth of a second longer.

Stephen Graham Jones is the author of sixteen and a half novels, six story collections, a couple of standalone novellas, and a couple of one-shot comic books. He's been an NEA recipient, has won the Texas Institute of Letters Award for Fiction, the Independent Publishers Award for Multicultural Fiction, a Bram Stoker Award, four This is Horror Awards, and he's been a finalist for the Shirley Jackson Award and the World Fantasy Award. Next up are The Only Good Indians (Saga) and Night of the Mannequins (Tor.com). Stephen lives in Boulder, Colorado.

ELECTRIC STALKER
Rebecca S.W. Bates

When lightning struck, it hit Lindsay like a bomb exploding in her face.

There'd been no warning other than a thick bank of dark clouds roiling across the horizon, where a greenish glow leaked from Denver. She'd been lifting her old aqua Schwinn into the bicycle rack at the front of the bus, bound for her temporary job at a landscape center in one of the suburbs, when the flash and the boom detonated around her.

The power of the blast struck her with crushing pressure, the weight of a sandbag dropping on her skull. The force wrenched the bike frame away from her hands and hurled her backwards onto the sidewalk. A blanket of twinkling floaters fluttered around her, coloring the air sepia.

She woke up in a white room surrounded by gray instruments and blinking pinpoints of colored lights. A shadow shifted beside her, and a voice broke through the burping, swishing sounds of machinery.

"Welcome back," said the voice. It sounded whispery and husky, like breezes rattling cottonwood leaves.

The brightness of the room fractured into a blur. Lindsay blinked furiously.

"We were so worried about you." The voice—a woman's, perhaps—quavered. "Thank God you had plenty of help right away."

It took a beat for Lindsay to summon her own voice, which scraped up through the rawness of her throat. "Who...are you?"

The heat of a flush crept up her neck. She wasn't entirely sure who *she* was, either. There was something urgent she had to do. Somewhere to go.

The shadow touched her arm, sending a spark of warmth through her. "I'm your Big Sister, silly. Amanda. Don't worry, you're going to be OK. I'm going to take care of you just like I used to, remember?"

Lindsay jerked away in a tangle of cords. It wasn't a question of not remembering. The truth was she didn't have a sister. She knew that for sure, because... because... Why did she know? Well, for starters, she lived...

Where did she live?

Alone.

She had no one, not anymore. There *had* been someone, though. Hadn't there?

When the blur finally flushed from Lindsay's vision, she decided Amanda looked nothing like a shadow at all. Probably in her late thirties, Amanda had a few strands of gray that shimmered like wires in her flaming red hair. It curled around a freckled face, unlike the pale brown wisps of split ends in a tangle against Lindsay's shoulder. Amanda had high cheekbones and rounded eyes, and Lindsay realized she didn't remember what her own face looked like. The more she tried to think, the less she could remember.

She lost all sense of time as hospital routine moved around her. She couldn't recall ever having a sister, but why would anyone lie about a thing like that? A predator might, but Amanda couldn't be one; she seemed like a truly nice lady who cared about Lindsay. *We were so worried about you!*

So, she chose to believe that Amanda was who she said she was. It was nice to have someone who cared about her. That hadn't happened since... Oh God, what was his name? He'd died, but she'd always kept a piece of him in her memory. Without even that much, he was gone forever.

As the stream of medical personnel flowed in and out of her hospital room, it was nice to have a sister she'd never had, someone who could handle all the paperwork.

When it came time for the nurse's aide to wheel Lindsay downstairs to the hospital's front door, Lindsay's chest tightened. She was basically leaving a safe environ—letting a *stranger* take her—although Amanda would laugh at her if she knew about her doubts. Should she resist? Where else did she have to go? There was somewhere important, but she couldn't remember.

She closed her eyes and furrowed her brow and thought so hard her veins felt as if they might burst.

All too soon, the nurse's assistant buckled Lindsay into the front seat of Amanda's Subaru.

"You're going to live with us for now," Amanda said. "The doctors say you need some time to recover, and you shouldn't live on your own for a while. Luckily, you hadn't signed a lease yet for that new place you were looking at. Good thing, considering..."

A faraway look crossed Amanda's face. Her hand shook as she put the car into gear and pulled into traffic.

"Considering what?"

"Ohhh...nothing." Amanda's gaze flicked to the

rearview mirror. She frowned and bit her lower lip.

Lindsay looked over her shoulder, but she didn't see anything behind them except three lanes of cars. "Clearly, it's something."

Amanda laughed—a nervous, high-pitched sound—and went on, rushing her words before Lindsay could press her further. "Do you know how many people on that bus knew CPR?"

"No."

"You were so lucky this time."

This time?

Lindsay didn't feel very lucky. She shivered and squeezed her eyes shut and saw in her head, one more time, the bomb exploding.

Amanda reached across to pat Lindsay's arm. "We're third generation, which is pretty special around here. Most people haven't lived in Boulder longer than a year or two. Just ask anyone on the street. Sometimes they'll tell you Niwot's curse has brought them back."

Lindsay's eyes popped open, and she whipped around to study Amanda's profile. Her face—half of it, at least—looked serious.

"You don't remember Chief Niwot, either? The Indian whose curse says you can never leave Boulder, and if you try to, you'll always come back."

Lindsay shook her head. They drove in silence while she tried to process what Amanda was saying. And *not* saying. The air felt charged between them inside the boxy space of the car.

"Sorry," Amanda finally said, breaking their silence as the car swerved around a corner. "I can't help myself. In the old days, you would've laughed at me and told me I'm doing my big sister thing by worrying so much."

Lindsay focused on the passing scenery. Older houses and cottonwood trees lined the streets, and a wave of calm washed through her at the sight of permanence. She tried to laugh, but it came out sounding more like a cry. According to Amanda, she'd lived here all her life. Niwot had never let her go.

She didn't have a sister, either.

Amanda steered the Subaru into an alley wedged between wood-framed Victorian houses. They stopped beside a post where a dented, aqua Schwinn was chained, and something triggered in the back of Lindsay's mind.

"I remember!" she shouted with glee, pointing at her bike.

Amanda crumpled over the steering wheel. Her shoulders heaved as she sobbed. "Thank God," she said, sniffling. "We were hoping the family home would help you remember. You gave us quite a scare, you know."

"Us?" Who else lived here?

"Hannah, Carl and me, of course."

"Carl?" Lindsay's heart lurched in her chest. That had been his name, the name of the memory who lived somewhere deep inside her. But he'd died.

At least, she thought he had.

Amanda sighed and pushed open her door. "It makes sense, doesn't it? If you can't remember your own sister, why would you remember my daughter and husband?"

Lindsay swore her Carl had died. Amanda's Carl couldn't possibly be the same person.

Except, how would Lindsay know for sure?

She didn't, but she knew the way upstairs to the second floor. The house *did* bring back memories, and now she felt certain she was who Amanda claimed she was. The bedroom where she'd grown up was in the turret room, although the flower quilt was all that remained of her old decorations. Amanda followed her upstairs with her water bottle from the hospital, chattering about the last time Lindsay had lived in this room during college. She'd stayed with Mom during her last illness.

Her name had been Hannah, too.

After Mom had passed, Lindsay moved into her own apartment in the basement of a house on the north side of Denver. That's when Amanda, Carl, and their daughter took over the family home. Wasn't it wonderful? They were all going to be together again.

Lindsay wasn't sure how she felt about that. "What about Carl?"

"What about him? He usually works late at the firm, but tonight is special—now that you're home—and he's going to join us for dinner."

"No… I mean… When did you guys…get married?"

"Sixteen beautiful years ago. I was a child bride, can't you tell? And you were my maid of honor. Don't you remember? You were still in high school." Amanda turned away. "No, I guess not."

A wedding rang no bells for Lindsay.

Her head hurt, long after Amanda went away to let her rest. She was trying to understand how Carl could still be alive. Not only that but married to her own sister. Was Amanda's Carl the same Carl who'd been Lindsay's boyfriend?

Impossible!

Or, could it be…

Had the lightning somehow split reality and jolted her into an alternate world where she had a sister named Amanda?

Sitting around the mahogany table at dinner that night, Lindsay felt certain she'd never met this Carl before, either here or in an alternate reality.

This Carl was a financial planner who brought in the big bucks and rarely made an appearance at the dinner table, Amanda explained. Tonight was a special welcome-home dinner in Lindsay's honor. After the long hours of his day of meetings, Carl was still clean-shaven with an agreeably woodsy scent of cologne. The silky shine of his gray suit and perfectly knotted cranberry-colored tie confirmed in Lindsay's mind she'd never seen this man before in her life.

She remembered her Carl now. He'd been a long-haired biker before heading to Iraq, where he'd been killed by a bomb. If she strained hard enough, she could almost hear him laughing, teasing about her beloved girl's bike. Straining to capture the elusive memories made her head hurt even more.

A board creaked somewhere in the house, maybe on the stairs? Lindsay looked up from her plate of pasta.

"That's just our ghost," her niece said brightly. Around twelve years old, Hannah had her mother's freckles and Carl's sandy brown hair.

"No, it's not," Amanda said with a laugh. "The house is settling."

"But it's true, there's a ghost!" Hannah bounced in her chair. Her ponytail swung, its ends brushing her shoulders. "Grandma used to tell me about the crazy old lady who used to live here before them, and—"

"Hush!" Amanda said. "It's just a story."

Hannah stuck out her lower lip. "They said she made the lightning come."

Lindsay's heart skipped a beat.

Carl and Amanda exchanged a worried glance, and then he said, "Why don't you tell us what you did in school today?"

Hannah's fork clattered to her plate. "Well, in computer lab I looked up about lightning, because, you know, Aunt Lindsay…"

In the distance, Lindsay heard something rumble. The ghost? Thunder, more likely. She stiffened in her chair.

"Eat your dinner," Amanda said.

"And what did you learn?" Carl said.

Amanda glared at Carl.

Hannah beamed. "Did you know there are five hundred *thousand* lightning strikes every year? Right *here!* We're third in *all* the states for deaths by lightning."

"That's enough," Amanda said.

"But Aunt Lindsay should know."

"Nonsense."

"I think she's right," Carl said, reaching across the table to lay a hand on Amanda's arm. "Considering that—"

"It's nothing," Amanda said.

"Considering what?" Lindsay looked back and forth from Amanda to Carl, who lowered their glances over their plates.

Hannah bounced again, kicking the legs of her chair. "Once you're hit by lightning the first time, you draw it to you like a magnet."

"That's enough," Amanda said.

The first *time?*

"The lightning keeps chasing you," Hannah said, "until finally—"

"I *said* that's enough!"

Carl interjected. "You heard your mother."

"But that's what happened to Aunt Lindsay!"

A clammy coldness washed over Lindsay. Pasta weighed like a lump of dough in her stomach. "Wait a minute. Did you just say that...I've been *hit* before?"

"Next time you might not be so lucky," Carl said.

"Carl!" Amanda said.

The room fell silent. Only thunder rumbled in the distance.

Lightning flashed all through the night, firing the windows of Lindsay's turret bedroom. She huddled under her bedcovers and squeezed her eyes shut, but the glow from the explosions penetrated through her eyelids and into the dark of her mind. The booms of thunder rattled the glass panes, shaking them as if howling to be let in.

It was searching for her.

Someone—or some*thing*—creaked the wooden boards of the stairs outside her room. Hannah's ghost, bringing the lightning.

Lindsay lay stiff and alert in bed, counting the beats of her heart. The next thing she knew she startled awake, feeling exhausted and also surprised sleep had somehow taken her.

At least the storm had passed.

Climbing out of bed, she struggled to breathe. Her skin felt clammy. She needed some fresh air. She padded across her room to the window and wrestled the sash up. The warped and peeling wooden trim made it difficult to open, but she'd always been strong. A faint memory of lugging heavy buckets, building her muscles, flitted through her mind. Had that been her memory or someone else's?

Outside, a massive, old cottonwood tree grew close enough to her window she could've reached out to touch it had the musty screen not been in the way. It was a barrier to keep her inside. And it wasn't the only one. Beyond the wooden fence that separated her from the house next door, the jagged line of Front Range peaks glowed in morning light. They stood like another barrier between the Rockies and the plains. The opposites of high and low, hilly and flat, forest and desert, cold and hot produced instabilities in the air. Was that why the lightning had lashed out? But why at *her*? She'd somehow disturbed its air space where the sky unrolled from mountains and stretched away forever.

After breakfast, Lindsay fled outside to the gloriously shining light of a clear day, unchained the Schwinn, and pedaled away. She spent the morning exploring the old, stately neighborhood. Following the signs for bike paths, she eventually made her way to the creek path. With no particular destination in mind, she chose west, the direction of the mountains. The natural beauty of sandstone slabs leaning against forested slopes drew her on, toward the mountains, as if…in the same way that…

She drew lightning to *her*.

That's what Hannah had blurted out the night before, and it had happened twice. It must be true, since Amanda had tried to stifle her daughter.

Lindsay bicycled on. Closer to the mountains she found the statue of Niwot, the streaming-haired chief who'd claimed these lands first. The long tangles of his hair and the beak shape of his nose reminded her of someone. She stopped the bike, lowering it to the ground while she probed the depths of her memory she couldn't quite reach. She thought she saw him there—Carl?

Not Amanda's Carl.

But *her* Carl was dead.

Back on the bike, she headed out of town into the canyon. Clouds piled up to the south, jamming against the mountains like spitballs caught against a wall. She pedaled harder, but the clouds moved faster, racing as if to catch her. The creek babbled below her spinning tires, and her breath grew more jagged. Her thighs burned and goosebumps prickled the back of her neck. The wind picked up, moaning through the branches of towering Ponderosas.

She thought she glimpsed movement through the pines a short way up the rocky side of one canyon wall. It reminded her of streaming hair—like Niwot's—but she told herself it was just pine needles shifting in the wind. Maybe she'd gone far enough. Another storm was brewing, and after all, this was the season of atmospheric instabilities. The air was almost too volatile to breathe. She could smell it coming, the clash of fire and ice in the form of lightning and hail.

She stopped the bike and checked her phone, but there was no signal. Tipping up her water bottle to drink, she noticed the clouds, plunging lower, closer to her. Their underbelly looked like iridescent fish scales. The clouds growled, and she knew lightning couldn't be far behind. It was looking for her.

Shit!

She slid her phone and bottle back into place, lifted the frame of her bike, and turned it around, all in a matter of seconds. She sprang onto the seat and pedaled hard downhill. Her focus stayed on the path alongside the creek, but it was impossible not to notice the flashes of light bursting around her. Blasts echoed back and forth on canyon walls. Loose rock shattered from above. She pedaled faster, dodging around the rocky debris that fell onto the path. The wind pushed her from behind, expelling her from the canyon.

She didn't slow down until after she'd passed back inside the city limits. When she reached the park and Niwot's statue, she realized nothing was flashing around her anymore. No sounds boomed.

Unsettled, she swerved the bike to a stop beside Niwot, jumped off, and breathed deeply. Her heart raced. Heat flushed her throat and sweat slicked her skin where wispy strands of hair pasted themselves. She felt dizzy as she gulped in the sweet air of spring. Cautiously, she glanced over her shoulder. The clouds had broken apart, and the sky had cleared.

As if there had never been a storm at all.

As the days passed, and pieces of Lindsay's memory returned, she grew eager to go back to work. It was only a seasonal, temporary job at a landscape center in Denver, but still. She felt incomplete not having a daily, specific task. Besides, she didn't want to be a burden to her family. Amanda scoffed, reminding her of the trust fund their parents had set up.

But Lindsay didn't remember any financial details.

Amanda told her it wasn't necessary for Lindsay to go to "that place," hauling flowerpots and digging in the soil, working hard, the way manual laborers worked. It just wasn't necessary.

"Carl is a good provider," Amanda said. "He makes enough to support all of us, while the trust fund keeps the house running."

He didn't mind, but then he never did, did he?

He hadn't minded when he went to Iraq. Got blown up.

No, wait, that wasn't this Carl. Even though Lindsay knew better by now, an alarm flashed through her, sending an electrical signal. The truth of the matter was that *her* Carl was dead.

And Lindsay was still healing.

Both Amanda and Carl thought that a job away from home was not a good idea. Not yet.

Lindsay wasn't sure she liked the idea of being cooped up inside, healing.

"No worries," Amanda told her. No one would have to stay inside much longer, because all of them would be leaving soon for Hawaii. Vacation for the gals; business for Carl. Didn't Lindsay remember? She'd already bought her tickets before the accident. She had to travel separately on account of *that job*. If she'd have quit, she would've been able to travel with the rest of them.

But Lindsay didn't want to quit her job. Frankly, she couldn't wait to get away from Amanda's nagging. Lindsay understood her sister only meant well, but... worry felt contagious.

For instance, there was the matter of transportation. She would have to ride her Schwinn to the downtown station where she would catch the bus to Denver. She tried not to think about how things had turned out for her the last time she'd hauled her bike on a bus. She tried to convince herself not to worry.

It wasn't easy.

Her boss made it easier, having told her to take all the time she needed. She'd gone through a traumatic experience, and the job could wait. Her boss was generous, but Lindsay was so ready to go back to work.

When that day finally arrived, Lindsay tried not to check the weather app on her phone every few minutes while she dressed. The nearest lightning strike was hundreds of miles away.

She checked once on her bike and four times on the bus. Each time, the lightning remained far away.

On lunch break, she heard the first rumble. Now her phone reported that lightning was fourteen miles away. So, it was coming. Time to seek shelter, her phone advised, but no one did. Customers and staff kept moving through the graveled rows between beds of plants without glancing up at the netting enclosure.

The mesh overhead made it difficult for Lindsay to watch the clouds, but she thought the air darkened a few degrees.

Thunder grew louder, sounding like an angry growl, coming first from one direction, then another. Lindsay checked her phone. Nine miles.

Why wasn't anyone concerned? Where was her boss? She ran along each row of plants, telling customers she passed to get inside quickly. She had to find her boss, convince her to close the garden center. Lightning was coming for Lindsay, and she didn't want to think what would happen if anyone else got in its way. The air felt thick, like a greenish-gray soup, and she struggled to breathe.

The screen of her phone glowed brighter relative to the dark air.

Four miles.

The flash and the crack of the boom came at the same time, shaking the mesh and rattling carts. Wood creaked, splintered, and snapped. A crashing sound exploded around her, and the mesh collapsed, entangling people and plants.

Screams pierced the air.

With that final crash, the storm stopped as fast as it had descended on the garden center. In the aftermath, Lindsay crawled out from under torn netting and toppled trays of plants. She followed the sound of sobs and wails around one corner of the building where she'd tried her best to herd the customers inside.

A century-old cottonwood leaned against the building, crushing its wall. Broken branches speared up from the hole that gaped in the side of the building.

Several people knelt there, sobbing, frantically clawing at the debris that partially covered a pair of legs. The legs weren't moving.

The lightning had been meant for her, Lindsay was sure. The tree had stood in its way. And a customer had died instead of *her*. Amanda told her not to blame herself, but she did, anyway. Because at home, later that day, she found out there'd been no storm. No wind. No lightning.

Maybe Amanda was right. Big sisters usually were,

weren't they? Lindsay phoned her boss and told her she wouldn't be coming back to work. She hadn't been ready, after all. Her boss understood.

The vacation would be exactly what she needed. Amanda told her to change her ticket so they wouldn't have to travel separately, but Lindsay resisted being told what to do.

The two nights she spent by herself in the old Victorian house passed quickly. She wasn't really alone, as the ghosts of the family kept her company. She was beginning to absorb in her mind the family photos and Amanda's stories. Now the family felt like a real part of Lindsay's personal history. She believed now who she'd been told she was.

The day of her departure arrived, and she locked the family ghosts inside the Victorian house and took the bus to the airport. Not even the clouds gathering round the airport could douse her spirits as she waited in line to board the plane. She settled into her window seat, and her fingers shook so hard with excitement she could barely buckle in. Her spirit soared along with the plane as it took off, nosing toward the clouds.

Something grumbled, perhaps a man's voice. She whirled around, but the woman sitting in the middle seat next to her had closed her eyes and appeared to be sleeping. She looked over her shoulder, but the only heads she saw were bent over their devices. No one had spoken to her.

She turned back to her window and watched thunderheads loom. The plane bounced each time its wing slid through wispy puffs. The engines revved up, droning louder. Then a flash sparkled outside, touching the wing with a bolt of fire. The air itself snapped, and a stream of sparkles sprayed so fast that for a minute it reminded Lindsay of some wild person with a mane of fiery hair. The plane lurched. It felt as if her seat dropped from beneath and the air had been sucked out of the cabin. Nearby passengers gasped.

During the moment of heavy silence that followed inside the cabin, the plane leveled, and then the pilot spoke over the intercom. "Well, folks, we've just encountered a mechanical issue due to an apparent lightning strike. We're going to have to circle around and return to the airport, get things checked out before we can get you on your way again. Sorry for the delay, but your safety comes first."

When they landed, an audible sigh of relief rippled through the plane, while some passengers clapped and cheered. Luckily, they were instructed to disembark rather than remain entombed inside while mechanics worked. They would need to await the arrival of a new aircraft.

This time, Lindsay felt lucky.

She slipped away from the waiting area and kept going. She didn't stop until she made it safely back to the Victorian house in old Boulder, where she closed and bolted the doors behind her, sealing herself inside with only the family ghosts. Staying home would be better. A staycation was just what she needed.

Niwot had tried to tell her not to leave—or was it Carl?

Lindsay didn't know whose voice it was on the phone that told her about the accident. There'd been a massive pile-up on the interstate, triggered by a sudden downpour following an extreme electrical storm. Amanda, Hannah, and Carl had unfortunately been caught in the crush on their way home from the airport. Amanda and Hannah had been taken to an area hospital. Sadly, Carl hadn't made it. The voice paused, and then offered condolences.

Lindsay blamed herself in the taxi all the way to the hospital. It had been an accident meant for *her*, and no one else. Would the lightning never stop until it found her?

But, *why?*

All she could think of was she'd dared to leave home.

In the back seat of the taxi, she twirled her thumbs in her lap and mumbled a prayer to the lightning gods; she promised she would listen to Niwot and never leave home again.

She brought her sister and niece home, and they buried Carl. Again.

This time, she was the one taking care of her family. They needed her all the more now that they'd lost Carl.

Because of *her*.

When all along, the lightning had wanted *her*.

As the days of summer passed, Lindsay almost kept her word. She hadn't meant her promise literally, after all. She had to leave the house occasionally for groceries and other necessities. And exercise, for goodness sake. As long as she stayed close to home, not leaving the city, she should be OK.

Each time she left the house, she always checked her weather app first.

Four hundred eighty-seven miles away, her phone assured her one morning when she unchained the Schwinn, bound for the grocery.

The flash and the boom exploded around her at the same time. The blast threw her backwards, slamming her against the trunk of the old cottonwood. Her world turned sepia. And then dark.

"Oh!" said a voice, penetrating the dark. "Thank God!"

She opened her eyes, uncomprehending. She didn't recognize the woman who bent over her, the flaming red hair that spilled around her worried face.

"He called 911," said the woman, "and the ambulance is on the way."

"Who…?"

"Carl called. Don't worry, they're coming for you."

Coming…always coming…for her.

Rebecca S.W. Bates lives in Colorado and writes speculative fiction and mystery under a variety of pen names. She is the author of the Centauri series and several dozen short stories, including Sharing Sol, a collection featuring characters from the Centauri world. Sample first chapters and stories at www.dmkregpublishing.com.

GAZE WITH UNDIMMED EYES AND THE WORLD DROPS DEAD

Carina Bissett

With the temperature hovering just below zero and the hotel grounds buried hip deep in snow, I spent my first evening in the small Colorado town at the lobby bar. Dark, sticky wood kissed my elbows and the slightly sour scent of rotting fruit burrowed deep in my throat. Rocky Mountain National Park in the summer might be a tourist's playground, but I was no tourist and it sure as shit wasn't summer. Even winters in Anchorage had been warmer than this.

"Well hello, dollface."

I caught a glimpse of red plaid and a bushy beard before I averted my eyes. The comment was obviously aimed at me because the only other customer sat at the end of the bar, and that old coot was firmly engaged with the sports feed rolling across a flatscreen. The TV tilted in a haphazard way just above a makeshift wine rack. Suspended from their stems, the upside-down goblets were furred with dust. There was more than one reason I preferred whiskey over wine. I ran my tongue over my teeth and shifted my weight on the barstool, presenting a back as stiff as a board to my would-be suitor.

Battered wooden legs protested as the man pulled a stool out to encompass his broad frame. The bartender slid a brimming, wide-mouth tumbler across the bar. Out of the corner of my eye, I watched the stranger shoot the amber liquid as though it was sugared water, not 80 proof.

"Another," he said. "One for the lady, too."

I decided to ignore him and stabbed at the candied cherries lurking under layers of ice and whiskey at the bottom of my Old Fashioned. A note chimed as though I'd stirred the clapper of a small silver bell. I frowned and jabbed again. One of the cherries broke free from the others. It rose at my prodding, a beady eye emerging from the amber liquid, a black imitation of life's spark hidden behind the lens.

I gasped and pushed away from the bar, nearly toppling in my haste to stand up. The glass eye jittered in my drink, clinking against melting ice as it tried to stay afloat. It spun drunkenly, bobbing along until its weight pulled the glass sphere back under. As if that wasn't shocking enough, another black orb fell out of nowhere right into my drink.

"What the fuck!"

I pushed back from the bar and shifted to stand.

The man sitting next to me laughed a deep rumbling sound like a bear. "You got the lucky seat." He pointed to a weasel-like creature chained to the ceiling right above my spot at the bar. "That's Lucky. He loses those damn eyes of his maybe two, three times a week."

The critter's fur bristled in warning, skin awkwardly bunched as though there hadn't been enough weasel to cover the taxidermy form. I should have found relief in the cobwebs stretching between tattered ears, but the way the fur splintered around the empty eyeholes left me dizzy and unmoored.

"Excuse me," I said. A reflex response.

"I don't think he minds much." The man in red plaid chortled. "I know *I* don't. Means I can buy you a *proper* drink."

He leaned over and fished the taxidermy eyeballs out of my glass. He prodded the wooden screws with a serrated spoon. The handle looked ridiculously small between the man's fingers.

"The eye sees a thing more clearly in dreams than the imagination awake," he said.

"What?"

The man wrapped the glass eyes in a handkerchief and stowed the bundle away in his flannel's breast pocket. "Leonardo da Vinci." He polished the spoon on his sleeve and slipped it next to the folded-up kerchief.

He waved a hand at the barkeep, who removed the remains of the ruined drink and replaced it with two dull glasses and a fresh bottle of high-end scotch. Scotch, not whiskey. I couldn't abide the stuff.

"No, thanks." I gathered my purse and fumbled for my room key. "I was just leaving."

The man stopped me with a hand roughened by hard weather. "I insist."

I froze, trapped by his touch. But before I could react, he released me and uncorked the single malt. His callused fingers stroked the bottle as though it was a living thing. In spite of myself, I felt a thrill at the chase. It had been a while since I'd been the object of a man's desire.

"You'll love this." The scent of peat and smoke unfurled as he poured.

He nudged a glass towards me and picked up the other. He tilted the tumbler and paused expectantly.

What did I really have waiting for me in my hotel room, anyway? The tavern might not have many amenities, but it did feature a big, brick fireplace that shed warmth. My hotel room was cold, decked out in the impersonal white linen expected in even the shoddiest of lodges. I hated white. I hated the cold. So, I slid back into my seat.

"Just one." I clinked his glass with my own. The sound echoed for a moment like a trap springing in the snow and I winked up at Lucky. *Who's lucky now?* The scotch burned all the way down.

I loosened up a little after that first measure. My companion kept my glass full as he told me tales of the Colorado wilderness and the animals that lived there. With a glint in his eye, he talked about the demons that roamed on four legs through the woods, devils that hid in the guise of simple animals.

"You can tell them from normal critters by the traps they lay for people." He wagged his fingers and began counting them off, one by one. "Bears, lynx, cougars, wolves, foxes."

I thought he looked like a bear and told him so. He laughed again. I held out the tumbler, eager to switch the conversation. Anything to keep from discussing foxes. Anything to soften the sharpness lodged like claws in my spine.

It worked, too. A little while later, the combined heat of the fire and the scotch made me desperate for cool sheets. My new friend helped me down the maze of long halls patterned with a faded floral print that looked more like animal entrails than elegant vines. The white doors seemed to stretch on forever. The bearded man at my side kept me upright, and I leaned into his strength. He might have told me his name, or maybe not. I didn't care. First names were slippery devils. I called everyone "Darling." Much easier all the way around.

That night, I dreamed I was back in Alaska. A span of a year I preferred to avoid thinking about. But at night, the eye does indeed see things in dreams more easily suppressed in the waking hours.

I remembered the full-length fox coat I'd coveted juxtaposed against the gritty reality of a vixen choked in a snare glittering against the snow. I remembered the sound of the creature's claws scrabbling on the tailgate when it regained consciousness. I remembered the wet thud of an empty wine bottle connecting with flesh and fur. My ex had only smiled when I told him I'd changed my mind. *You'll love it*, he'd said with arrogant confidence. *Wait and see.*

Sometime last night, when I'd laughed about his stories of evil bears and malicious foxes, the bearded man in the red shirt had said the same thing, *Wait and see.*

I woke up in a foul mood with a fouler mouth. After a couple of nightcaps, I had the habit of forgetting to brush my teeth before passing out. And last night, I'd lost count after four. Or was it five? Absently, I ran my tongue over furred enamel. The feeling that I was forgetting something gnawed at the jagged edges of a hangover, but I pushed the uneasiness aside. I reached for the tumbler of water I always kept near the bed, but my groping hand encountered something unfamiliar, something that shifted at my touch.

Sleeping mask hastily shoved aside, I gaped at a mound of marbles stacked on the nightstand. Not marbles, eyes. They gleamed in various shades of gold, brown, and black. The pupils set deep within each of the glass orbs watched me as I scrambled backward, nearly toppling off the far side of the bed in my haste to escape their judgment. The carpet crunched under my weight. Bits and pieces of wood and dried moss had been scattered across the floor. Someone, *something* had been in my room while I slept. I couldn't catch my breath, so I just stood there counting seconds with each inhalation.

The phone rang, a shrieking sound oddly reminiscent of a fox sounding an alarm. As if in response, the pyramid of eyes shuddered and then collapsed in a bouncing clatter of glass hitting glass. I didn't answer, didn't have to. A quick check of the vivid orange numbers glaring from the clock told me everything I needed to know. My first day on the job and I'd overslept.

I did my best to ignore the bark and moss and eyes, focusing instead on getting my ass out the door in hopes I would be able to keep my job. By the time I made it down two flights of well-worn stairs and a long white corridor flooded with fluorescent lights, my headache had reached epic proportions.

Pre-made excuses sprinted for the finish line as I slipped into the boardroom. Migraine. Stomach flu. Power outage. Suicidal friend. Dying parent. They rolled and tumbled over each other in a mad rush to win the day. But my false smile slipped when I realized only one person was waiting for me. Worse yet, I knew the man. The stranger from the tavern. He was wearing jeans and the same red flannel I'd pressed my face against last night in the hall. I was intimately aware of the nip marks scattered across my skin and tenderness between my legs.

"What are you doing here?"

The bearded man leaned back in his chair and looked me over, from head to toe.

"Feeling a little rough, Ms. Kingston?" The chair tipped back on all fours. The man poured a healthy measure of French roast from a coffee carafe and gestured to the chair on his left. "Have a seat."

Little details clicked into place. My questions about the pile of glass eyes and the mud-stains on the bedroom carpet slipped away with the sudden realization of who I was facing.

"You're Bruce Boston." Was he grinning under that thick beard? Of course, he was. "This is your hotel."

"I had my staff let you sleep in this morning. I figure you needed your rest."

Smug shitbird. Two could play that game. "So kind of you," I said, adding a little Southern drawl to the vowels for added emphasis.

I slid into my assigned seat. "What's on the agenda today, boss?"

"Cream or sugar?" he asked, polite. Distant.

"No cream." I used a pair of delicate silver prongs to count out five sugar cubes. Bruce didn't say anything, so I added a sixth cube just for the hell of it. "Do you have a spoon?"

He pulled the serrated spoon out of his breast pocket and slid it to me across the table. I made an attempt at nonchalance as I stirred the dissolving sugar cubes, click-clacking the silver against the rim while trying not to think of glass eyes.

"We'll start with a tour of the hotel and then finish up with a review of your duties."

I bristled. If he thought I was going to add sexual favors to my list of *duties*, Mr. Man had another thing coming. "I'm well aware of your expectations, Mr. Boston. I already signed the contract at the agency."

"Humor me," he said. "Tomorrow is soon enough to introduce you to the rest of the staff. When you're feeling better."

He stood up, and I followed him, cup in hand. When he wasn't looking, I slipped the silver spoon into my own pocket.

The original hotel had been added on to multiple times over the last fifty years. The result was a twisted maze of hallways and levels. In some places the seams of the floors didn't meet, resulting in a whole series of strange staircases and ramps. Even without a hangover, I strongly doubted I could find my way back to the lobby without directions.

Bruce didn't seem to mind the long hallways and ghastly floor coverings, but the fluorescent lights and twisting patterns made it difficult to keep my coffee down. Stuffed animals were everywhere— the ballrooms, tavern, tea room, dining room, lobby, conference rooms, and even in the enclosure dedicated to an indoor pool. The critters looked older and more mismatched than the hotel. And they watched everything. By the time we made it back to the boardroom, I was trying to figure the easiest way out of my contract. Management position and full benefits be damned.

Grateful to be off my feet, I settled into my abandoned chair and wondered if I should attempt another cup of coffee on a sour stomach.

"Any chance of getting tea instead?" I asked.

My would-be-employer nodded and picked up the receiver of an old-fashioned phone. I took the moment to take a better look at my surroundings. Wood paneling covered the walls, a gleaming golden expanse broken only by inset bookcases at either end. Books that appeared to have been selected and sorted by the color of their covers filled the shelves and, in one corner, a ratty stuffed beaver hunched over a branch on the uppermost shelf. It took a minute before I realized the creature was watching with hollow eyes.

Bruce placed an order for a tea service. Just as he hung up, a loud clattering rattled down the fireplace. A glass eye, larger than a silver dollar, dropped from the chimney and into the fireplace where the wooden screw attached to the glass began to burn in the hot coals.

Bruce leaned against the credenza. "Interesting."

"Interesting? Are you serious? What the actual fuck?'

Its companion rattled the metal on its way down before plopping in the flame next to its twin. I thought of my dreams and the look of that damned fox back in Alaska. Those eyes had been amber, not black like Lucky's. Had there been a glint of amber in the glass spheres stacked near the bed? I couldn't remember.

"Are we done here? I think I need to lie down."

My new employer rewarded me with a curt nod. "A word of advice, Ms. Kingston." He glanced at the fireplace and then back at me. "Don't go wandering off. The woods can be dangerous in winter."

"I have no plans to go hiking, Mr. Boston." I stood up abruptly, irritable and ill all at once. "Good day."

But once I was out in the hall, I realized I had no intention of going back to my room. What if the glass eyes were still there, or worse, what if they were gone? I crept from room to room, taking the long hallways from one side of the hotel to the other in search of absolution. Wherever I roamed, there were dozens of taxidermy animals waiting for me. I found everything from squirrels to bears, but one creature, in particular, eluded me. I moved my search to the other buildings on the property.

Outside, everything became clearer. My breath escaped in little clouds. The cold cut through my clothes and I couldn't help but wonder how much warmer I would have been in the fox coat I'd been promised. The snow blazed in the bright light. Paths had been carved from door to door. In other places, the snowpack revealed tracks—the swooping half circles of a rabbit loping, long scratches cut from a bird hopping from one tree to another, the deep paw prints of a predator stalking its prey.

It had been a day just like this one when my ex had found the fox caught in the snare. Up until that point, I'd never seen a fox in the wild, but there it had been, red fur shining like a stain on the snow. I remembered looking the other way. There was nothing I could have done, I told myself, even though I knew it was a lie.

But that had been years ago. That trapped fox had never been skinned. My ex had let the carcass freeze under the covered truck bed where it had stayed all winter. I'd only looked at the dead beast once, just before I left Alaska for good. The dead fox stared back. It still watched me in my dreams, but maybe that wasn't enough anymore.

In winter, the sun sets early in the North. That baleful eye cast an orange-tinted glow on the snowbanks. Black tree limbs stretched like a fence separating the hotel grounds from the forest beyond. And animals, surely more than I could imagine, paced that line between my world and theirs. Did they lament for their brethren, those brittle faded sections of skin and fur clinging hopelessly to wooden forms? Did they see us living our hostile lives through the glass lens screwed into the eye sockets of those taxidermy animals? I wasn't sure.

I walked a little farther, pushing out along a trampled path only wide enough for one person to pass. It led away from the shoveled walks into the wilder places, drawing closer to the bleak forest beyond. I felt more like I was wading than walking, but I persisted. Just a few feet further and I'd turn back, I promised myself. The fresh air would do me good. Although I couldn't see bird nor beast, I felt certain they watched me from the screen of black tree limbs menacingly tangled at the edge of civilization.

A crow screamed. The rasping caw was taken up by dozens, if not hundreds of other black-winged voices. I stopped and covered my ears as I searched the trees for the murder. I should be able to see them, shouldn't I? Or was it possible I couldn't see the birds in the trees, the beasts slipping through the underbrush, because my eyes were not my own?

The sun dipped a little lower, its light partially obscured by the trees. The amber glow deepened. Frantically, I looked around. Snow and cold surrounded me. The only hint of civilization was a section of the hotel roof I could see in the distance behind me. Everywhere else, the snow shimmered like a mirror cobbled together from millions of fragments of silvered glass. That's when I heard the delicate sounds of approach, a furred song played from the contact of swift feet on frost.

A blaze of red and white crested the snow-covered slope just off to the side of the path. The vixen stopped and stared, the dark empty sockets accusing the damned.

"It's not my fault," I protested.

The fox grinned, her teeth sharp as filed accusations.

I slipped a hand into my pockets and wrapped numb fingers around the handle of the silver spoon. It was small, but precise.

"I couldn't do anything to stop it," I said, one last attempt.

The fox opened its mouth and laughed.

The crows joined her in a raucous display, taking wing by the hundreds in a billowing cloud of feathers. Did those birds have eyes, or had they been replaced with glass, too? I couldn't tell. I couldn't feel my arms or feet. The cold chewed on my face and nibbled on my bones. No fur coat for me. Not now, not ever. The fox moved closer, mouth agape as I lifted the spoon. My eyes weren't black like a crow's or gold like a fox's, but they worked just fine and that would have to do.

Carina Bissett is a writer, poet, and educator working primarily in the fields of dark fiction and interstitial art. Her short fiction and poetry has been published in multiple journals and anthologies including Hath No Fury, Gorgon: Stories of Emergence, Mythic Delirium, NonBinary Review, and the HWA Poetry Showcase Vol. V and VI. She teaches online workshops at The Storied Imaginarium and she is a graduate of the Creative Writing MFA program at Stonecoast. Her work has been nominated for several awards including the Pushcart Prize and the Sundress Publications Best of the Net. Links to her work can be found at http:// carinabissett.com.

GRAVE MISTAKE
Joshua Viola and Carter Wilson

The baby kicked. Maybe it was a punch. A tiny little fist, pounding her womb, demanding attention.

Pregnancy and Stephanie didn't get along. Morning sickness, weight-gain beyond what she'd expected, and now, two short weeks before she was due, the relentless discomfort, the sleepless nights, the baby constantly shifting, turning, and rumbling inside.

Those were all manageable things. She could tough her way through them. What Stephanie struggled with most was the secret— a secret that began as shame and blossomed into horror.

Once she got past thinking of suicide, she did her best to accept her pregnancy as a good thing, no matter what the truth was behind it. But this Sunday's *Denver Post* headline changed all of that.

DNA FOUND IN CEMETERY
MATCHES MISSING DRIVER

The lie could no longer be ignored. Another kick. Or

punch. *What the fuck am I doing here?*

She stood with Elijah and Oliver at the Lafayette Cemetery entrance. Oliver was the equivalent of Scooby-Doo's Shaggy. Tall, thin and in desperate need of a shower. Elijah was his polar opposite. A former Homecoming King with a body that rivaled most Calvin Klein underwear models.

Elijah had become obsessed with the fact the baby's due date was Halloween. He was a horror fanatic, and having their first child be a *Halloween baby* put him in the holiday spirit like never before. When news broke about the cemetery disappearance, Oliver asked Elijah to join him on a midnight expedition to use his ghost-hunting equipment to talk to potential *witnesses.*

Maybe Oliver really could help find Brock, Stephanie thought. Not that she believed in ghosts or spirits or any of that nonsense, but maybe they'd find a clue. Something the police missed.

"This is so creepy," Elijah said. Stephanie heard the excitement in his voice, and she hated that his enthusiasm annoyed her.

He's trying so hard, she thought. *And the harder he tries, the deeper I bury myself. There's only so many times I can blame my mood on hormones.*

The aroma of wet grass hung in the air, and a nearby street lamp flickered over a swath of cemetery lawn, glittering with moisture from a heavy mist.

"Why would ghosts be in a cemetery, anyway?" Stephanie asked. "If you were a ghost, would you just hang out in the place you were buried? It doesn't make any more sense now than when we went on those drunken cemetery-crawls when we were kids. Stupid then, stupid now. And we're not kids anymore."

"Maybe not," Oliver replied. "But we're not looking for ghosts tonight."

"I thought you said that's why we're here."

"You didn't tell her?" Oliver said to Elijah.

Elijah shook his head. "Thought I'd leave the honor to you." Oliver smiled.

"Well, what is it?" Stephanie asked.

Oliver cleared his throat. "There's a special grave on the other side of the cemetery."

Stephanie peered through the gate's bars. "What makes it special?"

Oliver gazed at her, his eyes catching a glimmer of the moon. "What's buried there," he said.

"Enough with the bullshit, Oliver. Just spit it out. What is it?"

"A vampire," Oliver said in what he must have thought was a spooky voice.

Stephanie rolled her eyes. "A vampire? You don't really believe that, do you?"

"I do," Oliver paused. "And it's where Brock went missing. Where they found all that blood."

The headline burned bright in Stephanie's mind and she felt her insides lurch. They went to high school with Brock five years ago. They'd all partied together. Skinny-dipped at the lake. Rolled houses with TP. Even got wasted in a cemetery or two. Stephanie actually dated Brock for a while sophomore year. And now he was missing. They found his red Mustang in the cemetery parking lot and buckets of his blood spilled over some grave. The current theory was that he had been exsanguinated. Stephanie hadn't even known what the word meant until she Googled it.

The act of draining a person of blood.

But they never found a body. He might still be alive. And, according to Oliver, there was a chance they could find some answers.

"I read the article, Oliver. They didn't say which grave

it was."

"Theodore Glava's grave. The Transylvania Vampire. It's all over Facebook."

"And how are we supposed to find it? You wanna check every tombstone? That'll take all night." Stephanie looked at Elijah. "And we *aren't* staying here all night."

"Tell her," Elijah said, his face distorted in shadow and moonlight.

Oliver gazed at the numerous headstones beyond the gate. "There's a tree growing out of his grave. It sprouted from the stake driven through Glava's heart."

A gust of wind scattered leaves over Stephanie's feet, as if the cemetery itself had taken a deep breath.

"Well, that's not entirely true," Elijah said. "Rumor has it, the stake just grazed his heart. Didn't kill him, but did enough damage to keep him trapped down there."

"Yep," Oliver agreed. "He's supposedly still alive, whispering to those who'll listen."

"You two are idiots," Stephanie said. Elijah shrugged. "I guess we'll find out."

"They say Glava flows through the tree. From its roots all the way to its branches. If you get too close," Oliver clenched his fingers, "he'll snatch you up!"

Elijah chuckled and gave Oliver a friendly slap on the back. "Yeah, and apparently people have been coming here for years, offering animal sacrifices. They say once enough blood has been spilled, Glava will rise again. But, far as anyone knows, Brock was the first person ever murdered at the gravesite."

"If you're trying to scare me, it's not working. And Brock is missing. We don't know if he was murdered," Stephanie said and wrung her hands around the bars, ready to move the conversation away from Brock. "How do you even know Glava's from Transylvania?"

"His tombstone says so," Oliver said.

Elijah let out an excited giggle. "This is so creepy-cool! I can't wait to see it." He rubbed Stephanie's belly as if to coax a genie from the bottle. "Good training for our little Halloween guy."

"Please stop saying *guy*," Stephanie said and stepped away from the gate. "You know that bothers me."

They didn't know the sex of the baby, but Elijah always referred to it in the masculine. He never said *boy*, but used terms like *dude, guy,* and *little man.* Just to spite him, Stephanie wanted a girl. She should be happy one way or the other, but Elijah had taken all the fun out of the surprise. And now, after seeing the news, she was craving an Ambien cocktail more than ever.

"And anyway," she added, "why is any of this fun to you two? Brock's missing, and you're treating this like Disney's Haunted Mansion ride."

"Why are you so grouchy?" Elijah said. "Brock was a dick. He cheated on you back in high school, remember?"

Stephanie ran her hands along her arms, warming herself. "We shouldn't be here. It's cold and depressing and pointless. And that MVP thing isn't going to pick up anything other than whatever the two of you are planning to say under your breath."

"EVP," Oliver corrected. "Electronic Voice Phenomena. Picks up sounds made by the supernatural. But we'll start with an EMF meter, which measures fluctuation in electromagnetic fields."

"Like the PKE Meter in *Ghostbusters*," Elijah said.

"Exactly." Oliver removed the object from his jacket pocket. Stephanie thought it looked like a cellphone from the 90s. "If we detect something, we'll try to communicate."

Elijah pushed open the cemetery gates and they slipped through. The moment she passed beyond the safety of the parking lot, Stephanie was certain she didn't want to be there. She took a deep breath and held it, then slowly exhaled. This calmed her until the baby kicked again.

The orange glow of nearby streetlamps lit the area around the small cemetery, but inside, the only light guiding them came from the slivered moon. Stephanie pulled out her iPhone and noticed that she had no service. It really was a dead zone. She thumbed the flashlight app to life. The light swept over tombstones, some etched and weather-worn with age, others slick and gleaming like a polished coffin. All of them had names unknown to Stephanie, though she expected at any moment to read a familiar one, perhaps a distant relative who'd settled here before she was born.

Stephanie followed Oliver and Elijah to the middle of the cemetery through a copse of twisted trees, each of them decades old. Barren, bony limbs cut sharp silhouettes in the moonlight, and their fallen leaves crunched beneath Stephanie's shoes.

"Well, Oliver, it doesn't look like any of these trees are growing out of graves, now does it?" she said.

"This way," he said.

Elijah spoke just above a whisper, "Come on, Steph. Let's try to have a little fun tonight, okay?"

"Fun?" Stephanie said with a heavy sigh and picked up her pace, gaining some distance from Elijah. "How can you consider any of this fun? Our friend is missing."

"*Your* friend," he said. "I haven't seen Brock in forever."

Maybe Elijah was right, Stephanie realized. Maybe it was best that Brock was gone. Better if he never came back.

The baby kicked again.

"Here," Oliver said. They stopped at a small burial plot tucked into one of the cemetery's many corners. The light offered by the moon's crescent was just enough to see what lay before them: a large tree sprouting from the grave, casting tangled shadows over a small headstone that sunk several inches into the earth.

Stephanie squinted at the letters carved onto the surface of the stone marker and moved closer for a better look, stepping into a mound of mud at the base of the tree.

"Goddammit," she said and jumped back, scrubbing her shoes in the grass.

Elijah turned on his phone's light and shined it at the headstone.

"Theodore Glava. Born in Transylvania. Died December, 1918." He moved the light over the grave.

"What the fuck?" Oliver said. "What is that?"

Oliver pointed at Stephanie's shoe print in the mud.

"Holy shit," Elijah said.

A red liquid oozed from the grave, pooling in the shoe print.

Oliver turned on his own pocket flashlight and dipped a finger in the liquid, holding it inches from his face. "This is blood."

"Don't fuck around," Stephanie said. "Is this some kind of a joke? Did you guys do this?"

"No," Elijah whispered. "I swear."

Stephanie felt a surge of nausea rising in her throat, but she fought it back down.

"Do you think it's Brock's blood?" Oliver said.

Stephanie knew enough to know it wasn't blood bubbling up from the ground, but maybe this really was left over from the crime scene. Was that possible? Wouldn't the police have it cleaned up? Wouldn't it have soaked into the ground or dried up by now?

"I've had enough of this. I'm going back to the car." Stephanie turned, but before she had a chance to leave, Oliver held up the EMF meter.

"Hold on," he said. "Just let me see if there's a reading."

As much as she wanted to go, Stephanie knew they wouldn't budge until they had their results.

Oliver scanned the area with the EMF meter, and Stephanie thought he looked like some geek at a Star Trek convention. Yet her anxiety was persistent, and her mouth watered with nausea.

Little red and yellow squares flashed on the device, but it didn't make a sound.

"Anything?" Elijah asked. Stephanie could hear the goddamn schoolkid-excitement in his voice, as if all this death was nothing more than a playground diversion.

"Maybe," Oliver said. "I don't usually get a signal on the first try, but I'm definitely picking something up." He turned slowly in a circle, raising and lowering his arms a few inches as he did.

"Meaning what?" Stephanie said.

"Maybe nothing. Could be interference. Could be noise pollution. Wait here."

Oliver walked into the distance until his shape disappeared in the shadows. He returned only a minute later, but it was a long, lonely minute, even though (or perhaps *because*) Elijah stood next to Stephanie the entire time.

Oliver held the device up, and again red and yellow lights danced on the display.

"There was nothing over there, so that rules out interference or noise pollution."

"So now what?"

"Now we walk a little, see if the signal is stronger anywhere else."

The baby kicked again, this time hard enough to take Stephanie's breath away.

"What is it?" Elijah asked.

She rubbed her stomach. "Just another kick."

Elijah placed his hand on her shoulder and Stephanie almost recoiled at his touch. "I'm telling you, little guy's gonna be a soccer player."

"Jesus, Eli, would you just *stop*?"

"What's your problem tonight?" Elijah said.

Stephanie couldn't clearly see his face in the dark, but she could in her mind. Narrowed eyes, bunched eyebrows, cheeks tightened in annoyance.

"Maybe it's being eight-and-a-half months pregnant in the middle of a fucking cemetery at midnight."

"I thought you wanted to have fun."

"Being surrounded by dead bodies and bleeding graves isn't my idea of fun. It's yours."

He started to say something but stopped. He'd done that more and more lately. A year ago, he would have kept arguing, told her how much she'd always loved Halloween and the macabre. But lately he dropped arguments quickly. He said Stephanie was more irrational since she was pregnant. Arguing had become pointless.

As she turned away from Elijah, the article flashed in her mind again, as it had with maddening regularity all day. Brock's face on *The Denver Post* website. His deep-blue eyes, his full lips drawn into a tight, dry line, traces of a smile. The same look he gave her at the high school reunion earlier this year.

That stupid fucking reunion.

She followed Oliver, who picked his way through tombstones and tree limbs in search of something otherworldly. What was once the aroma of moist earth now seemed more like decay, the rot of everything around her. Elijah trudged behind, grumbling under his breath, probably something like *shouldn't have brought you*. She couldn't agree more. He was right—a year ago, she would have loved this, and five years ago Brock would have been right here with them.

But it wasn't five years ago, and even last year seemed like the distant past. She couldn't go back, none of them could. The lives they led then, and the futures they hoped for, were gone.

"Okay, let's try this again." Oliver lifted the device once more, but the red and yellow lights were gone now. "Nothing," he said, then continued on through the grave markers.

They repeated this exercise three times, and each indication of something supernatural was weaker than the last. They circled back until the lights flashed and danced at Glava's sinking, lopsided headstone. Oliver stood next to Stephanie's bloody shoeprint and said it was time to use the EVP recorder. Time to stop looking and start listening.

The nausea surged, and Stephanie fought to hold it down. "Okay, it's recording, so we need to be totally quiet." *I'll try not to puke*, Stephanie thought. She was well past the point of morning sickness. This nausea rippled from a horrible reality.

They stood in silence, the weight of the night cocooning them. Other than the cars in the distance and the gentle rattle of leaves in the wind, her world was devoid of noise, and because she could hardly see anything, she was left with what existed in her mind, and that was the last thing she wanted to be alone with.

It was at that moment the terrible thought came. The same thought she had months ago.

Kill the baby.

Those three chilling words struck her and began looping in her mind, a soundtrack in the back of her brain.

"I'm going to play it back now," Oliver said, pulling Stephanie into the moment. The thought was still there, but it faded a bit, relaxing its grip on her mind.

Elijah shuffled his weight back and forth with nervous excitement.

Oliver played the recording of the past minute or two, thumbing the volume so what emitted was the faint, static hiss of background noise. Amplified silence. Stephanie heard the traffic on Baseline Road, the rustling of leaves in the cemetery. But then, after a long lull, there was one other sound on the recording. Two seconds of noise, just before the recording ended.

It sounded like a voice. A voice whispering nonsense: *Feedeetee.*

Sounds like baby talk, Stephanie thought.

"Holy shit!" Elijah said. "What the fuck was that?"

"Hold on, let me play it back."

Oliver restarted the recording about five seconds from the end.

Feedeetee.

Stephanie gasped and placed a hand over her belly as the baby kicked harder than ever.

"Again," Elijah said. "Play it again. I can almost make it out."

"This is amazing. Clearer than anything I've ever picked up," Oliver said.

Stephanie turned away as Oliver played it once more. Even in the darkness, she knew she couldn't hide the horror on her face. Stephanie braced herself for the words. Even the baby stilled for a moment, as if straining to listen through her belly. Then the voice came, garbled and spongy, like it was speaking through mud.

Feedeetee.

The baby went into a frenzy, and it seemed like her stomach had turned into a nest of hornets. A million stings inside her, each one injecting more poison than the last.

Stephanie screamed and dropped to one knee. The

moisture from the ground spread into her jeans like blood.

Elijah rushed to her. "What's wrong?"

"The baby. I-I have to get out of here."

Stephanie stood up and Oliver lifted the EMF meter toward her. The red and yellow lights danced faster.

"There's something here," he said. He took a step toward Stephanie and lowered the EMF meter to her belly. "Right *here.*"

"Knock it off, man," Elijah said.

Oliver hit record on the EVP device and Stephanie slapped it from his hands. It landed with a thud at the base of Glava's headstone.

"Hey, that was expensive!"

Elijah put a hand on Stephanie's shoulder but she swatted him away, the most aggressive gesture she'd ever made in their relationship. "Don't touch me!"

Elijah's voice registered not anger, but deep concern. "I'm sorry, Steph. I...I guess I didn't realize how upsetting this was to you."

"Of course, it's upsetting! This is the place where he went missing. Where Brock was probably killed."

If only he knew, she thought. If only he knew how much closer she'd been to Brock than just an old high school friend.

Another kick.

Oliver walked to the headstone to retrieve the device while Elijah tried to console her. Stephanie felt something inside her tear open. She screamed as loud as her lungs would allow. Screamed louder than she ever had in her life. Screamed in pain and rage and at the fucking inability to rewind time, to make different decisions, to have a normal, happy life with a normal, happy family.

"Oh my God," Elijah said and yanked off his jacket. He put it on the ground next to the tree sprouting from the grave and told Stephanie to sit down.

For a moment, Stephanie thought she felt the earth rumble beneath her. But that sensation was soon replaced by pain, one so profound she had no voice to even scream against it.

The ground was soft, comfortable even, and through the pain she remembered the blood she stepped in. This cemetery, this exact spot where Glava was buried and where Brock went missing, was an open, festering, bloody wound.

"Oliver, the fire department's a block away." Elijah jabbed his finger to the west. "Get help."

But Oliver didn't seem to hear him. He held his equipment out and walked closer to Stephanie, mesmerized by the kinetic, dancing lights.

"I've never seen anything like this," he said.

Stephanie drifted into a place where pain and fear were softly numbed by some kind of acceptance. She couldn't define it, but it felt a great deal like a night of pills and vodka.

Oliver leaned down to her, his arm outstretched, gripping the recorder, holding the microphone steady.

Stephanie felt the ground shift again. Loose soil. Heavy stench of rot.

She held her hand up to Elijah's face and looked at him in the moonlight. He looked as he had before all of this shit started. Simple, cute, innocent. He didn't deserve any of this. She had to tell him.

"Eli," she said, fighting through the agony boiling inside her. "Eli, you need to know something. The baby... the baby isn't yours."

He pulled away and her hand fell from his face. "What?" "At the reunion...I was with...I was with Brock."

Stephanie turned her head in shame. There was nothing else to say. No further explanation needed. No excuses.

Elijah stood. "You're in shock. You don't know what you're saying."

She shook her head. "No, it's true. I'm so sorry."

"Holy shit..." Oliver whispered.

Elijah's words were tight and fierce, "I'm going for help," he said. "And when this is over, we're done. Oliver, stay with her until I get back."

Stephanie felt the ground shake as Elijah ran through the cemetery, weaving around the silhouettes of trees and tombstones, until he was gone. She thought she felt Brock's presence as soon as Elijah left. And in a way, he *was* here, inside of her, his blood coursing through the veins and arteries of their child. A baby that now felt as if it was trying to claw its way out of her.

Oliver stood motionless.

"Play it back," she told him. "Whatever you just recorded, play it back."

Oliver fumbled with the device, but finally managed to play the recording.

She heard a voice. Different than before, but familiar.

It was Brock's voice, and it played clearly through the recorder: *I woke it up.*

Oliver shrieked and dropped the EVP recorder. He stumbled back and tripped over a headstone, cracking his skull on another.

"Oliver? Oliver, are you alright?"

He didn't answer.

Stephanie closed her eyes and listened to the rest of the recording until it ended.

The earth shifted and she felt the coolness of freshly turned soil on each side of her. She tried to move, but the pain scorching her insides kept her down.

Rough, icy fingers like the brittle twigs on a branch tugged at her pants, pulling them off. She was naked from the waist down now, but she wasn't cold. Heat seared through her lower body, and she felt herself widen to the crowning of the baby's head. She breathed through the pain.

Brock's voice, now low and guttural, spoke to Stephanie again, but this time it wasn't through the recorder.

Feed the tree, he said. *We have to feed the tree.*

Not baby talk at all.

The fingers were on her, pulling the baby from her body. A hard tug tore the child free and the sounds of new life echoed through the cemetery. For a brief moment, relief washed over Stephanie. The child's cries gave her a sense of accomplishment. She'd struggled and suffered through the entire pregnancy, often unsure if she'd make it to the end. And now she finally had. But as soon as the cries began, they became muffled and distant.

Stephanie fought against the pain and forced herself to sit up. She looked down and saw the fingers that delivered the child weren't fingers at all, but roots reaching out from Glava's grave, taking her child into the ground.

"My baby!"

No. Not yours, Brock said as Alexa was pulled down into the fetid earth to join him.

We are Glava's family now. And family feeds the tree.

Joshua Viola is a three-time Colorado Book Award finalist and co-author of the Denver Moon series. His comic book collection, Denver Moon: Metamorphosis, was included on the 2018 Bram Stoker Award Preliminary Ballot for Superior Achievement in a Graphic Novel. He edited the #1 Denver Post bestselling anthology, Nightmares

Unhinged and co-edited Cyber World—named one of the best science fiction anthologies of 2016 by Barnes & Noble. His fiction has appeared in numerous anthologies, including D.O.A. III – Extreme Horror (Blood Bound Books), Doorbells at Dusk (Corpus Press), and Found (RMFW Press), and has been reprinted by Tor.com. He is the owner and chief editor of Hex Publishers in Erie, Colorado.

Carter Wilson is the USA Today and #1 Denver Post bestselling author of six critically acclaimed, standalone psychological thrillers, as well as numerous short stories. He is an ITW Thriller Award finalist, a three-time winner of the Colorado Book Award, and his novels have received multiple starred reviews from Publishers Weekly, Booklist, and Library Journal. His latest novel, The Dead Girl in 2A, was released in July 2019 from Poisoned Pen Press. Carter lives in Erie, Colorado in a Victorian house that is spooky but isn't haunted...yet.

THERE IS SOMETHING UP THERE

Joy Yehle

"I knew that tour company was asking for trouble opening that third mine," he said. "There's a damn good reason there are no trails, and nobody goes there. Listen to me, girl, there's lots of people who went to that area and never came home. There's something up there."

My elderly neighbor had insisted I come over to his place after he saw me packing up my SUV and found out I might have to go to the backside of Guanella Pass. I thought maybe he had maps or something; this was totally unexpected. I held a bulky scrapbook of newspaper clippings dating back many decades, all about hikers, fishermen, and hunters who had gone into this particular area never to return.

"When I was a boy, my dad took me hunting up there. We had our dog, Daisy, with us. Something crashed into our camp the first night, grabbed Daisy and ran off with her. I only caught a glimpse of it, but the sound it made," he shook his head. "It screeched like the devil himself. Poor Daisy, I ain't never heard a dog yelp like that. We never found any sign of her. I spent the rest of my life looking for proof of what we seen that night."

I'd lived next door to this man for two years. When I first moved here, he befriended me right off. It was obvious that I was in a bad way, my arm was in a cast, and both eyes were still bruised. He never pried and had always been straight with me, so I tried to listen with an open mind.

My phone vibrated, and I checked the message. "Look, Mr. Kleland, I appreciate the heads up, but I've got a job to do, and I have to go." I put on my Silver Plume Search and Rescue cap and pulled my ponytail out of the opening in the back. The 'standby' call had just turned into a 'call out'.

He nodded solemnly. "Hang on a second." He stood up and rummaged around in a desk in the dining room. When he came back, he held his hands out to me. "Take this. Please. For me."

I took the ivory handle jutting out of the deerskin sheath. The long blade that followed shimmered in the light and made me think of a miniaturized sword that might have belonged to a medieval knight.

"Um, OK, Mr. Kleland. Thanks?" I said.

"You keep that close, Lilly!"

I rushed home and finished loading my gear into the back of my SUV. The knife Mr. Kleland had given me sat on the rear bumper. I glanced over and saw him standing on the porch of his house. Slipping the weapon into my rucksack, I held it up to him. He nodded with approval.

I whistled, and eighty pounds of German Shepherd goofball came galloping around the house and leaped into the back of the SUV. His tail swatted everything in reach, his ears twitching excitedly. He knew we were going to play the *Find It* game.

I rubbed his big ears. "Let's go, Pulaski. We got work to do."

There were only three things my town was known for: fishing, perfectly restored Victorian houses, and the narrow-gauge railroad. Colorado Train Tours ran restored steam trains along a fifteen-mile loop through the mountains. Tourists could get off mid-way, have lunch, and tour two silver mines left over from the 1800s.

What I knew of the current situation was that a crew had hiked up from that location to a new site that the company wanted to open. They were tasked with breaking a trail so that folks looking for a little more adventure could backpack in, camp overnight, and explore a newly discovered mine. It was a primitive and rugged area, and one of the crew had gone missing.

A staging area had been set up at the boarding platform just minutes from my front door. When we got there, I put Pulaski into his harness and clipped on the leash. He'd work off-leash but not until we hiked to where the tracking dogs lost the trail. Air scent dogs are trained to find general human scent carried through the air, unlike trail dogs that follow a particular scent.

We walked to a canopy tent where several rescuers, sheriff's deputies, and other volunteers hovered over a table spread with maps.

When I commanded him, Pulaski sat, but he protested with a whine. He was ready to play. I shook hands all around and met Mason, the leader of the trail crew. He looked a few shades paler than healthy, and his eyes were red as if he'd been crying.

"TJ is the only female on the crew," Mason explained. "We hiked all day the day before, we'd been digging and chopping for a few hours. I sent her ahead to check out the terrain, you know, so she'd get a little break without the guys giving her a hard time. Goddamit!" He suddenly exploded with emotion. "Why did I let her go alone!"

Pulaski twitched at the raised voice and looked up at

me to see if he should be worried. I rubbed his ears, and he settled down.

"It's all right, Mason. Just finish," a man in a deputy's uniform said.

"So, I send TJ ahead, she was barely out of sight when we heard a howl or a screech coming from her direction. It wasn't like anything I'd ever heard before." He lifted a water bottle to his mouth, and it splashed on his chin because his hands were shaking.

"Was it her?" I asked.

He shook his head vigorously. "No! It was some animal. I only caught sight of it for a second."

I looked into the faces of the others. I wasn't sure where this was going, but if we were tracking a predator, that changed things for my dog and me. "I'm sorry. If you guys called us out to track a mountain lion or something that's not what we do," I said.

"Let him finish. If you and your dog can't work it, fine," the deputy said.

"I only saw it for a second—from behind, but I could see it was massive and covered in hair," he squeezed his eyes shut for a second as if it would force the memory into focus. "It was standing upright on its hind legs! TJ was hanging over its shoulder like a too long scarf. She lifted her head and looked right at me." He pointed two fingers at his eyes. "She said 'help me.' Only I couldn't because the thing moved way too fast. I tried to run after them, I swear," his voice cracked and his shoulders slumped.

"It's OK, Mason," the deputy said. "Go sit down for a minute." Once Mason was led away to the tailgate of a truck, the deputy turned to me. "I don't know what happened. Couldn't be a bear. I mean what kind of bear throws a person over their shoulder and runs? Has to be a person. What do you think?"

"Maybe he misidentified a bear or mountain lion in

the panic of the moment," I offered.

"Still. Over his shoulder? Has to be a person," the deputy said.

Mr. Kleland's warning echoed in my memory, and I considered going home. This was either an animal or a criminal of some sort. I was good with lost people. Killer predators and bad guys, not so much.

Against my family's advice, I moved to the big city of Denver from the small mountain town where I grew up. I thought it would be exciting. I was there less than six months when I came home and found two guys robbing my place. I didn't fight back; I was too scared. They broke my arm, my nose, sexually assaulted me, and took my belongings. The victim's advocate told me that not fighting back probably saved my life, but I'll never know because they'd never been caught. I moved back to the mountains within days.

I didn't move back to my hometown, though. She didn't come right out and say it, but I heard the 'I told you so' loud and clear when I told my mom what happened. I can't say I was surprised, she'd never been particularly warm and supportive. Neither of us made much effort to connect since. It was sad to think only real family had four paws.

"Pulaski is big, but he doesn't attack. What if it is a man and he has other ideas for us? Or hurts my dog before we reach him? And if it is an animal, we don't track predators," I debated.

"You'll be tracking the girl, and you're not going alone," the deputy said, tapping his sidearm. "But it is a risk."

I looked down at the search sheet for the girl. *TJ Wilson, 22, 5'3", 115 lbs., brown hair, green eyes, dark blue hoodie, jeans, and black work boots.* Something familiar stirred in my heart, something I knew was just magical thinking, but it made sense to me. Coming to someone else's rescue would somehow make up for the fact that I failed to come to my own rescue when I was attacked. It was the main reason I started working search and rescue shortly after my ordeal.

I looked at Pulaski. All his muscles strained against his skin, his nose already sniffing at the air, he was ready. I certainly wouldn't be alone.

"What do you think, Pulaski?" He wagged his tail and he made a soft woofing sound with his cheeks. "OK, we're in," I said.

We had to ride the train to the mine stop and hike to where TJ was last seen. I stuffed my rucksack into my overnight backpack and checked to be sure I had enough food and water for us both.

I thought Pulaski would be freaked out by the noisy chugging train, but he hung his massive head over the side of the open car letting his tongue flap in the wind. We'd never done a search like this before, and I was more than a little nervous. Pulaski seemed to understand my thoughts and pulled his massive head in long enough to lick my hand.

Deputy Switzer from the command post, Ethan and Dan from Search and Rescue, and a Jackson with the train company were going to hike up with us. Several others would set up a base camp at the train stop.

When we got there and unloaded, I gave Pulaski some water. I slipped on my pack, and we started our ascent. The trail started easy enough, the ponderosa pines and Douglas firs were a comfortable distance from each other. The biggest obstacle was the knee-high grass.

It was only an hour long hike to the place where the crew had been working. The scattered tools corroborated Mason's story of panic and chaos. We went a few yards farther and found an area where the brush was matted down, and branches hung broken from several trees.

"Mason said the guy carried her off to the north-east," Deputy Switzer said, pointing with two fingers on an outstretched arm, as if he were directing traffic.

We proceeded in that direction and could tell by the damaged foliage that something big rumbled through. We walked until the growth thinned out and signs of the culprit became difficult to see.

"Time for my boy to do his thing," I said, bending down and touching Pulaski's forehead to mine. "OK, buddy, let's play. Find it!" He wagged his tail and pranced excitedly. I took his leash off, and he darted ahead, disappearing into the willows.

Jackson looked shocked. "Won't he get lost?"

I shook my head. "No. This is how we do it. He'll try to find the scent and will keep checking in with me. Just make sure you stay behind him. I don't want him to scent on one of us."

As if on cue, Pulaski bounded out of the bushes and yipped, then turned and darted back the way he had come.

"This way," I said, and we followed him deeper into the woods.

It was as if nature was trying to keep us from going any further. Trees, bushes, and boulder fields slowed our progress to a crawl. The change in terrain had little effect on Pulaski. I could hear him just ahead of us giving an occasional, excited yip. We walked single file with Dan leading the way. I bumped into his back when he suddenly stopped. A hard lump under his jacket told me Switzer wasn't the only one carrying a gun.

"Listen," Dan said as he stood stock still, scanning the surrounding trees with his eyes.

I listened. There was nothing at first until I heard the distinct sound of something hitting the ground directly behind me. I spun but didn't see anything, then a small barrage of stones rained down on us from the direction we had just come.

Deputy Switzer leveled his rifle and swung it back and forth, but the trees were so thick there was no way to see anything.

My thoughts jumped to Pulaski. Again, as if he could read my mind, he appeared just to the left of us, tail wagging.

"Come!" I commanded, he immediately came to me and sat on my feet.

We all stood still, listening and scanning the trees.

After several moments of nothing, Deputy Switzer hung his rifle from his shoulder again. "Stay sharp," he ordered, and he started to walk in the direction that the rocks had come from.

"Hang on. Pulaski alerted that way," I said pointing the direction we'd been going.

"I'm going this way. You guys follow the dog," Deputy Switzer said. "I'll go a couple miles. If I don't find anything, I'll follow behind you and meet up at the crew's camp."

We watched the deputy disappear into the woods. I commanded Pulaski to "find it," and he dashed off with gleeful abandon. I wanted to find this girl and get the hell off this mountain.

After more grueling terrain we finally came to the remnants of the crew's overnight camp. Everything stood in disarray. Not one tent stood, and all their gear had been thrown around as if someone had rummaged through it.

"We should let Switzer know we got here," Dan said.

"Yeah, I think you're right," Jackson agreed.

A stench like rotting meat and skunk spray wafted over us.

"Holy crap! What is that?" Ethan asked, pinching his nose shut.

Jackson unclipped his walkie. "Switzer?"

Static answered.

He pressed the button harder as if it would help. "This is Jackson. Switzer, do you read?"

The walkie cracked to life. "Switzer here. What's up?"

"Where are you?"

"I'm about two miles from where I left you. Why?" Switzer said.

"We just got to the camp, and it smells like something is dead up here."

We all startled when the bushes, layers into the forest, rustled. I expected Pulaski to come bounding into the clearing, but he didn't. The vegetation moved again. Not the small swish of a deer or dog, but a pull-it-out-by-the-roots shake. I sucked in my breath.

"What the hell?" Ethan exclaimed. "Is that the dog?"

Before I could answer, it stopped.

"That sounds like something big," Dan said, and he reached into the small of his back and pulled out a small sleek handgun.

"Hey!" I shouted. "Put that away! I don't want you to accidentally shoot my dog!"

He dropped his hand to his thigh, his finger not on the trigger, but the weapon still in his hand.

"Look!" Ethan said as he pointed off into the distance.

I scanned the woods around us. Far off, some birds were screeching a warning to each other, but other than that it was silent.

"The treetops," Ethan specified.

Then I saw it. The tops of the tallest pine trees, about two hundred yards from us, were swaying as if something huge was pushing between them.

"Whatever it is, it's moving away from us," Dan said.

Before we could breathe, the bushes behind us rustled again and we all turned, ready for the devil himself.

Pulaski bounded out and came right to me.

"Good boy!" I gushed and rubbed his neck.

"Let's take five and then get back on it," Dan said.

Jackson radioed Switzer to let him know our plan. Switzer hadn't seen anything but had met up with a group of law enforcement that was searching behind us. They'd try and meet up with us before dark. The terrible odor was gone, but Switzer warned us not to touch anything more than necessary.

"We need to get going. Let's not spend the night up here, huh?" Ethan said.

We all wholeheartedly agreed and hiked again in the direction that Pulaski was set on. Once we were far enough away from the camp, I reluctantly unhooked his leash.

"Be safe, buddy. Now, find it!"

He pranced off blissfully unaware of how uneasy I was becoming.

We followed Pulaski for about an hour. I knew he was onto something by the way he stopped and sniffed the air and then darted off again and again. Abruptly he froze, and so did I. His nostrils flaring and his chest heaving more than before. Relief flooded me, and I was sure he'd found her. He took off at a full run, I was about to go after him when a volley of rocks crashed down on me.

I ducked, covering my head. A large stone crashed into my middle back, and I yelped. As quickly as it happened, it quit. Taking quick stock of my body, I was glad to find that my only injury seemed to be my back.

I turned back to the rest of the group and saw Dan down on one knee clutching the side of his head, blood oozing from between his fingers.

"Dan!" I shouted as I ran to him.

Before I could even begin to evaluate him, an ear-splitting guttural screech pierced the air. My heart pounded in my ears, and my veins swelled with adrenaline.

"What the fuck was that?" Jackson cried, his eyes as wide as saucers.

Dan opened his mouth, but no sound came out. The others were shouting, but I couldn't make sense of it. A dark figure entered my peripheral vision, and a giant hairy hand shot out and covered Dan's face. There was a cracking sound like dry twigs being broken up for kindling and Dan collapsed.

I stared at Dan's face, trying to understand what was happening, but then something hit me. Something big. I was suddenly aware that I was moving fast, and the wind was knocked out of me.

Bent at the waist, draped over a broad shoulder, my face was bouncing into long red-brown foul hair, *or was it fur*? I could see the rugged terrain streaming past me. My backpack slid onto the back of my head, but not off, the weight of it pushing my face into the inhuman bristle. The thing let out a terrifying roar, and my grip on reality and consciousness began to slip away. My last thought before the darkness took me was of Pulaski and the way his warm tongue felt on my hand.

I came to on the ground just inside a mine opening. This mine had long ago collapsed, and I was only about seven feet into the tunnel. The sun was creating predawn shadows, and birds were beginning to welcome the new day. The stench of the thing clung to me and made me gag and choke, bringing back the reality that couldn't be happening.

The creature hadn't killed me, and maybe I still had a chance of getting out of this alive, but I didn't know where my dog was. A pang of sorrow stabbed me in the gut at the thought of never seeing his beautiful face or feeling his soft fur again. I squeezed my eyes shut. If I was going to have any hope of surviving this, I could not afford to lose it.

When I opened my eyes again, I noticed the figure of a person pressed against the rock wall, curled into a fetal position.

"TJ?" I whispered.

A pale face with wide green eyes turned to look at me. She had a deep gash across her forehead, her blood dried a rusty brown.

"Oh my God! I thought you were dead!" TJ said.

I shook my head, "Not yet. We have to get out of here before it comes back. Can you walk?"

TJ turned slowly on her hip to sitting position. "It doesn't matter."

"Let me get my bearings, OK?" I had no idea where we were or how far the thing had carried me.

"Don't you know what it is? We can't outrun it!" TJ's voice was shrill. She was on the edge of hysteria.

"TJ, I need you to take a deep breath. I'm Lilly, I'm with Silver Feather Search and Rescue; we're going to get out of this."

"You're doing a great job on the rescue part," she spat. "It's a freaking Bigfoot for fuck's sake! Did you hear me? Bigfoot!"

I held my hand up to her, "Sh, sh! It's just a man! Deputy Switzer said so!" Now I felt close to hysterics. "There's no such thing as Bigfoot!" I said, my voice shaking despite my efforts to keep calm.

As if to answer me, a low growl rumbled from behind me. I turned slowly; every system in my body on red alert. A massive dark figure crouched only a few feet from me in the shadows. It leaned forward. Dark brown eyes glinting with intelligence stared into mine from a gray, wrinkled face. It wasn't a human face nor that of an ape, but something in between, something impossible. Fear paralyzed me, but my brain started flipping through every data file on board trying to make sense of it.

"It can't be," I whispered.

Its giant mouth opened to reveal sharp fangs, and it screeched at me. I gagged, its breath was a rancid mix of feces and putrefied meat. Propelled by pure terror, I scrambled on all fours out of the mine entrance and into the small clearing. It crawled after me and crouched only a few inches from me.

I began to cry, and my body went into an uncontrollable trembling. It moved toward me. It reached out a long arm to my face, and I let out a banshee cry from my very soul. I heard TJ whimpering, and I was sorrowful that this was how our lives would end.

Without warning, a blur of black and tan fur launched from the trees and a row of flashing white teeth sank into the outstretched hairy arm. The giant let out a yowl of pain. It stood to its full height of well over eight feet. My beloved Pulaski hung from the outstretched arm by his jaws.

Snapped out of my paralyzing fear, I scrambled backward. Pulaski making an unfamiliar and deadly snarling sound. The monster was grabbing at him with its free arm. Everything around me seemed to go into slow motion, but my mind was whirring. I realized I still had my backpack on and inside it was my rucksack, and God Bless him, the knife Mr. Kleland had given me.

I tore the pack off and yanked the nasty blade out. Holding it out in front of me like a battering ram, I let out a battle cry and charged the monster. Because of my height, the knife entered the Bigfoot's groin area. I lunged with everything I had, burying the blade up to the handle. I couldn't lie to myself any longer, it was Bigfoot.

It yowled and grabbed the back of my jacket with his dog-free arm and tossed me as easy as if it'd flick a fly. I hit the dirt and felt a dangerous shift in my ribcage, and I made a wheezing sound when I tried to get air back into my lungs.

Pulaski released the creature's arm and dropped back. He barked furiously and snapped at the creature, spittle and blood flying from his mouth. The Bigfoot screeched and yanked the knife from its body. Blood sprayed from the wound and I realized I must have hit an artery. It roared at me and then at Pulaski, then suddenly it darted into the trees, the ground shaking with its footsteps.

Pulaski hurried to me and licked my face. My tears and snot mixing with his saliva. I felt his body and legs with my hands as best I could; moving was excruciating. I almost fainted from relief to find nothing broken. There was some blood on his chin and around his mouth but I couldn't tell if it was from him or the creature.

I trembled, hearing a whimper behind me. I'd almost forgotten about TJ. I stood and tried to take a deep breath, but the sheering pain in my chest would not allow it. I gingerly moved to her. Pulaski was already licking her hand in an attempt to coax her to get up.

"We gotta go!" I gasped at her, and she stood up, as wobbly as a newborn fawn. I scooped up the knife and said, "Just in case."

TJ nodded.

"Pulaski, home!" I wheezed. He knew that meant to find my truck.

He wagged his tail, yipped at us and began to trot into the woods as if nothing had ever happened.

The going was slow. We drug each other along as best as we could. TJ did her utmost to keep moving, and I worked to not pass out. I tried to keep us concealed, and we stopped every so often and tried to listen for any noises that weren't us.

I couldn't tell how long we hobbled along like that. Maybe forever. Neither of us spoke. Physically, I could barely breathe, but it was dread and shock that stole our voices.

We reached the edge of a vast boulder field, and I hesitated. We'd be out in the open. I knew it wasn't logical, but I envisioned the beast leaping from rock to rock, and all hope of escape left me. It had to be dead, but that thing or more of its kind could be steps behind us for all I knew.

I pulled TJ down next to me in an attempt to hide and decide what to do. Thinking we were taking a break, Pulaski came back to us and laid down beside me, his mouth was still bleeding and I pulled my sleeve over the heel of my hand and wiped gently at his wound. It took everything in me not to weep.

My breath hitched when the air was split by what sounded like an ax hitting a tree somewhere near us.

"What was that?" TJ breathed.

I knew it was the creature or its kin. There was no outrunning it. Sweat ran in icy beads down my back.

"His name is Pulaski, like the ax. Hold his harness he'll pull you along," I said, bitter tears choking me.

TJ shook her head firmly. Pulaski whined at me as if he knew what I was planning.

"You have to get my dog out of here, please," I begged.

Again we heard the cracking sound, this time it sounded closer. We clutched each other. Pulaski sat up, his nostrils flaring. I was about to shout at TJ to run, but then I heard something else. The steady beating of helicopter blades.

Forgetting about the thing seeing her, TJ leaped onto a large boulder and began waving her arms. Pulaski yipped excitedly and nudged me with his nose. I squinted up at the sky and the bright orange rescue helicopter hovering overhead.

I shivered for a few moments, even though I wasn't cold. The motion didn't hurt my ribs thanks to the meds being pumped into me through the IV. I shifted my feet under the warm body of Pulaski, and he was so tired he didn't even stir. The hospital staff agreed to let him stay with me since he was a hero and all. The big dog was no worse for the wear over the ordeal. He had a cut on his chin that took several stitches but he'd heal.

The helicopter that found us was equipped with a thermal camera and only saw us because of our heat signatures. They reported seeing four other signatures not far from us. Law enforcement was searching the area for our kidnapper and Dan's murderer. I knew they wouldn't find anyone, not human anyway.

TJ, was down the hall for observation. She told our rescuers that a large man with a long beard had abducted us. Pulaski and I fought him, and he ran off.

"They'll never believe us," she whispered to me, and I knew she was right. "Lilly and that gorgeous dog saved me," she gushed.

The truth was, we saved each other.

When the nurse asked if there was anyone she could call for me, I gave her Mr. Kleland's phone number, so I wasn't surprised when he entered the room later. I needed to take care of this first, then I could deal with calling my mom. He had a handful of daisies wrapped in grocery store plastic. I pointed him to the chair next to my bed.

"I told you, girl." He reached out and patted my hand.

"My stuff is in that closet. Could you get it?" I asked.

He nodded and did as I asked.

I unrolled the bundle and pulled out the weapon he'd

given me. It's once pristine blade now stained brown with dried blood. His eyes grew wide.

"You were right," I said holding the knife out to him.

"Is this what I think it is? They said you stabbed it. Kicked its ass, I heard." His eyes sparkled with excitement.

"I don't know, but maybe you can have it tested or something and prove what's up there."

He leaned in and hugged me gently around the neck and left with the blade wrapped in his jacket. Pulaski lifted his head at the sound of the door closing.

"It's OK," I said, and despite what I knew we shared our world with, for the first time in a long time, it was.

He wagged his tail twice, plopped his head back down, and resumed his soft snoring.

Joy Yehle is a Colorado native and currently a Castle Rock based horror writer. Her mother was Native American/Hispanic and her dad was Scotch/Irish, so she grew up hearing folklore and otherworldly tales and have always been fascinated by such topics. She's been an IT professional and an educator, but next to being a mom, sharing her love of the darker things in life is her passion. Her first novel DREAD was published in October of 2016. Her short story "Yankee Sierra Seven" won Pandora's Box of Horror Dystopian Challenge and is now being worked into a series; one of many WIPs. She has a spooky photo of the Stanley Hotel published in Stanley Hotel, a Chilling Interactive Adventure by Allison Lassieur, published by Capstone publishing.

SCRAPE
Gary Robbe

An ever-present fog surrounds the house. I press my face and hands against the cool glass of the bedroom window, trying to see if there is any movement or sign of life within any holes in the fog. Disjointed memories flash inside my head. I have no control over them, when they come or how long they last. I don't know which ones are real, or not.

The old house is being scraped. Mom, Dad, Rachel and me standing by the curb on Downing Street watching the bulldozer close in for the first ceremonial punch to the bricks and wood structure. I like the old two-story house. It has many rooms, nooks and crannies, places to explore and hide, overwhelming smells of must and caked dust, hints of decay. It is extraordinarily empty. A perfect place for an eleven-year-old boy.

But Mom and Dad have other ideas. This house will come down, and a new house will go up. They only bought the place for the desirable land in a desirable neighborhood.

It's a hot summer day, no clouds in the sky, and although there are many trees on the street, all the ones on our property have already been taken down. The sun gleams off the yellow tractor until a plume of black smoke covers it. Dad coughs. Mom laughs. Rachel picks dandelions. I turn my attention to the house.

The reflection of a dark cloud crosses the second story window. But it's not a cloud. Something is moving inside the house. I glance around just to be sure. No planes, birds, giant insects, nothing. Maybe it's an optical illusion, or possibly a couple of workers doing last minute preps inside before the bulldozer makes contact.

I return to the window. And I see a figure, no, figures in the window. The figures are small, children, I guess, and I can barely make out faces resembling a boy and girl. Standing behind the window, with the light hitting it, makes them seem transparent. Unreal. The boy raises his hand.

I scream. That catches the attention of Dad, who quickly motions for the bulldozer to stop.

I shout over the rumbling, idling engine. "There's somebody in there!" Then point to where I can still see the vague, but undeniably human faces behind the glare streaking across the window.

Dad looks that way and squints. "I don't see anything," he says. He walks to the bulldozer where several workers mill about, says something to them, and all of them go into the house. I keep my eyes on the window until Dad appears, waving with a big grin on his face. Of course, the house is dead empty.

Six months later we are in our new house, a two-story box with transplanted trees and a rooftop deck. I can't remember a thing about the construction. We are simply there, inside, looking out new windows with the stickers still on them. All the furniture is new. It smells like a new house.

But that memory of the new house is brief. A tease.

I scratch the peeling window frame and wait for more holes in the fog to appear.

Dad screams downstairs. He has found Mom. He knows he is the one who stuffed her in the fireplace, a window of sanity, open for only a few moments, long enough for him to anguish and tear into his eyes and pound up the stairs to look for Rachel and me. He won't come into our rooms; he can't come into our rooms. The house stops him from that.

Is this happening now, or is this just another too real memory slice? I close my eyes. I see Dad, beneath the kitchen table, his head bashed in, Mom sitting down calm as can be with an empty cup before her as if she is pretending to have tea. A broken baseball bat on the floor next to her. When she looks up at us with those eyes that don't belong to her, Rachel and I run up the stairs to our rooms.

Eyes closed, or open, it doesn't matter. When a dream memory comes, I am there and it is real, however discordant, or *wrong* it may seem. I imagine time means nothing. I imagine there are multiple versions of me across all kinds of planes of existence, and that everything I remember, or dream, did happen. I've thought about this stuff. I am twelve. I am thirty- five. I am dead. I was never alive.

Did I grow up in the new house, leave for college, meet a sweet girl I fell in love with, marry and have kids, two of them, Delilah and Matthew? I have memories of those things, but I have never left this House, never once made it past the desolate yard and the fog that surrounds us.

Every now and then, when I stand at the window, I see glimpses of what might be the real world in the holes of the fog, and in between the memories I think there is a chance to escape and maybe meet the me on the other side.

The first night in the new house. Everyone is excited, especially Dad, who sees this as his finished project. Mom is everywhere at once, smiling and dancing and singing like she is on a honeymoon cruise.

Mom opens my closet door a dozen times. "I can't believe how much room you have in here," she says.

"It's not that big," I say. It's just a normal step in step out closet with a bar to hang clothes and a couple of wire shelves. Mom makes a big deal out of everything.

Then she disappears into the closet, closing the door, the room becomes very quiet as if she stepped into another world. She pops out like she is playing jack in the box entertaining a two-year old.

"Mom, stop, I'm not a baby."

Later I look in the closet. It seems even smaller than I remembered. I can't figure out how Mom, who is a big woman, could even fit in it. There's a musty smell too, something I hadn't noticed before. It reminds me of the original house that had been scraped to make room for this one. I step inside. Nothing strange. Boxes stacked to my chin, a few shirts and pants hanging on the wooden rod. Wait. The rod is supposed to be metal, not wood. And the wire shelves are gone, replaced by well- worn wood ones. This is the closet I popped into before the house was scraped. The house that is gone. Gone.

The door swings shut. Everything is pitch black.

"Damn it, Rachel!" I yell. I push the door, but something pushes back, something stronger than me. "Mom? Dad?" Whoever it is stays silent. Then, a faint scratching, starting at the bottom of the door, moving upward and getting louder. The scratching grows in intensity, as whatever it is digs its nails into the wood of the door. I back away, expecting to stumble into the boxes.

I don't.

I swing my arms around in panic. It's not a closet anymore. Whatever I am in is immense, my voice echoes as if I'm in a deep cavern. I run, but I'm not sure I'm running. I can't see. And I can't feel my feet strike the floor.

There is no memory of getting out.

"Do we know anything about the people that lived in the house?" Mom directs this at Dad, who is busy rolling spaghetti around his fork. It's taking all his concentration.

"What?" The question sinks in. "An old couple, I think, lived there for thirty or so years.

Don't know anything about anyone before them. The house is a hundred years old." He lights up.

He is proud to tear down something that old.

"I like it the way it is," I say.

"It does have character," Mom says.

"Ha! Character means it's a money pit. Besides, everyone is doing this in Denver.

Tearing down old wrecks and putting up new homes. Half the homes in Platt Park are scrapes.

We'll save money in the long run."

"I'd rather stay where we are. All my friends are there." We are living in an apartment in Golden. My school is in Golden. My friends are in Golden. I don't want to be in Denver, having to make new friends all over again. The thought of being in a new school makes me sick.

"Tomorrow's the big day," Dad says.

Rachel, wearing her spaghetti like mod jewelry, says, "What about the children who live there?"

"No one lives there, honey," Mom says. "It's our house now. It's been empty for years."

"I've seen them," Rachel says. "A little boy and girl. They play hide and seek."

Dad laughs. "Nobody is there. Maybe some of the kids in the neighborhood sneak in – damn dangerous thing to do. And Mom and I have always been there when you kids were there. We never saw or heard anything. Come on, eat. Forget this nonsense. When the new house is built you'll forget there ever was an old house on that spot."

In my new bed, in the new house, unable to sleep, staring at the ceiling. Faint light from the moon filters in through the curtains, enough to make out multiple stains, cracks and plaster folds in the ceiling. I imagine the stains taking on the shapes of snakes. I count them. Somewhere in the back of my mind there is an unsettling awareness that this is not the fresh smooth ceiling of a new house.

Two, three, four, a boa constrictor, there a western diamond back, coiled, big snakes, small snakes, seven, eight, nine... The diamond back uncoils. It slides effortlessly into a confluence of tangled snakes, all of them quivering and moving, bubbling from the ceiling as if they are about to drop.

I curl under a ball of sheets and covers and a squeal escapes from my mouth. No one hears it.

Dad stands at the front door with his briefcase in hand, befuddled, as if he can't understand why he's there. Mom comes from the kitchen and asks why he hasn't left yet, is everything all right? He tries to form words, but nothing comes out, his hand on the doorknob moving to his hair to figure things out. Mom tells Rachel and me to go upstairs and get ready for school.

The next thing, I'm in my room looking out my window, fog coating everything, and it's getting dark.

Mom stares at the ceiling and the peeling wallpaper, wallpaper that doesn't belong here in our new house. We are in the living room, except for Dad, who hasn't moved from his bed in a long time. She spins, slowly, counting the stains and the cracks and the plaster bubbles trying to convince herself that simple arithmetic will change everything back.

Her eyes grow wide and wild when I tell her about

the snakes on my ceiling coming alive.

She has seen them too.

Rachel sees and hears children all the time. She tells me about it, but won't tell Mom and Dad because she knows they'll get mad. They hide under her bed and in her closet, which is pretty small. She hears them playing inside her walls.

"That's impossible," I say. But deep down I know it's possible. This is not the same house anymore, the one Dad and the architects designed, the one we are supposed to be living in. None of us can even remember what that house looks like anymore.

"They're here and can't get out," Rachel says. "Like us."

I don't say anything. I see a faraway spark of fear in her eyes, the eyes now of a much older girl. Somehow, we are holding on. How long have we been here? A few days? A week? Months?

Everything is a blur to me, and I'm sure it's the same for Rachel. Mornings we get up and get ready for school but that's as far as we go. Sometimes I am suddenly in the cold black closet that seems to go on forever. Or in the living room, staring at a bloody mess of human meat. I found Rachel once, not all of her, but recognizable parts in the refrigerator. I'm sure she has stumbled across me as well.

"I wish I could see them," I say.

Every night I count the snakes. Every night the snakes change position.

There is a dream I have frequently. Holding June's hand, looking down into a crib where Delilah, a fresh squirming baby opens her big blue eyes. I have never felt prouder. Matthew cries in the background. June squeezes my hand. One of us will have to leave the beautiful eyes to see what he is wailing about.

I wish it was a dream.

We've tried every imaginable way to get out of the house. Once I managed to slip out the front door, or was let out, only to re-emerge in my closet. Today I am in the attic, a stuffy and thick-dusted room with one window facing the street. There are several old boxes and pieces of broken furniture that have been here forever.

The casement window is cracked and caked with grime. It is so filthy I can't see anything but I know the fog is still there, always. It's quiet downstairs, too quiet, and at the same time a thumping crosses over the roof right above me. The thumping is terrifying because it's coming from *outside*, but it moves on, as if it was oblivious to whatever is beneath it.

With a screwdriver I pry the window. It gives after my hands become numb with the effort. I push the window open. The fog mist rushes in, then settles on and mixes with the dust creating a sparkling carpet for an instant. I don't waste any time.

I squeeze through the window and scramble onto a sloped roof, holding onto the mushy rotted frame with one hand.

The frame snaps, silently. I tumble off the roof. There

is no time to scream.

Rachel bends down, stares me straight in the eye. "What are you doing under my bed?" she asks.

Dad uses hammers against the doors, and the windows. Wood splinters. Glass shatters. Blood spills from his arms and hands. But in a blink, all is as it was.

The first night. The first week. The first month. Maybe years. We scramble and huddle and scream. Odd dreams and images assail us. I remember bits and pieces of school, friends work (somewhere sitting in a cubicle before a computer), all these things stop action pictures of our lives out *there*, moving on, while we are imprisoned *here*.

Dinner. Mom makes spaghetti, and we sit around a little oak table in the kitchen. I don't know where the table came from—it's not the one I remember Mom and Dad buying at the furniture store, but no one says anything about it, so I don't either. Rachel refuses to touch her spaghetti, says it squirms like a nest of worms. Dad ignores her but doesn't touch his either. He stares at his plate.

Normally we are chatterboxes at the table but this time no one seems willing to talk. Like we are all holding in secrets.

Mom breaks the quiet, speaking to Dad. "Do we know anything about the people that used to live in the old house?"

Dad twirls a small bit of spaghetti on his fork, then scrapes it off onto the plate. All the while staring through

Mom like she isn't there. Dad is a tall man with broad shoulders and long arms, fit, but with a slight paunch. His black hair is thinning. He always wore a crooked smile like he knew something you didn't. Tonight, he isn't smiling.

"An old couple, I think, lived here for thirty years or so. I don't know what happened to them." He looks down at his plate. "Or the people before them. This place is over a hundred years old."

"We're in our new house," Rachel says, eager to correct Dad. Everyone turns to her, and she looks back and forth to each of us, wondering if she said something wrong. For an instant she is a teenager with dyed red hair and multiple face piercings, scarecrow thin, hostile eyes darting everywhere. Then, in a flash, the six- year old Rachel is back, a slight quiet moppet, the kind of kid that blends into any scene like a chameleon.

Mom smiles. Dad studies the table, looks at Rachel, and says, "Guess I forgot!" He laughs a forced fake laugh, and we all laugh.

Then Rachel says, "But I've seen the people who used to live in the old house. They live here now."

Mom puts her smile back on, a shaky one that threatens to fall apart. "Honey, I'm sure you're imagining things."

Dad shifts uneasily in his seat. "What do they look like Rachel?"

"Don't encourage her," Mom says through her teeth.

Rachel is beside herself. She wanted attention, now she is sorry for being the center it. "They are so white, like Mom's china dolls. And very, very old. They watch me when I wake up in the morning."

"Stop it," Mom says.

"Go on," Dad says.

"At first I was scared. Their arms sometimes go up

and down like they're scratching at me, or playing like they're cats, but they don't get close. I don't think they can get to me. I'm used to them now. I don't think they want to hurt me. I think they just want out."

"Enough of this!" Mom jumps from the table. She glares at Dad, fists clenched, shaking. "Don't encourage her! There's no one in her room!"

Mom flops out of the room like she had too much to drink. Dad doesn't say a word. When I look at my spaghetti it does look like worms swimming in blood.

I wake up and see the ceiling, all wrong, and the walls, covered with wallpaper, spirals and strange geometric shapes. A lamp by the bed on a night table I don't recognize. And the bed itself is not the one I laid in last night when I went to bed. Did Mom or Dad somehow carry me to a different room while I was asleep? I throw off the quilt. Where did that come from?

It's a strange, unfamiliar room. When I go into the hall it's obvious—this is not the new house we moved into. I recognize features from the old house that had been torn down, except everything is fresh, as if we had been transported back in time to when the house was well taken care of. The wallpaper is not torn and hanging in threads, the wood floors are not water damaged, the rugs covering them are fresh and not reeking of mildew.

It is early morning. The hallway is dark but there is enough light filtering in from downstairs that I can see many closed doors, and the stairs. I know there are four bedrooms, and a closet, and a door that leads to the attic. I explored the place many times, only now the place is fixed up clean, and I wonder if I am still asleep, dreaming each step I take.

I go downstairs, moving agonizingly slow. Trembling. No sounds come from the kitchen. Someone should be up. I know I am in a dream. Something is shadowing me, I can feel it, something just at the corner of my eye, a blurred movement, a disruption of light and space.

Whatever it is mimics my moves, and each time I whip around to look it whips around at the same time so that the image, the feeling, is always out of reach at the edge of my vision.

The feeling of being watched and having something close to me that doesn't belong is overwhelming. I hustle into the kitchen, expecting it to be empty, but it's not. Mom and Dad are at the table. Empty glasses and utensils are all over the room, on the table, the counter, on top of the refrigerator and stove, even the chairs. It's as if they had a party during the night and never bothered to clean up. There's no food. Anywhere. The glasses are empty and dry.

Mom notices me in the doorway. She gives a little wave with her fingers, along with a vague smile. Dad's fingers are in his mouth. He's chewing, fresh lines of blood streaking down his chin, dripping onto the table.

We keep to our rooms, Rachel and me. Dad screaming. Mom screaming. Things crash downstairs. A lot of thumping and screeching as if all the furniture is being moved and tossed about. After a long silence there is a knock at my door. The door opens a crack.

Dad says, "We can't get out."

I think early on we all knew that something dreadful had happened. We razed an old house to make room for a new one, a modern townhouse style home with four bedrooms, three baths, open space design with a spacious kitchen and living area, and a rooftop deck with a view of the mountains. I can't remember anything about that place except the stickers on the new windows.

We are in the original old Tudor style house, with casement windows, a small functional kitchen, three modest bedrooms and a living room with a sooty, neglected fireplace. It had never been torn down. It was, and is, and always will be.

And the new house? I believe it's still here too, only out of reach. Perhaps inhabited by the parts of us not drawn into this world. That explains the unexplainable memories that slip in my head. We are trapped here, in these bodies, in a house that shouldn't exist, while we are at the same time moving on with our lives. Out there.

Rachel asked once, only once, if we were dead. Like the people she sees. I don't think so. I don't think the dead can feel pain. And we can feel. I can't explain how we come back after dying in gruesome ways. Rachel and I have talked about that, but we just don't know. Mom and Dad are too far gone—there is nothing human left behind their eyes. They die and come back repeatedly, but the House has taken something from them that it hasn't taken from Rachel and me.

There is no food in the pantry, hasn't been for a long time. We are ravenously hungry, and have devoured every edible thing in the house until there is nothing left but each other. I don't know if the distant memories of killing each other for food are real or not. I don't want to know.

It doesn't matter. We don't die anyway.

Rachel disappears for long periods of time. I don't know where she goes, and she won't talk about it. She is always empty when I see her after these disappearances, and it is only after a long while that she becomes herself again. I suspect she has a place, like my closet, where she falls into a black abyss.

Mom and Dad pop out of nowhere. Sometimes they seem normal. Sometimes they are monsters beneath the skin. We avoid them whenever possible.

I can't avoid the images that are fed into my brain. They are waking dreams. I am sure what I see and remember is real. Dad murdering Mom in the kitchen with a large butcher knife. Dad hacking at Mom with a hatchet. Hitting her with his fists. Mom catching Dad from behind with a baseball bat, the swing connecting so well and so hard his skull caves and splatters like a rotten pumpkin. Mom slicing Dad's throat like she is carving the leg from a turkey.

Blood is everywhere in these soundless images. The killer, whether it is Dad or Mom, then turns their attention to Rachel and me. We run up the stairs to our rooms. The killer jiggles the doorknobs but they can't get in. They can never get in.

There have been a few times when we were caught. I can't think about that. It has become something of a game with Rachel and me, to see how close we can come to the murder action, to scamper to our safe rooms and shut the door at the last second. The killer pounds our doors and screams in frustration. Rachel giggles hysterically in her room each time.

I do the same.

Delilah climbs an old ash tree in the backyard. She is fluid, moves like a spider, a natural athlete. Matthew is downstairs playing video games. Every now and then I hear him laugh or shout. They are so young. And at this moment I feel so old.

June comes into the bedroom and stands next to me, watching our spider girl hang from a branch about ten feet off the ground. We are not concerned. Delilah is safest when she's in the tree.

June puts her arm around me, and I know she is smiling, seeing our little girl out there so happy and free. I think of mom and Rachel, long gone, how they would have enjoyed this moment too.

"We should take pictures," June says. "Show them to your dad the next time we visit."

"Yeah," I say. "As if he would recognize us anymore."

I turn and see her beautiful face, tiny worry lines sprouting from the corners of her eyes. I force a smile and give her a sideways hug. "Everything is going to be all right."

I let her go and turn back to the window. Delilah is gone. So is the ash tree. The few trees remaining in the window view are leafless and gnarled black against a gray sky. Everything is wrong. I gasp and spin, and June is gone too.

Scratching outside my door. I am still disoriented from the waking dream, but I go to the door and slowly, cautiously, open it to see what's making the noise in the hallway.

Dad is opposite the bathroom, not far from the stairs. He is groaning, as if in pain, and his hands are raised above his head while he presses in and moves along the wall. His hips move in and out. He is licking the wall.

The holes grow bigger outside. Rachel joins me at the window. I feel the heat from her body and listen to her shallow breaths, but I don't look at her.

I once found Rachel hanging in her closet. She used a rolled- up sheet and tied it to the wooden rod, then tied the loose end about her neck while standing on a metal folding chair. She must have kicked the chair out from under her and was apparently hanging there for some time. Her face swollen blue, the neck bent, swinging softly as if there was a breeze in the closet. I didn't scream or shout, simply held her limp body while I unwound the sheet and let her drop to the floor. When she did, her eyes opened, and she gurgled for air.

Now Rachel shuffles when she walks, as if she's carrying a great load on her back. Her voice is so hoarse it's almost impossible to understand a word she says. The words are bent.

I don't like to look at her this way. I wonder what she sees when she looks at me.

The fog is almost entirely gone now. Rachel presses her face against the window.

"Lorck," she says, pointing at something. There are people outside, in the yard. The sky is clear and blue, a light breeze disturbing the leaves of the trees across the street. A bulldozer is idling in the grass and dirt. Rachel giggles. I am tempted to run downstairs, get Mom and Dad, whatever their condition may be, show them what's happening out *there*. But I don't. If I take my eyes off what's happening outside, it will disappear.

Construction workers walk here and there. A family is gathered by the street watching the activity. The mother and father are hard to make out, but they seem young and familiar. A young boy, in shorts and tee shirt, about my age, with tussled blonde hair, watches the house. A little girl is sitting cross legged in the grass, preoccupied with dandelions.

Rachel squeals. The bulldozer starts toward the house. Everyone is watching the bulldozer but the boy. He stands straight and his eyes catch mine. I raise my hand.

He screams.

Gary Robbe is an educator and writer currently living in Denver, Colorado. He can be found on Facebook and Twitter under his own name

THE COPPER DOOR KARMA JAR
Cindra Spencer

As one customer exited, another regular entered Copper Door Coffee.

"Small hazelnut latte, extra shot!" Jess shouted over the whirring espresso machines.

"Wow." Tom leaned on the counter.

"Impressive, no?" She glanced up from the register.

He laughed. "It is for someone who cried her whole first day. What was that, just five, six months ago?"

"Oh god, I forgot about that. Seemed impossible to learn all the faces and names. Not to mention drink orders."

"And yet, here's my hazelnut latte."

Jess held out the hem of her apron and curtseyed.

Tom grinned and tucked bills into the tip jar. "See you Saturday."

"For a weekend mocha."

"Now you're just showing off." He shook his head, smiling, and moved down the counter.

Jess used the rare reprieve to adjust her ponytail. She liked being on register, and the other baristas liked having her there. After she started, tips went up nearly sixty percent.

The door opened, and Jess lit up again. "Kimmy! Haven't seen you in ages!" She leaned over the counter to give a hug. "River Rock blend, leave room for cream?"

"Damn skippy." Kimmy fingered the bright, green ribbon she'd personally wrapped around the tip jar, months ago, increasing visibility. "Hey, you still have it."

Jess beamed. "Of course."

"May I?" Kimmy pointed at the pens. "New idea."

"Sure. Why haven't you been in?" Jess tapped keys to ring her up.

Kimmy pulled off the pen's cap. "New marketing job, remember?" She gestured at her suit. "I rarely come this way anymore." She wrote, then turned the glass around to show Jess the added words, "KARMA JAR," in silver.

"Ha! I love it. I miss our chats. But I still see your sweet husband, obviously. Mark makes me write those cheesy love notes on your cup every day." Jess rolled her eyes. "I bought that sparkly purple pen, you know, after he said it was your favorite color. He said—" Jess stopped talking when she noticed how still and pale Kimmy had gone.

Kimmy's voice cracked, another betrayal. "So sw-sweet."

It was too late to pretend it was anything else. Jess's eyes softened, and she whispered, "I'm so sorry." She hit all clear on the register and closed the drawer as Kimmy ran out.

Jess tossed under the bed covers. *Too much caffeine,* she lied to herself.

Her head snapped up every time the door opened. When it was finally him, all the clever things Jess meant to say vanished. "Mark."

"Good morning!"

She winced. Her hand hovered over the pen canister.

"Um, how about, '*I love you a latte*.' And draw one of your little hearts."

Jess wrote the message, but her eyes never left his. She passed the paper cups back to the baristas. "Large coffee, large vanilla chai!" she yelled.

"Damn skippy," he confirmed.

Jess squinted. *Kimmy's expression.* "Have a good day, Mark."

He pointed to the tip jar and deposited a few coins. "Love it. With good karma, how could I not?" He winked, and her stomach lurched.

Jess threw the covers off, her body covered in sweat.

"Asshole," she muttered.

She got up and opened the window, inhaling the cool, Denver air.

Hannah turned the water off and wiped her hands on her apron. "If you keep filling the tip jar like that you won't need student loans."

Jess laughed. "Hardly. That might buy one textbook. This is my last semester, anyway."

"You're at CU, right? Major?"

"Criminal justice."

"Aw Jess, making the world a better place. I wanted that too when I was your age." Hannah lugged a sack of beans into the back.

The door flung open. "Good morning."

He walks too light for his weight, Jess thought. "Morning, Mark." She pulled out a pen. "What will it be, then?" Her tone was clipped.

"Ready? '*It's in The Cards*.' And draw a little heart."

Jess raised an eyebrow, pen poised. "In the cards?"

Mark grinned. "Inside joke. She'll know what it means."

Jess grimaced and passed the cups to the baristas.

His pocketful of coins clinked into the jar. "Get some sleep, Jessica. You look tired."

Jess kicked the covers off and sat up. When her eyes adjusted, she looked at her son, hunched up, sleeping in a crib he had long outgrown. *I'll have to get Aiden his own bedroom, and soon.*

The clock blinked 3:25 a.m. Too late to get quality sleep, too early to rise. She tip-toed to the window and leaned out, relishing the cool night breeze. The streetlamp flickered on Federal Boulevard, and that final night with Aiden's father, standing under such a light, flooded back.

"*How could you?*"

He shrugged. "I don't know. I'm sorry!"

She pointed to her stomach, ballooned with his child, as if that was touché enough.

"*Baby, I know. I'm so sorry.*"

"*Do you love her?*"

"*I—*"

It was that pause that did it.

Jess rubbed her head. Best not to revisit that ugly memory.

Except...it all turned out just fine, in the end. He'd hardly made any noise. The phone cord she'd snuffed him with dug a deep, satisfactory purple line into his neck—and cheap to replace.

She thought of Mark and his stupid message. Jess smiled. Perhaps it was in the cards to turn out fine for Kimmy, too.

Hannah glanced at the clock. "You're a few minutes late. That's a first."

"Sorry." Jess clocked in. "Got held up. I'm so sorry."

Hannah laughed. "You're my best employee. There's no demerits."

Jess retrieved the bright green ribbon from her apron pocket. It proved to be strong. Stronger than Mark, that was for sure. Even better than a phone cord. Before rewrapping the tip jar, she reached into the canister of pens. She drew a little heart, and tied it back around, making sure that Kimmy's "KARMA JAR" lettering displayed proudly.

Cindra Spencer has an affinity for dark mysteries so she is often on the road inspecting Colorado's health facilities. She occasionally dusts off her keyboard and pretends to be a writer.

BLOCK 12
Thomas C. Mavroudis

Adrienne and I became friends through a writer's retreat, bonding over morbid fascination. Her current fancy was gravestone symbolism, and I was happy to oblige her. So, on a mostly sunny morning, she came down from the mountains and I took her to the old Riverside Cemetery. I planned on making these expeditions a habit.

The nearly nameless place is buried in the exact part of town you would expect the nucleus of a classic zombie picture, hemmed in on three sides by factories. It was the sort of industry sprawling with red caution lights, towers wrapped with spiral iron staircases, and smokestacks discharging plumes of emissions acrid with cooked minerals and the putrid tang of pet food being processed. On the remaining side, the north, the burial grounds are safeguarded by the steady confluence of a plains tributary, the sandy bars on the far end frequented by deer and smaller wildlife, a reminder of long-gone tranquility.

I had been there once before, seeking a pioneer

relative. After a handful of U-turns in more than one industrial dead end, we reached the cemetery gate. Opposed to how I remembered it, the grass was green and maintained, and the dirt road was neatly graded. Some historical group must have made it their cause, as no one had been interned there for decades. We parked near the closed office, wetted our mouths with coffee, and began our discovery.

"Should I lock the car?" Adrienne asked.

I looked across the landscape, the unmoving graveyard and billowing factories. "I think so."

Unconventional Adrienne was dressed in full black, including lace gloves, and with three fingers of calf exposed between the top of her boots and the hem of her dress. Her face was occluded by both a wide-brimmed parson's hat with a black lace band and sunglasses like black river rocks. I was surprised she didn't wear a veil.

We left the road, plunging immediately into the sea of granite and marble. Adrienne was a kid on Christmas morning, distracted by urn, obelisk, and angel, and every chiseled decoration. Each grave was not marked so fancifully. There were many basic stones, and several made of inexpensive blocks of poured concrete, the names and dates drawn in with a stick or finger. Some were gone entirely, the missing headstone's concrete foundation the only indication anyone rested below.

Occasional birds alighted on the warm stones, others pecked at the grass. Pollinating insects traversed wildflowers and the rare perennial, generations old. Rodents scurried in the shadows of stone and shrub, and a train blared its crossing through the steel and smoke wasteland. Otherwise, we were alone.

On the verge of the mausoleums, I suggested we attempt to thoroughly absorb one row of graves, study the details that made them the same and different. But

Adrienne couldn't do it, anchors, tree stumps, and winged hourglasses plying her attention. Then something else distracted us both.

There is no mistaking an infant's shrill cry, not the sort from hunger or need for attention, but that sound uttered from the icy hot frustration of wordlessness. I cringed at the detestable sound. "What is that?" I said.

We craned ourselves to find the source, but it was beyond our scope, down behind the mausoleums toward the river. The chance of a baby by itself was unlikely. We could hear no consoling voice under the wail, no *Shhh* either gentle or frantic. We continued onward, inevitably to the heated sound.

A rabbit darted from an antique rosebush to its warren beneath a bare concrete base. "You know," I offered, "rabbits were considered witch's familiars because they could mimic a baby's scream."

"I don't think they sounded this good," Adrienne replied.

We came to the mausoleum-lined ridge, a necropolis skyline, then down the hill. At the bottom, across the road, was a meadow marked by only a few common blocks, and further on, a decrepit fence at the edge of the river. What we supposed was an old woman in a dusty habit crouched over one of these simple markers, and the inconsolable child.

"Hello?" Adrienne called.

The woman lifted slightly, a curtain of grey hair obscuring her face. We ambled steadily to the scene, measuring the situation.

"Something bad's happening," I said. "Something's wrong."

The scream grew more dire and demanding, but we couldn't see what was happening, for the shape of the crone blocked our view. Adrienne quickened her pace, and instinctively I grasped for her hand, grabbing nothing.

"Are you OK?" she said. "Do you need help?"

I wanted to stop. I wanted to pause everything, and rewind. I faltered alongside Adrienne just as she reached the woman's back. I could tell she wanted to touch her—I shook my head. *Don't.*

"Hey," I called to the crouching shape. I'd had enough of this mystery. "What are you doing? What's going on here?"

Then it turned around and stood up, rising over seven feet, no old woman. There was no baby, either, just this cadaverous and ancient man, the infant's incessant wail flowing from the blackness of a smile that fractured across his craggy face.

Of course, your instinct is to run—if you can avoid the instinct to merely fall down, to collapse into insanity. My instinct was to grapple Adrienne around her midsection and wrest her away, far enough away to reset her so we could run together. I stumbled and fell, dropping her. She vomited, either from shock or my squeezing. And behind us, the man continued to scream.

When I scrambled to my feet, I grabbed Adrienne by her arm, pulling her up. We ran to the hill, her boots inhibiting our best efforts. By the time I yanked her up to the crypts, the man and his vicious sound were gone. We panted. There was a cramp in my side, and it was my turn to throw up.

"Fuck," Adrienne said, taking off her sunglasses, a wild smile on her face.

We strode quickly back to the car, paranoid, looking sideways and behind each other's backs. The cemetery seemed to stretch without end. Bright clouds converged overhead, locking in the heat of the day, enveloping the landscape with a dull white coating like gauze, and the flies and midge clouds roared with an electric, mindless drone.

As we finally approached the car, the stagnant air began to stir with returning freshness and color. There was an older couple in the rows near the front gate, contemplating history or an ancestor. They didn't appear concerned about us. We rinsed our mouths out with a warm bottle of water, rolled down the windows, and I started the car.

"Should we drive down around there on our way out?" Adrienne's smile was fixed.

"Hell, no," I said. She laughed at me and put her sunglasses back on. I drove out the furthest from the river that I could.

Originally, we had planned lunch, but I couldn't eat, and Adrienne was too giddy, so I drove her to her car, and we made our goodbyes.

"Overall, it was a good day," she said.

"I guess so." I smiled awkwardly and hugged her. Her ribs and spine felt exaggerated and left a repellent sensation in my arms.

Over the course of the following days, I tried my best to shake off the experience, but it was hard to ignore. Some might think it childish, but I kept the lights on in my apartment. I watched game shows and talent shows and read entertainment news in bed; anything to soften my anxiety.

Likewise, I was unsettled because I didn't hear from Adrienne. It wasn't unusual, weeks had gone by in the past where we were not in contact. But why was it happening now, after such an extraordinary event?

Then a day or two later, the emails began to show up. Links to articles, blogs, images. Ghost stories mostly, accounts of banshees, kappas, and La Llorona—all things that would have thrilled me in a pleasant way a month ago. Below each link was Adrienne's signature and a little black heart with vampire's fangs. With trepidation, I read them all.

Her correspondence continued with a batch of peculiar information hardly connected to our incident. Spirit boards, automatic writing, grammomancy. *AllMusic* articles about obscure, out-of-print neo-folk and death-jazz records. The general lack in association allowed me to appreciate the details as though I was an uncommitted party. Gradually, I was able to relax once more with a single lamp on in the living room.

On the weekend, Adrienne texted me: "In town. Coffee?"

I knew she wanted to go back. There was no stopping her, so the only thing I could do was try and stop myself.

She was already at the coffee shop, mohawk tied into a ponytail, gargantuan eyes and smile, her fingers tapping away at the table as if playing some invisible keyboard.

"What?" I said, easing into the chair opposite her.

"I couldn't email this stuff to you." She pulled a composition book from her bag and flipped over leaves blackened with her heavy script to a middle page. "Block Twelve."

The designation was written prominently on the top margin. Below it I could see questions she'd written, lines of bullet points, and words bolded or underlined. On the opposite page was a rough but detailed sketch of the graveyard, and on the side, the shrieking figure.

Her diligence dried out my mouth and throat. "You've been busy," I said.

"It's all I can think about. You?"

"No. Not really. I've actually been trying to think about it as little as possible."

She smacked me in the shoulder, as she would her

brother. "This is pretty amazing. I'm surprised you're being so reserved about it."

"Reserved? It scared the shit out of me, Adrienne. It really did. I didn't like it."

She closed her book, marking the page with a finger I noticed was newly raw with fidgety chewing. "Don't be scared. Look, we shared this experience, and I need you to help me work it out."

Although Adrienne was more than just a creative acquaintance, the rawness of the cemetery had bared a new vulnerability between us.

"Were you scared?" It was the sincerest thing I'd asked anyone in some time.

"Yeah, I was. Of course! But I'm not now. It was a show, right? A secret message. That's what we went looking for. Secrets. Hidden, forgotten things. So, don't be afraid, be excited. We're on to something."

Her enthusiasm was infectious, and I struggled to cling to immunity. "OK," I decided. "Tell me a little about Block Twelve."

"OK!" She smiled and her teeth reminded me of those age-worn blocks of marble.

Traditionally, Block 12 was the potter's field, although a few memorialized remains were laid therein: a dozen Japanese frontiersmen and some others. Adrienne relayed a short list of ordinary historical facts, which I was content to hear.

And then she said, "But here's the payoff. Most of Block Twelve is occupied by babies. Mostly newborns. Some days or only hours old." A change in my expression must have mirrored my dreadful turn of thought. "Come on," she said. "This is cool!"

In fact, if it had not happened to us—or even me—it would have been very cool. I was, after all, the instigator of the exploration. But a mentor of mine, another comrade in the curious, warned me long ago that when you deliberately seek out the weird, it tends to notice you back, attach itself, and never let go. In our case, the line between thinking and doing were not necessarily solid or static. I didn't believe Adrienne and I had actually *done* anything. But I could tell she was driven to do something.

"So?"

I didn't know if continuing the conversation would encourage her more, or if there was a chance I could keep her from doing whatever she was formulating. She tapped the sketch of the man. "So. What about him? What's your theory?"

"It's got to be a baby, right? Or..." She hesitated. "The whole mass grave."

I nodded slowly.

She kept the conversation going with herself, asking questions and answering them; posing an idea, then building on it or debating it. I was quiet. I nodded or raised an eyebrow, tested a smile if it seemed safe. It all headed to the declaration I was dreading to hear: "We need to go back."

I'm not superstitious. As far as I'm concerned, black cats and broken mirrors are not catalysts of doom. I'm not sure what I would call the incident at Block 12. On one hand, it defied reason, and therefore, within reason, there was nothing to fear. Yet, as impossible as the occurrence was, it happened, and what does that do to one's definition of reason? I guess ultimately, that was what Adrienne sought. I wanted to abandon the whole pursuit, but I couldn't humanely allow her to be a part of it alone.

"All right," I yielded. "But not today. This is only coffee." I wasn't ready.

"Not today," she agreed. "We need to do some more thinking."

The emails Adrienne sent next turned darker. A video about a medium who admitted to being a fraud and a follow-up article about the man who murdered him. Then there was a bulletin board discussing enigmas in closed-circuit television feeds. It was tolerable as long as I never clicked links to any of the actual footage. The index of haunted dolls I had to completely ignore.

My nightly routine changed, settling into bed with a volume of straight fiction, nothing supernatural, nothing uncanny. Drowsy, lamp off, and turned on my side, I was fast asleep.

Just as suddenly, or seemingly so, my phone buzzed with a text. I had been out for at least four hours, according to the clock on the screen which was bright and washed the room with a sanitized whiteness. The message from Adrienne read "Hi."

"Are you OK?" I fumbled with sleep addled thumbs, my heart hammering at my sternum.

"Do you know who this is"

I turned the bed lamp on. I typed, "Adrienne."

"This is an anagram of Adrienne"

Anagram. Or amalgam? Neither made rational sense. And whatever it meant, it didn't come from Adrienne as I knew her. I powered down my phone, trying to think of what to do for the remaining hour until dawn, trying to think of nothing at all.

The following workday was consumed by thoughts of Adrienne and the non-Adrienne. I hesitated to check my personal email for fear of what puzzles might have been left there. Around mid-day, I relented to turn my phone back on. There was a scroll of messages; none from Adrienne, all of them from meaningless five or eight-digit numbers. I deleted them all without reading a single one. In the courage of my work station, I called her.

"Hey!" she answered. "Can you hear me? Something's wrong with my phone."

"I know," I said.

"Have you been calling me?" She sounded on the far end of a profound gulf.

"No. Have you been texting me?"

She paused, or the phone cut out. Then I heard, "Are you alright? What's the matter?"

"I'm glad you answered," I said. But then the call truly failed.

That evening, the dread gained greater weight. Twilight fading, I pulled the switch on my living room lamp and the dated tungsten bulb popped, cradling the space in murk. Fumbling with the television remote, I eventually generated some mood light. Alex Trebek and the blue *Jeopardy!* board. The lead contestant burned through the category "Superstitions." I knew every macabre answer.

At the commercial break, I sensed the presence of a fluttering, unwanted guest holding in the gloom. The only reasonable thing would have been an insect, but this was bird-like. I watched the spaces between the wall and couch, the corners where the walls meet the ceiling. I looked into the shadows. No rodents, bugs, hint of anything. The category for Final Jeopardy was "Disasters," so I flipped channels until I hit a baseball game. It might have been soccer—something normal, non-threatening. Still, the sensation persisted, like a rash on one's sixth sense.

I looked over to the corner again, the dim crack of shadow, and looking directly at the angle, saw nothing. But, from the rim of my eye, the space continued to twitch. It flickered and fluttered, and I tried to ignore it as you would an itch, until the crack moved. It scuttled from the corner across the wall to a place within, spilling from my peripheral vision into full view. My bowels cramped with a sharp heat. I edged slowly, deliberately away from the scuttling, until I was off the couch, reaching for the ceiling light switch, never trying to look at the thing, because I wouldn't see it anyway. It dissipated in the light, as shadows do.

I kept the light on. Kept the kitchen light on too, and somehow—through half a bottle of gin I hadn't even realized I had—I was able to sleep in my darkened bedroom, light from the rest of the apartment seeping under the door.

On Thursday, Adrienne sent me an email with the subject heading "Breakthrough-of sorts." Her message stated that her phone was dead, and she asked if she could stay with me through the weekend. Her closing remark was, "We have to do this now." Her tone, however, was not of terror, and that horrified me even more.

Friday night, Adrienne showed up in black shorts and tank-top with everything in a cobalt blue sports duffel, and I teased her about its contrast with her usual ensemble.

"Wait until you see my pajamas," she said.

We could still banter like paranormal investigators whose highlight of their career was a garbled EVP. At least she could still act that way. I, on the other hand, was merely a puppet, completely terrified beneath my casing.

She set up her laptop and composition books on my dining table. "It's a spirit," she began, "just not a human spirit."

"Hold on. I've got to eat something. Nervous stomach." But really, I was trying to postpone everything. We ordered delivery that arrived faster than I hoped, and I couldn't eat it—something more than a nervous stomach. I opened a bottle of wine I'd been saving for some unknown, special occasion, started receiving its sustenance. Adrienne wouldn't drink.

"I'm exhausted," she said. She didn't look it. She looked wired. "Remember when I told you Block Twelve is all I can think about? It's true. I haven't been sleeping."

"What happens when you try to sleep?"

"Oh, I don't try to sleep. Really. I've had this drive, pushing me through the night. And in the day? I don't know. Not sleeping, I don't think."

All the while, she typed away on her computer, notebooks open on either side. She tapped a note in one book with her pen, cross-checked it with the other book. Some awareness would unveil in her mind, and she would type away again at the keyboard.

I watched her work this way, manic, for a few minutes. Then I said, "You have to be sleeping." The wine helped. Helped me. Half of the bottle was gone, and I tried to think how I could get Adrienne to have some.

"I haven't been sleeping. I know this." She smiled that broad, increasingly vacuous smile. "You know how it goes, one thing leads to another, to another, to another, an endless catalog of ideas and half ideas. The apocalyptic Google hole. Like cramming for a test."

"You have to take a break," I said.

"I can't...I can't stay awake much longer. I mean I can. I don't have a choice, is what I'm saying."

If I grabbed her hands, would they stop? If I held them gently, if I guided her away from her work, would she rest? Or would she break?

"Look at this. Look at all this. *Tsukumogami, rusalka, drekavac*, unclean spirits. It's none of these or all of these. We don't know. No one knows. See? That's the problem. That's the problem, right there. This conglomerate spirit."

I pulled my chair beside her and looked at her screen. There must have been at least forty windows open along the bottom toolbar, as though the machine had a virus activating infinite pop-ups. She went from one tab to another, cycling mechanically so the screen images were viewable for a handful of seconds, gleaning bits of information; or nothing at all, trapped in a circuit of monstrous visuals and sinister knowledge.

"Adrienne." I said her name again. I was afraid to touch her. Instead, I took a risk and folded her laptop closed.

She stared at the empty space, then her eyes rolled around, maybe reading the after images, or reading something only she could see. When her expression went flat, she turned to me and said, "Thank you."

At last, she appeared tired and hoary; what I mistook for eyeshadow was fatigue and her lips were bloodless. Her large eyes themselves had collapsed into cheap replicas of eyes.

We ate some, talked little. Adrienne had a sip of wine. I finished the bottle. Washing her face in the bathroom, I could hear her sigh and groan over the water. I straightened out my bed, opened a bedroom window to let out the unexpected heat.

We lay on the bed covers in the night breeze, and soon Adrienne's body shuddered with sleep. Dizzy, but not tired, I peered at the whorls of paint on the ceiling, hoping they would stay still. I tried to compare the anticipation for the next day with some other experience. This was neither a holiday nor vacation; closer to a medical exam, or the results of one, and still not like that at all.

Adrienne shifted around, exhaling in fitful huffs. I was leery to watch her. As I began to drift off, she settled down, and I had the feeling she was looking at me. She had rolled onto her side, but when I turned my head to look at her, her eyes were shut. A trick of the lamplight and the fatigue of her face. I looked back to the ceiling and could see from the corner of my eye that her eyes were indeed open, wide and moist. Again, they were closed when I looked at her directly. I resolved to doze on the couch before that hideous smile emerged and joined those abyssal pits for eyes.

Adrienne woke me in the dreary morning. The apartment was humid and the sky outside was the color of dead skin. I hoped some cheerful sunshine would accompany us again, but the forecast for the day predicted worse. Adrienne had not improved, either. Since I had so easily broken her connection to the apparition—entity, whatever it was—her body quickly succumbed to the effects of starvation and insomnia.

"Let me make some coffee," I said. I'd slept just as bad, and could have used the caffeine, but really, I was stalling, hunting for alternatives.

"No," she said. "We better just figure this out."

I didn't like the hopelessness in her voice. Could a doctor or priest help? A shaman or Obeah Man? A physicist or astronaut were just as likely. It could have been that the experience *was* the message. Regardless, I was committed to following through, rigid with the common sense I was close to abandoning, and courage from an Arrowhead water bottle filled with Irish whiskey. Considering the booze I'd been consuming recently, I recognized I hadn't escaped total bodily harm myself.

We drove in silence on uncannily empty streets. The few pedestrians and motorists we passed appeared oddly shrouded, with obscured faces. Not rain, but heavy, damp air collected on the windshield, beading in thick droplets. We turned onto the service road along the highway and passed under the railway bridge that represented the gateway to the industrial wasteland. The whole landscape was a dead, alien city. I took a long sip of whiskey, then reached over for Adrienne's hand. I imagined touching fragile bones, but what I grasped instead was repulsive, a mass combined of roots and tallow. She pulled her hand away first. I didn't want to look at her.

I pulled the car to the side of the road by the open postern, as the main gate was barred. Adrienne got out before me and passed through the postern, drifting between the gravestones like a blackened spirit. I wasn't sure I could get out of the car, my hand still and solid on the door handle as I watched her. I took a deep breath, drank the rest of the whiskey, and caught up with her before she was lost.

"What are we doing?" I asked.

"Finding out what it wants."

I suspected what it wanted it already had.

I stopped, hoping she would halt with me. "I mean… do we have a plan? A smudge stick or something?"

She looked back at me with a tiny grin. "Yeah. Smudge stick." She kept slowly walking. "I'm thinking, if we allow it to present itself again in its own space, we need to stand it out. I think we disrespected it. We need to let it finish its message."

"That sounds right." But I didn't believe it. The rules of movies and fairy tales did not apply to this world. This was a snag, an unraveling in the weave of human order.

"Look at this place," Adrienne said, as if she read my thoughts. "It's a world outside of order." She waved her skeletal arms, conjuring. "The chemical pollution of the factories in the air and ground, nature unbounded, the river continuing its millennial course aware or unaware, and this hallowed ground filled with crossing cultures… all of it forced together.

"Take into account the nameless dead of Block Twelve. Think about it! There've got to be pockets like this all around the world. Strange things happen, they really do, but only in these little concentrated spaces.

And these stories leach out, they decay and change, and become myths and urban legends and campfire stories. This thing is one of those roots, see?"

Conglomerate spirit—she named it. And I knew it was true, yet naming something didn't define it at all.

We approached the hill of mausoleums. If we watched ourselves on a black and white drive-in theatre screen, we would have rolled our eyes and laughed at the hackneyed scene: Tor Johnson stumbling out from behind a wooden crypt façade. Instead, we stood above Block 12 beside a grey mausoleum that resembled a Slavic cathedral. Adrienne's face was all eyes and mouth. As for me, the Irish whiskey was ready to crawl from my guts and throat.

I scanned the long potter's field. Adrienne's gaze fixed on a spot that seemed vacant to me. Then I peered through the bars of the crypt, seeking something to manifest in the darkness.

"Where is he?" Thinking of it as *he* made the thing practical. I irritably rolled chunks of old concrete from the foundation under my shoe. The whole platform was webbed with cracks and pocked-marked with animal burrows.

"Just wait," she said. "Wait."

Instantaneously, the black line of her mouth drew up into a smile and expanded as before—unlike the old, towering man and unlike her. Like something new.

I could have called her name, I could have grabbed her. I could have pushed her down the hill. I stepped back, away from her and the sound that never came, the sound I never wanted to hear again. I stepped away from the growing disorder, and stepped into soft earth and worn cement, my feet shifting to maintain balance and traction, each graceless step hammering the frail foundation and loose earth until it gave way and swallowed me.

I awoke furrowed in dirt and decomposed vegetation. Minutes or seconds passed. I recall looking at the walls of the crypt, confused, and at the too bright spot, the hole in the crumbled concrete and earth where I had apparently tumbled through. The brightness made my stomach churn. The side of my head where it had smacked the vault throbbed and a red glare pulsed at the side of that eye. I've had concussions before, so I remembered not to stand up too fast. I called for Adrienne, but the sound was whispered, mumbled, could have been imagined. I thought I was pissing myself, but it was my phone buzzing.

"Adrienne is here and no longer here," the text read.

I looked back at the hole, watched it slide down a long shadow-crowded tunnel.

The next time I woke up, I was slumped with my back against the vault. It was night, or simply dark. What I guessed at first was blood trickling from my head felt more like a finger drawing designs on my scalp—which it was.

I came fully awake when the whole hand clutched a patch of my hair. I felt the space of a wide mouth descend next to the swelling at my right temple. Then I heard in a gritty whisper, "Can you hear me?" It snickered, its slimy hair lapping my ear. I hyperventilated in sync with its display of amusement.

It slithered from its perch on the vault into my lap, holding my face in its muddy, desiccated hands. Its face was a richer black in the darkness, its breath dirt and spoiled milk.

"Adrienne says you can leave now," it told me. "Adrienne says to tell her story."

Denver Horror Collective member Thomas C Mavroudis is the host of horror literary event Frights and Flights at Denver BookBar. Under the direction of Stephen Graham Jones, he completed an MFA from the University of California, Riverside-Palm Desert and was the Horror Writer's Association 2019's Scholarship from Hell recipient. Tom sold his first short story to Turn to Ash and since then, has appeared in Weirdbook, The Year's Best Body Horror, Terror in 16-Bits, and Behold the Undead of Dracula. His novella, Bergdorf & Associates, is due in 2020 from Omnium Gatherum Books. He was born in the Mile High City, and lives near its heart with his wife, daughter, and too many dogs.

A PLACE FOR CADY
Melinda Bezdek

Cady's grandmother cradled the phone between her ear and her shoulder as she held the door open and shooed Cady out. The little girl crossed her arms over her chest and planted her feet.

Her grandmother covered the speaker and hissed, "Go!"

Cady stuck out her tongue and stomped onto the front porch. She let the screen door slam behind her and stood against the wall to listen.

"Sorry, hon, your daughter. Now, tell me again what the doctor said. Is there anything else they can do?"

Cady plopped down on the top step of the porch and unloaded a pocketful of rocks. She eyed a stream of ants crossing the walkway. Their little legs hustled across the pavement, some of them carried crumbs of food. They were clearly planning to take over the world. Any minute soldier ants would come bursting from the dirt on the attack, and if they succeeded, they would turn Cady, her family, and everyone into their slaves. Humans would have to carry the ants' food and do tricks for them. They would lock everyone up in separate cages and only let them out to work.

She picked up a rock and threw it at the marching insects. It landed close enough that they scrambled to get out of the way. "Take that, you evil ants."

Overhead, the bare branches of an old cottonwood held several monsters, roundish creatures made of sticks that poked out in all directions. Their arms and legs were skinny and they had big eyes that moved across their bodies so they could stare at you no matter which way they turned. They were easy to mistake for squirrels' nests if you didn't look closely, but Cady knew better.

They were her spies, watching every movement in the neighborhood and the city. They told about the giant blue horse that killed its creator and a spider-man who hid in a lady's attic for months. They also spied on her brother lying in his hospital bed. They said he was faking, that he just wanted attention. If that was true, he was a good faker. Her parents hadn't called her once the whole week.

The wind blew. The monsters bounced on their limbs and groaned. They were such whiners. "At least you guys aren't alone."

They laughed. *Neither are you. We are just above you.*

Cady looked out to where the mountains should be, but they were hidden by rain and distance. The thunder grumbled. This was the kind of day Cady loved: The sky was heavy, the air was charged, and the colors were electric. She inhaled—rain on hot pavement. One of the monsters swung from its branch and landed on Cady. It scratched her with its pokey body. Luckily, it was light or she would've looked like someone had thrown a porcupine at her. She shook it off and said, "What are you doing?"

Get the ants, it said.

She charged them, stomping her way through their

bodies, crunching and scattering them. She shook off the ones that crawled up her legs, and all the monsters cheered. She ran out to Alcott Street.

A is for Alcott, the street Grandma lives on.

B is for brother, butthead, boils, and banished.

C is for Cady and Calvin, too, even though he is the butthead.

And D is for Denver, where I'll live forever.

The houses on Alcott were old. Cady liked that. It made them mysterious. The monster pulled at her shirt. *You should go to the McKay house.* She turned left. The McKay house was her favorite. Built with red bricks, it was a puzzle of several houses stacked and attached to each other. Fish scale siding embellished the many peaks and carved wood trim lined the roof.

Cady's grandma said it was built by a Scottish man trying to lure his beloved to America. Cady was sure it had worked. They got married and probably had a little girl who they adored more than anything in the world. They would've given her the room with the biggest window and the softest bed, probably a canopy bed with posts made of jungle trees. The branches and leaves tangled across the top and vines hung down to the foot of the bed so each night the girl could swing onto the mattress. Then her parents would tuck her in with a story and a kiss. In this house, no one was sick and no one was sent away because they were just too much to handle right now.

"When Calvin gets better," Cady said, "my parents are coming back for me, and we're all going to the zoo."

We like zoos, the monster said. "The best part of the zoo the otters. I love how they swim around having so much fun swooping and swirling. I wish I had friends that I could just play with all day." Cady swerved across the sidewalk, bobbing her head up and down like an otter. She twirled until she fell and watched the sky spin above her.

We are your friends.

"I know," she said. "Calvin likes the penguins. He's a penguin expert. He knows all the types of penguins that live all over the world, or most of them anyway. Anytime he sees one on TV or in real life, he walks just like they do." She jumped up and stiffened her arms and tottered in a circle. "Sometimes that kid just kills me."

Cady picked up a stick and dragged it along the sidewalk. The scraping echoed against the houses.

It's very quiet.

Cady nodded and looked around. Not a single person, dog, or bird. It was like nothing lived there at all. She looked at her grandparents' house. The other monsters were gone, and even the line of ants had disappeared. Cady turned to go back when a cold wind whipped through the street. It flung her hair into her face, and she fought to clear it from her view. She turned into the blast and it flung her frizzy curls behind her head. She opened her eyes to find the wind had somehow pushed her at least thirty feet down the sidewalk to the McKay house.

She parked her stick at the edge of the lawn and looked up at the impressive structure. It was empty and had been ever since she could remember. The windows were midnight dark as if the glass consumed any light that tried to get in. There was a small *No Trespassing* sign off to the side.

Go to the door, the monster said.

Cady hopscotched up to the porch and waved at the long-faced gargoyle guarding the entrance. Its smile grew wider, exposing its stone teeth. Cady watched closely to see if she could catch the creature move again. It became a contest: the little girl with the frizzy hair versus the gargoyle with the stretched-out face. Young versus old, flesh versus stone. She was sure she would win, until shuffling in the house grabbed her attention. She stepped closer and claimed victory when the gargoyle's smile grew again.

The wood of the porch sunk beneath Cady's feet. She moved closer to the house. Inside, there was something moving, something tall like her grandpa and wide like him, too. It passed by the window and disappeared. Cady pressed her face against the glass with cupped hands to block the outside light. The figure crossed again and went upstairs.

Follow it, the monster said.

Cady ran to the side of the house where she found a pine tree next to a rooftop balcony. She grabbed the lowest branch and pulled herself up. She was an expert climber. She'd been teaching Calvin her tree-climbing moves before he got sick, and he was getting pretty good. He would've been able to climb this tree without any problems.

She wondered if people forgot how to climb trees when they couldn't do it for a while. If they did, she would teach him again. She was an expert big sister, too. If he were here now, he'd be racing her to the top of the tree, telling her to be careful not to get her hair tangled in the branches. He always made fun of her hair. She would tell him the tree was full of squirrels. He hated squirrels. They made him scream louder than the whistle her gym teacher used.

Halfway up the tree, Cady was level with the balcony. She inched across the thickest branch to reach the railing, but her hair got snagged. Calvin would've died laughing. As she pulled at it, she felt something watching her. She looked up at the window but saw only black.

With a yank, she pulled herself free and toppled over the railing, landing with a thump. She yelped. This wood also bowed under her weight. She scooted toward the house and peered in. She could tell the thing was standing directly across from her in the darkness. Goosebumps rippled up her arms.

It turned to look at her and its breath fogged the window. In general, she liked monsters, but this one didn't seem as harmless as her little friends. Her heart thumped in her chest and echoed in her ears. She took a step back. The wood sank. This adventure wasn't fun anymore. She wished she was sitting on her grandma's couch, watching *The Price is Right*. She tried to run, but her legs were frozen with fear.

A dim light filled the window. Cady saw the thing standing in front of her. It was all her little monsters piled on top of each other. Their eyes stared at her. They blinked and smiled. Their spiky arms reached for her. She should've been comforted by the fact that she knew them, but she wasn't . Cold sweat shivered through her skin and she took one step back and then another. Her foot caught on something and she fell. The wood cracked beneath her. She hit her head as she went through the balcony, through the yellow cloud of insulation, through the ceiling, and through a coffee table.

The world was hazy and made of greys when Cady opened her eyes. Something dark and sticky surrounded her. It covered her, the coffee table, and the floor. She gingerly wiggled her hands and her toes, then moved her legs and her arms. Everything seemed to be working, but there was no pain. There should be pain. It is supposed to hurt when you fall through a ceiling. Maybe she was in shock. Her mom said that happens sometimes. She was in shock when Calvin first got sick. She said she was numb.

Cady scrambled to stand, but the ooze surrounding

her clung to her body like tiny hands. She fought to lift herself, and as she did, she expected to feel the floor beneath her. Instead, she floated.

The big monster made of little monsters watched her and then they each looked up toward the monster at the top. Their eyes moved up their body and congregated in the middle of their forehead. Their mouths reached toward each other until they combined into a gaping smile with crumbling, yellow teeth.

Cady gasped, but the air was empty. She looked up at the hole she'd made and tried to inhale the oxygen that filtered in.

This isn't the right place for you anymore.

They were right. It wasn't the right place. None of this was right. She needed to get out, to escape, to get away, to go. Cady tried to run, but the gooey stuff held her. She flung herself toward the door.

It won't open.

The monster's voice was deep and edged in a giggle. It picked her up and lifted her over its head. Her body was suspended at the end of its long arms so when she kicked, she hit nothing but air. The monster opened its mouth and tipped the top of its head back like it was on a hinge. Its mouth grew into a hole bigger than its entire body. The walls of the chasm were maroon and faded to black in the center. Cady felt herself being lowered toward the pit. She flailed, but the thing's grip was solid.

You will like your new home. You will never be alone.

The monster dropped her into its mouth. Cady fell through the darkness toward a pinprick of light. Her hair whipped against her face, so she knew she was moving fast, but it felt like she was drifting. As she moved towards the light, it grew bigger. There were roots sticking out of the walls, and a pair of spiders stood on one of them. They blinked at her with all their eyes. She reached for the root, but her hands brushed past it. She tried to swim through the air, but she stayed perfectly centered until she was spat out onto a carpeted floor.

A ring of children sat around her. They were about her age and stared with empty smiles. Each one wore a matching dress or suit of a different color. Cady looked down. Hers was yellow. She hated yellow. Yellow was Calvin's color. Teal was her color. Her dress turned green, and then blue seeped in until it was the perfect shade of teal.

The children welcomed her in unison and a girl in blue stood up. "Hello Cady, do you want to play with us?"

Cady looked up. The hole she fell through had turned into a chandelier bolted to a solid white ceiling. She looked around for a table or chair she could use to climb up to the dangling crystals. Maybe if she pulled on the light fixture, the hole would open back up and she could climb out.

The room was full of toy chests, doll houses, and stacks of games, but there were no chairs. On the far wall, however, there was a bookshelf. It would make a good ladder if she could move it. She used her whole body to pull it toward her, but it didn't even sway in her direction. She looked closely to see that wall seamlessly extended forward to create the bookshelf. The shelf was part of the wall, and so were the toy chests and doll houses. Everything was one thing.

The children stood there watching Cady pry, kick, and tug all the objects in the room, seemingly indifferent to her efforts.

When she gave up, the girl in blue said, "Maybe you would like us to show you around before you try to escape."

All the other children nodded.

The girl reached for Cady's hand. Cady pulled away

but followed her into a dining room where there was a table longer than her entire house. On top of it were candelabras and fine china and forks and knives so shiny they bounced streaks of light around the room. Cady bent down to see the wood floor stretch up into table legs.

In the next room, a spiral staircase led up to two doors at the top: one yellow and one teal. The girl in blue took Cady through the teal door into a room with another grand chandelier, and there were clouds painted on the ceiling. The walls were all glass. This was the biggest window she had ever seen. To the right was a bed with posts made of jungle trees and their leaves and branches tangled over the top to create a canopy. Thick vines hung from the end.

"It is just what you wanted," the girl said.

It was what Cady wanted, but also nothing like anything she would've ever wanted. She felt weird in this space, like she didn't quite fit between the molecules of air. She walked to the window. There had been hours of daylight left when she hopped off her grandparents' porch, but here it was the middle of the night. The streets and the yards were covered in the same ooze she'd found at the McKay house, the other McKay house, the real McKay house. Stick monsters floated by in groups, and several stopped to stare at Cady. A little one pointed at her. Cady cocked her head to the side and the small stick thing mimicked her.

"Don't worry. It won't always feel so strange," the girl said. "You will never be alone here, you will never be sick, and you will never be sent away." She smiled. Her eyes closed slowly and stayed shut a moment too long before popping back open. She seemed to stare through Cady. They all did.

Cady missed her brother and her parents and her grandparents. Their photos appeared on the dresser. She missed the sound of barking dogs, and a distant recording of yipping chihuahuas played. Five of the children began running in circles and bobbing their heads like otters. They twirled until they fell to the ground. The other two tottered around with stiff, penguin arms.

"See," said the girl in blue. "Everything you wanted."

Cady pushed past the swirling, tottering children and ran down the spiral staircase. She went through the dining room and through the playroom into the foyer where she grabbed the golden handle of the front door and pulled. The door didn't budge. She yanked, flinging her body back and forth as she tried to get it to move even a little bit.

"It's not a door," said the girl in blue.

"It just looks like one," said a boy in orange.

"You can't go out there, anyway," said a girl in purple.

"It isn't the place for you," said the girl in blue.

Cady pulled at the handle one last time before examining the edge of the door and realizing they were right. It wasn't a door. It was continuation of the wall just like the bookshelf had been. Escape was an illusion created by the carved outline of a door. She flung her body against it and peered out its window. Outside, shocked stick monsters gaped at her. Some covered their mouths with knobby fingers while a few laughed and imitated Cady's flinging body. A parent covered its offspring's eyes and ushered it away from the traumatic scene.

Across the street, other houses were lit up from the inside. A group of children played tag in one. In another, some adults played a boardgame. Beyond the houses, the world was dark and dripping with muck. Cady turned and looked at the children. She'd never felt so alone.

Do you want us to bring your brother? He's on the edge. We could get him here soon.

The last time Cady saw Calvin, he wore a thin

hospital gown with tiny blue diamonds. Tubes grew from his arm and his nose and attached him to the machines that walled in his bed. He was tired, but he still laughed when Cady puffed out her cheeks and crossed her eyes. She could always make him laugh. He laughed so hard he gasped, and the beeping of his monitor grew intense. Their mother looked at their father and their father pulled Cady out of the room. Cady's parents were so worried about losing her brother that they sent her away.

Cady looked at the white walls trimmed in gold, the stiff, brocade chairs, and the heavy, swooping curtains. Calvin would hate this place as much as she did. Maybe even more, since he didn't care about big windows or a bed made of trees. She would be a terrible sister if she brought him here, trapped him with her in a fake world where creatures gawked at them. She would be a terrible daughter if she stole her parents' favorite child. It would be selfish and mean and horrible.

But—if she did, they would be alone instead of her.

Melinda Bezdek got her MFA from New Mexico State University and taught English composition at Fort Lewis college before becoming an instructional designer. Her mother filled her childhood with myths, legends, and scary stories.

TASTE
Henry Snider

An October breeze filled the air and its bite tasted of decay. Mason Wells stared through the '72 Mustang's cracked windshield as the first snow of the season fell. Snowflakes, innocently white against the stark countryside, danced on the wind before they succumbed to the pull of gravity. Thirty miles east of Denver felt like another world.

His mind drifted back to the orange VW bus that blew by a few minutes before, and way over the speed limit. The type A in Mason screamed to put the pedal to the floor and teach the driver that classic muscle cars trump old hippie buses every time...but the greasy-haired little girl in the back window distracted him. Unblinking pale blue eyes stared out the rear window as the vehicle pulled away and disappeared over a slight rise, appearing as little more than a dot on the next hill as he peaked the first. Then they were gone.

Only a powdery landscape cut with a razor of a county road lay before him. Mason shook his head and focused on the task at hand. "Get Harmony."

This was the third time they fell off the wagon to drugs. Parties and the fast lifestyle of the elite stock trading up-and-comers drew them in. A little nose candy fell into a habit that cost them six years-worth of savings, the last of which went to pay for a stint in rehab.

Mason down-shifted and slowed around a corner. Barren fields allowed the snow to drift. Armies of flakes accumulated on the road and filled the ditches. A hazy sun hung low in the sky and glowed dull through the storm.

The odometer ticked off another mile and Joes, Colorado faded in the rearview mirror.

"Not much farther."

Both stayed clean for over a year, until the Christmas party in Cherry Creek. With all the holiday spirit and goodwill, neither thought ill of a little holiday blow. Three months later they were in the middle of an eviction and jobless. A five-year trading suspension landed on Mason's shoulders for being caught in the middle of a line while the floor was still open. Harmony begged a loan from her parents to get out from under their addiction's merciless hunger. Mr. and Mrs. Krenshaw relented, as loving parents of an only child tend to, and paid for a second trip to the "cleaners."

"Damn it...c'mon!" He slammed the shifter back into fourth and felt the Mustang slide. Teeth gritted, his foot eased off the gas and let the car work itself out of the impending fishtail. A couple of seconds passed before tires gripped the asphalt's slick surface. Farms drifted by, their bounty harvested for the season.

Mason's foot danced with the accelerator again and pressed harder where opportunity allowed.

Following the second stint at rehab, they got matching rose tattoos after spending the day window shopping used bookstores on Broadway. Mason's was on the inside of his wrist and Harmony's on an ankle. Petals lined in black peeked from the edge of his jacket's sleeve. The artist went too deep with the needle and the artwork's detail ended up hazy, like a testament to the last several years. Hers turned out better but still not worth the money they paid.

The Mustang's odometer ticked off mile forty-one. He slowed and stared hard at the two farms paralleling each other.

"Lady or the tiger...lady or the tiger." Fingers strummed on the steering wheel as he weighed which driveway to turn into.

This time they both stayed clean for over a year. Mason took a job as a bookkeeper's assistant, unable to return to the stock market until the suspension expired. Harmony pulled in fantastic tips at a local bar, averaging five times his meager salary. The uniform's short skirt didn't hurt matters, either. A flash of upper thigh and a smile easily made the difference between a dollar tip and a ten-dollar tip.

Then the tips stopped coming home.

Two weeks ago, an amber vial rolled out of her jacket. Harmony just stared at him and waited for the argument which lasted all night. Tears and cold-turkey promises flowed like water. Then the accusations fired back and forth. Mason lost control and slapped her. It was the first time he ever hit her...first time he ever hit a woman, for that matter. The tiny container disintegrated under an unopened soda can he smashed down, sending glass shard-peppered powder all over the kitchen table. He left her there trying to pick out enough glass to allow for one last snort.

Mason selected the farm on the right, the one with the double-wide mobile home spearheading a century-old cluster of buildings. Recent tire tracks marred the thin sheet of snow and sporadic tufts of yellowed weeds added a nicotine tint to the otherwise pristine landscape. The driveway went straight as an arrow past the side of the mobile home to the homestead's remnants. Barn and paddock fence lay colorless against time's embrace. A splash of color pulled his gaze to the same parked VW bus that passed him earlier.

For the last week he searched for Harmony and followed a spiral trail, first from regular connections made at the bar to seedier dealers who didn't just trade for money. A pistol-whip delivered from a lowlife named Eddie cost Mason a tooth. Now, two hundred bucks later, he brought his own gun to level the playing field. A distinctive lack of quality reflected the price paid. Rust ate at the .38 Special and after two hours with a brush and solvent, he was confident the hunk of metal wouldn't just blow up in his hand.

The Mustang pulled to a stop behind the bus and Mason got out. The little girl still stared out the back window, greasy blonde hair framing a grime-smeared face. He left the car door open in case things turned sour, which, considering his luck as of late, was a distinct possibility. The child's eyes stayed on his car, without so much as a glance in any other direction.

She's not moving.

No breath fogged the rear window.

Stomach-churning reality set in as what he took as pale blue eyes were actually clouded green ones. Mason staggered back, butt knocking the driver's door closed before he lost his footing and fell, the pistol digging into one hip as he struck the ground.

The child's forehead pressed against the back glass. An unfocused stare looked to Mason's right and panic caused him to pull the gun for the second time in three days and, still seated on the frozen ground, he thrust the revolver in several directions in as many seconds.

Convinced he was still alone for the moment, save for his audience of one, he got to his feet.

"Son of a bitch!" The words fell lost in the snow and he crept to the back of the bus to look at the young corpse.

The girl appeared to be seven or eight–pretty in a sad sort of way. A bungee cord attached on either side of the glass anchored her in place like a demented ornament. Dusty-purple lips remained parted and revealed a missing front tooth, mirroring his own. Mason stepped forward and saw a massive brown stain across the lower portion of her t-shirt, the kind of brown that only comes from dried blood. Sickened by thoughts of what kind of torment the child went through before death, Mason started to look away.

Her eyes were different.

The death-faded eye pigment vanished all-together during the last moment. Now one eye, the right, seemed more reflective than the other. She still stared in the same direction but somehow didn't appear quite so dead. His gun hand shook as he backed away.

Mason had drawn his gun for the first time the day before at an east Colfax fleabag apartment. A twenty got him the same address given to Harmony. The two guys there freely admitted she left just a few hours before. Then they talked about how the cute little brunette was short on money. A laugh and a nod from the smaller of the two directed his attention to the far wall thumb-tacked with dozens of panties. The red spray-painted words "Wall of Shame" added a bit of color near the ceiling. Shock set in when he recognized a sheer pair of pink underwear from the white iron-on letter "M" Harmony put on the butt for Valentine's Day. The pistol ended up in his hand, thrust in the dealers' general direction. Mason left with her panties and the dealers' lock box containing a little over eleven grand–enough to start a new life somewhere else.

Another day of questions and nearly a grand in payoffs bought him here.

Nothing moved on the farm, save thefalling flakes. He gripped the pistol tighter and crossed the yard toward the mobile home's back door. Midway across the backyard, he altered direction, wary of being in the dead child's gaze. After one glance over his shoulder, Mason climbed the stairs and stood at the back door. Music thrummed and vibrated one glass pane into a sad mimic of an angry hornet. Seconds ticked by as Mason stood on the stoop, half waiting for someone to open the door on their own and see who was there. Inside, an empty kitchen, filthy with grime and dirty dishes, gave testament to the squalor just out of sight.

"Dead Cat," he murmured, recognizing The Doors' song as it blared. He reached out and tried the doorknob.

Locked.

"Shit." Heat rose in his cheeks.

Mason backed down the steps and walked to the front of the manufactured home, ducking under each window just like the cops on Harmony's favorite crime shows. He stopped at the front corner of the house and surveyed the scene. White snow covered the front lawn and a "Welcome Friends" sign hung cock-eyed on the front door.

Each step felt heavier than the one before and left Mason ready to drop by the time he got to the small deck. One clay jug, overflowing with cigarette butts, lay toppled by the door. A handful of the scattered filters were chewed midway along the shaft just like Harmony did when she was nervous. He grabbed the knob, turned it and swung the door open.

A wall of marijuana smoke hit him in the face, the smell tickling his senses. The television cast a blue glow inside the living room. The misadventures of a cartoon deer danced across the screen. Entangled in a mass of sheet lay an unconscious man, beard and long hair giving the impression, if only for a second, of a drugged-out Jesus complete with caked white smear over his upper lip. Harmony's jacket served as a wadded-up pillow for the junkie. Mason kicked the door closed with his heel.

Through a door to the right rhythmic sounds of ecstasy ceased, replaced with a man's scream of rage and pain followed by, "What the hell?" A smack of fist against flesh, audible over the music, followed. The bedroom door ripped open and a man, built heavy and wearing only a jutting pair of boxer-briefs stepped from the bedroom. Blood ran down the hulk's chest as he pressed down on a nasty neck wound. He saw Mason and bellowed, "Who the fuck are you?"

The man on the couch coughed, getting everyone's attention, then rolled over and returned to snoring.

"You come for him?"

Mason's eyes narrowed as he recognized the hulk as Eddie, the scum who'd knocked out his tooth. His gaze fell from the man's face to the protruding underwear then over to his wife's jacket. "No. For Harmony."

As the name passed his lips Mason raised the gun and fired. The hulk's underwear dimpled between waistband and jutting member. Its depression darkened and blood spewed low in the man's abdomen, the inflicted injury still higher than he'd aimed. The muzzle flash lit the room up for an instant.

A nasally grunt came from Eddie as he fell over, hands clutching at the bubbling wound. The erection deflated in a purge of blood that underwear failed to contain and a small crimson pool spread.

He stared at the gunshot victim for several seconds as shock set in for both of them.

"Oh, God," Mason muttered. "I didn't...I didn't mean

to."

More noise came from the bedroom.

"Harmony," Mason whispered, then yelled. "Harmony!" He ran to the doorway and stared into the bedroom.

Murky light wept around the edges of a tacked-up blanket serving as a window curtain. The room lay barren except for the queen mattress and a nude woman sprawled face down on its sheetless surface.

"Ha...Harmony?"

The figure stirred, rolled over and exposed a bloody face and torso. A Chinese dragon tattoo emblazoned across the stranger's left breast, its mouth frozen in the midst of biting down on the areola. She stirred a second time, but beyond that appeared oblivious to the gunshot just fired.

"Gawwwwd," the figure purred, "that was so goooood." Words drew out as she spoke them and hung in the air. The woman's hand slid across her collarbone, a single nail raked over the dragon's nipple, before sliding perversely lower. "Eddie...come back to bed."

"I'm—"

"You're not Eddie." Eyes snapped open and silver orbs focused on Mason. The sex kitten drone vanished. Blood, already drying, stuck the corners of her lips together.

"Harmony," Mason said again. "I'm here for Harmony."

The woman rolled to the right and propped herself up on one shoulder. "That brunette bitch?"

"She has a tattoo like this on her ankle." Mason extended his wrist and exposed the tattoo. A black stem with two thinly lined leaves bloomed into red petals. Any excuse to look away from those eyes was welcome. "Have you seen her?"

Locks of blonde hair, the same greasy shade as the little girl's, met the meager light. She's the girl's mom,

Mason decided and resisted the urge to tell the dragon-lady how he found her daughter. The dragon swayed, drawing his attention from her face.

"Oh, you like Puff?"

"Huh?"

"Puff. My magic dragon, of course." She pushed herself upright and stood on the bed and faced him. "Would you like a closer look?"

"I...no," he said, suddenly embarrassed. "I don't want a closer look. Harmony," Mason said again, raising the gun in her direction. "I'm looking for Harmony. Is she here?"

Dragon-lady stared with the same flat, unblinking gaze Mason thought her daughter had. "Come here."

His pulse danced as Harmony touched his hand for the first time.

At the party, he looked across the room and saw a brunette stealing glances in his direction.

Vertigo played with his equilibrium. In direct contradiction to the woman's demand, he stepped back, ankles inadvertently kicking into the calves of Eddie. "Don't." Mason's voice wavered in time with his gun hand.

"Gnuhhhhhhh," Eddie managed to mutter while clutching himself. Aside from the moan, he lay frozen in pain.

Mason chanced a glance down at his first gunshot victim. The man rolled onto his back and convulsed. A small amount of foamy spittle erupted between clenched teeth only to be caught by grizzled hair well on its way to being a beard.

"No running," a feminine voice said.

She suddenly stood right in front of Mason, clearing the ten or so feet from the middle of the bed to the doorway in a single blink. Breath, cold and metallic, puffed into his face as she spoke and brought forth an urge to vomit.

Mason staggered back and tripped over the legs he'd already kicked once. He landed hard; wind knocked from him in a single whoof.

The dragon-lady knelt by Eddie and drew in a long breath through her nose. Eyes closed, she looked like a person savoring the smells from a kitchen. One hand, the left, slid seductively down the man's chest, snaking its way back and forth as if in the midst of foreplay.

Mason backed up further, distancing himself from the scene as it played out.

"Hel...help," Eddie muttered.

Her pale hand met Eddie's crimson ones, moved up and over them, resting as if a spider ready to leap. She looked from the clenched hands to his face, then without warning shoved her finger between his and buried the digit up to its third knuckle in the wound.

The pair's eyes locked as gender roles reversed in the sudden penetration. His hips bucked in an effort to extricate the invading digit.

"Shhhhhh, baby." She moved her finger in time with Eddie's weak thrashing. Swaying nipples hardened and Mason saw in disjointed fascination that the dragon appeared to bite down on her breast.

"F...f-f-f-f—"

Her hand jerked free, drenched in blood. She licked the digit seductively, never breaking the locked gaze with Eddie. "Isn't this what you said you liked, Eddie?"

Mason kicked back further until his head hit the television with a loud thunk.

She looked over at him then, silver eyes reflecting the television's glow. A snarl escaped and the dragon-lady's crouched form went from erotic to predatory. Bared teeth, stained orange from blood and saliva, grinned with a savage fury.

Their eyes locked, then went to the mobile's front entrance.

Rather than trying for the door, Mason pushed himself up and jumped against the picture window. Thin drapes padded the escape and the window glass resisted, cracked, then gave way. A white-hot knife of pain shot through his side as he tumbled out the window, slid off the stiff branches of a fitzer bush and landed in a tangled heap on the snowy ground. Mason reached down and pulled a pie-sized shard of glass from just above his hip bone, the jagged slice ended no more than an inch from where he'd put the bullet in Eddie.

"Cosmic joke," he muttered, parroting Harmony's constant comment about ironic justice. With one hand gripped against his own bloody wound, Mason pointed the other, the one with the gun, at the gaping window. No figure moved in the black maw of an opening. He blinked against the brighter light and waited.

Nothing.

Silence.

Snow.

Then a click as the front door unlatched and swung into the relative darkness of the mobile home. The dragon-lady stepped out onto the small deck and shielded her eyes against the cloudy day. Natural light did nothing to compliment her. An addict's body, emaciated save for that of the silicone breasts, stood nude on the deck. Xylophone-like ribs protruded and she descended the steps one at a time, toes stepping carefully on the wood planks.

Mason got to his knees, bit his lip against the pain until blood filled his mouth. "Stay...back." The gun stayed pointed at the ground.

Dragon-lady walked onto the lawn and turned to him. Her skin seemed darker now and hue deepened by the second, the shades changing from milky to tanned leather. The hand shielding her eyes browned further and took on a mummy-esque appearance like he'd seen once on a special about hikers frozen in the mountains. Multiple splits along the palm and arm opened and showed a raw redness underneath beginning to char with exposure.

"Ow," she said in a small voice and looked at the fresh wounds.

Snow fell onto her shoulders and refused to melt, even where flesh glowed like embers.

That unblinking gaze focused on its prey.

Mason stared into eyes so reflective he saw himself.

She stepped closer.

Ten feet...Harmony was reflected in those eyes.

Five...Harmony waited for him, arms wide.

Mason's arm rose and he fired a single shot. The dragon lady's head snapped back and her feet kicked out, leaving her sprawled on nature's white carpet like a sacrificial snow angel.

"I...I warned you," he managed. Bile sat at the back of his throat, threatening to erupt at any second.

"Me-yuhhhh," the woman groaned and worked to sit. A neat hole sat just above her right eye, the surrounding skin ballooned as it kept the shattered skull contained. The right eye itself ruptured from the bullet's impact and the reflective orb wept clear fluid in an oversized crocodilian tear. A matted mass of pink and gray lay entangled with hair a few yards beyond her.

Mason fired a second time into her face and she fell again. Spasming legs kicked out a rhythm only she danced to. A third and fourth bullet struck her, all but obliterating her features from the nose up. Legs quit moving and Mason stared at the spongy mess that had once been a face — nose hanging on by nothing more than a flap of skin still attached to the cheek, one eye collapsed like a crushed grape while the other bulged in its socket from shattered cheekbone, palate splitting into an artificial harelip.

The dragon relaxed its grip on her nipple.

"Hechsssst," passed misshapen lips.

Then quiet hung as cold and heavy as the afternoon chill.

Staring at his handiwork, he felt the bile churn higher. It spilled from Mason's lips and onto his shirt. He gained shaky footing and looked at the blood-stained snow. The pattern took on the form of a Rorschach test print.

"Thuh-thuh-thuh," sputtered from the dragon lady.

Mason turned away, unable to witness the dying woman's last moment. He walked slowly back toward his car, but continued to look over his shoulder every couple of steps.

"Maaaaa–sonnnn," a whisper on the wind called.

Mason stopped with his hand on the car's door.

"Maa–son?" The whisper became a voice. Harmony's voice.

"Harmony?"

"Mason? Oh, God, Mason." Her lyrical voice echoed off of the cluster of structures and he had trouble figuring out what direction her voice came from.

"Where are you?"

"Here," she called out.

He turned, sure it came from the old homestead just ahead of the vehicles and not one of the other out buildings. Hope renewed, he walked past the cars.

Smack.

Mason ducked at the sudden sound and half-buckled from pain.

The VW bus driver's side window spider-webbed as a small palm struck it. The hand disappeared only to be replaced with the ravenous face of the dead child. She pawed at the window, pink drool falling from colorless lips. And there were those damned silver eyes again.

He was sitting with Harmony in the café where they had their first date.

The little girl shifted, eyes reflecting more.

They were throwing water balloons at her cousins' pool party.

The child's palm smacked the glass again, adding more intricate lines to the webbed glass.

"Blink damn it." Mason tore his gaze away and felt dizzy. Shaking the disorientation from conscious thought, he stepped past the front of the bus and chanced a backward glance. The child-thing scrambled to the front seat and kicked at the windshield. A collection of boot prints marred his view of the crazed figure who, luckily, didn't seem to understand the concept of a door handle.

"Mason!"

His head snapped to the left and Mason saw a low shadow shift through the original homestead's missing window. Decades of neglect showed in the frame's swelled wood, remnants of white paint flecked the building's empty panes. Inside, a figure swayed rhythmically back and forth, head and shoulder silhouetted before a stark wall.

Smack. Smack-smack-smack. The fourth impact with the windshield produced an audible crack.

Mason stepped through the doorway. Wooden planks, warped and separated from years of exposure to the elements, creaked underfoot as he went from the small alcove into the nearest room. Generations' worth of rodent feces–the consistency of dirt–covered the floor. Holes from some attempt to run proper wiring ran shin-height along the nearest wall while vandalism had torn through horsehair plaster on the other. A ten-foot-long gash exposed ribbed wooden backing, mortal wounds open to elemental infection.

Harmony sat on the floor with her back against the remnants of the wall, her condition paying homage its abused state. The waitress' pallor matched that of the dragon lady and her offspring, who still pounded away at the windshield. His wife wore work clothes, white blouse now stained with grime and the miniskirt exposed legs to frigid air. Shoes had been lost somewhere along her journey down this particular rabbit hole. A thin, pencil-sized length of silver dangled from one hand, its end sharpened to resemble an oversized hypodermic needle. Mason recognized it as the silver coke straw he'd given her before their troubles started. She bobbed her head and shoulders back and forth, almost imperceptibly, attention focused on her right forearm.

The length of sharpened tube lined up with the crook of her elbow and bit into flesh.

"Harmony!"

An audible sizzle ran the length of the tube and blood welled. Her head dipped with slow determination and a snort, the ferocity of which only a powder-lover could properly appreciate, shook her body. A second nostril-clearing sniff followed.

Harmony's head rose with obvious effort. A single trickle of crimson cut a path from her nose–through the clotted vestiges of former indulgences–and pooled at the corner of her mouth. An all-too-familiar shiver ran through her body, bare heels raked along splintered floorboards. The straw pulled free and smoke rose from a perfect round hole, one with four identical mates along her arm.

"Maaaaaaason," she cooed as euphoria took hold. Her eyes opened and orbs the same reflective silver as the straw focused on him. "Oh...Mason."

He stood just inside the room, frozen in place.

He was caressing the back of her hand while she slept.

A crash came from just outside the missing window, but Mason couldn't bring himself to look away from the scene playing out before him.

"I...I tried, Mason." She looked down at the self-inflicted wounds, breaking the trance. "Funny how they kind of look like cigarette burns."

"Honey, we can—"

"They don't hurt, though."

Harmony shifted, exposing both more leg and an amazing amount of mottled bruising along the underside of her thighs. He stared and a memory ripped him back to the age of fifteen - to when he found his grandmother sprawled half out of the tub, two days dead. Meemaw had the same purple-gray bruise–a discoloration of blood settling along her legs.

"Oh, God, it's sooooooo good," she drawled, ecstasy apparent in her voice. Sporadic convulsions rippled through her.

Mason walked over and squatted beside her. Smells of sex and burnt ham brought a surge of hate, disgust, depression, anger and love, vying for control in a swirl of emotional cacophony. Flashes of their first date, their first heated encounter on a friend's apartment building's roof, their first declaration of love to one another–all of these and a hundred other memories reflected in her mirrored eyes.

"Honey," he repeated. "It's going to be okay."

"I don't know where I am." Harmony's eyes closed and his love's confession spilled forth. "They kicked me out, Mason. She's the one who bit *me* and they kicked *me* out!" A second wave of pleasure took hold. "It wasn't so bad up 'til then...nothing we hadn't done before. But it hurt."

Guilt added itself to the whirlwind of emotions. "We can—"

"D-don't. They wouldn't even let me have my shoes." She clutched the gleaming metal in both hands. Underneath, the palms darkened, taking on an ashen look. "I came in here to try to get warm." Her eyes opened, then rolled back up into her head, lids closing once more. "When...when I woke up I was so thirsty. I cramped worse than the first time at rehab. So much worse."

"Come on." Mason reached for her and she knocked his hand away.

"I couldn't walk. I was so cold. Then the cat came in." An almost imperceptible nod to a bloody mess of orange fur in the corner. "And I wasn't cold anymore."

"God." The song playing earlier came to mind.

Confusion crossed Harmony's face. "I...I can't—I can't stop." She held the straw up, words falling in quick succession. "But it's better with this. You can feel it so much faster."

"We'll get you some help." He caressed her cheek. It felt like running his hand along a leather jacket left to the elements overnight.

Another, louder, crash came from the window. Mason looked up.

The little girl was in the midst of extracting herself from the VW bus, birthing herself from the vehicle in a bloody mixture of gouges and glass. She screamed as hair and a patch of scalp pulled free before jerking herself back inside.

Mason grabbed Harmony by the arm. "We've got to go!" When he pulled, he heard her lower back pull free of the frost.

"No."

He looked down at her as if the word had no meaning and pulled a second time to pull her up.

"There's no time!" Mason felt his bladder tighten, fear pressing the need to relieve himself.

The little girl pushed an arm through the windshield and smacked it down against the front of the bus. Flesh split against glass, bloodless. Just beyond, in the back yard, Mason saw the monstrosity that was the child's mother, complete with deflated mass serving as a head, stagger around the corner.

"Stay," Harmony whispered. She reached up, nearly pulled him off balance and said, "You swore we'd be together no matter what. I—" she sniffed again. "I can't go with you. I can't walk."

"Oh, Jesus. But...."

Her hand ran down the length of his arm and gently placed the metal tube between shaking fingers. She offered her perforated arm as one would a dinner roast. "Here."

"Harmony–"

"Just this once." She smiled the way she did the first time he said, "I love you." Her eyes pulled the cold from him and he felt the world tilt.

Harmony was squealing as he shoved wedding cake into her mouth.

They walked around the lake holding hands and not saying a word, content to just be together.

"I—"

"Shhhh."

Mason glanced back one last time as the child fell from the front of the bus, then gingerly took the straw and bowed his head to Harmony's outstretched arm.

Flesh sizzled and the world fell away.

Henry Snider is a founding member of Fiction Foundry (est. 2012) and the award-winning Colorado Springs Fiction Writers Group

(1996-present). For over two decades he's dedicated his time to helping others tighten their writing through critique groups, working as editor for various publishing houses, classes, lectures, prison prose programs, and high school fiction contests. He lives in Colorado Springs, Colorado with his wife, fellow author and editor Hollie Snider, son – poet Josh Snider and numerous neurotic animals, including, of course, Fizzgig, the token black cat. You can find out more about Henry at http:// fictionfoundry.org/members/henry-snider/

CHRONIC COLD
Josh Schlossberg

Alicia sat shivering on a folding chair at a card table in the middle of the dark, icy alley. The sole streetlamp cast a cone of yellow light around her and illuminated the snowflakes hissing down from the sky. Eight-foot snowbanks hemmed her in on both sides as if she were an Olympic athlete about to launch down a gigantic luge track.

She yanked off her mittens and checked the weather app on her phone: Eight degrees at 6:09 a.m. Snot leaking down her upper lip from her second stupid head cold in three weeks, she plucked a tissue from the pocket of her parka and angrily blew her nose. Her fingers chilled from the seconds of exposure, she slid them down the front of her snow pants—under her jeans but over her long underwear—to thaw them on her groin.

She had to use all her willpower not to be lured back inside to her warm, cozy bed, her bedroom window a snowball's throw away on the second story of her carriage house abutting the alley. But she had already paid the $150 for the right-of-way permit to block the alley, and there was no way she was letting that truck speed past again—as it had every goddamn weekday morning since she moved to Denver five months ago—no matter how cold it got.

The winter had started off mild with average temperatures in the mid-forties and only a single dusting of snow. But the first week of January unleashed a single digit freeze and negative wind chill that dumped thirty-eight inches on the Denver metro area. By the time residents dug themselves out a few days later, a second brutal storm unloaded two and a half feet more. After yet another three feet the following week, the city council allotted emergency funds for extra plowing to allow passage on side streets and alleys. Still, every two to three days for the next few weeks, anywhere from eight to twenty inches pounded the Mile High City. Embarrassed and slightly defensive weather reporters blamed it on the polar vortex.

By mid-February, even ecstatic skiers and snowboarders were praying for the white stuff to stop, with frequent avalanches from upwards of twenty feet in the Rockies forcing resorts to close—two disasters killing a total of six people—while I-70 and other mountain highways shut down on the regular.

As a freelancer working from home, Alicia wasn't too inconvenienced by the novelty of a harsh winter, especially with the grocery store a mere ten-minute walk across her trendy West Highland neighborhood. To the contrary, she had hoped the nearly nonstop snow would keep her neighbor from blowing through the alley in his rumbling, piece-of-shit pickup during his customary 6:10 to 6:20 a.m. window and let her sleep until her nine o' clock alarm.

Happily, the first two storms did effectively block the alley for a week, forcing her neighbor out on the street in the opposite direction—a far more convenient route he had no reason not to take every day, living as he did in the quadruplex on the corner. But then the plows came and, despite the ice, he was back to barreling through at the crack of dawn, vibrating her bed and jolting her from a sound sleep to which she was rarely able to return.

Though she had never seen the culprit, the beat-up Ford with the "Native" bumper sticker, fishing poles in the gunrack, and the breakneck speed at which he drove gave her a pretty good idea of what he probably looked like: a scruffy, stocky, ZZ Top listening plumber-type in a baseball cap and Carhart jacket, perhaps a bit younger than her thirty-five years. Today was the day she would find out for sure when she made him promise to either slow down or avoid the alley altogether. And if he said no? Well, then, she'd simply refuse to let him pass.

Sure enough, a rhythmic scratching from his end of the alley as of someone scraping ice off a windshield. As the crunching got nearer, her belly fluttered when she realized they were footsteps. Had he finally accepted how inconsiderate he had been all these months and was coming over to apologize? Or was he planning to bludgeon her with a wrench?

As she squinted into the darkness, a massive figure emerged from the shadows. Walking on all fours and no less than five feet high at the shoulders, it appeared to be a small horse. Had someone gone for a ride across Denver's arctic tundra and fallen off? But as it got closer, its colossal rack of antlers proved it to be the biggest deer she had ever seen. No, check that, an elk.

Even recent transplants such as herself were familiar with the majestic creatures grazing the meadows outside Evergreen or foraging by the road in Rocky Mountain National Park. She recalled recent news reports about desperate deer, elk, and even moose escaping the snow-choked mountains down to the Front Range communities of Boulder, Arvada, and Golden in hopes of finding something to eat.

Trudging along with its head hanging down, its ribcage and bony haunches protruding from its pelt like a scaffolding draped with a blanket, it certainly appeared to be starving. But what made her toes curl inside her boots were the dozens of barnacle-like black growths sprouting all over its body, ranging in diameter from grapes to navel oranges, including a fist-sized one on the side of its snout like a blind, misplaced eye.

She had never heard of elk attacking people, but if anything that big got spooked—despite its emaciated state it had to weigh at least 500 pounds—it could do some real damage. And something about those warts or tumors made her feel like puking.

She thumped her mittens together to get its attention, but either it didn't hear or ignored the sound and kept plodding towards her. Heart racing, she bit off one mitten, tore off the other, and clapped her hands once, twice, and again until it came to a shambling stop about twenty feet away. Lifting its huge head to peer at her with black eyes, it snorted a cloud of vapor into the air: greeting or threat Alicia was unsure. Seconds later, it lowered its head again and kept walking, its antlers jutting out like broken chandeliers.

Her thighs tensed involuntarily, telling her to get the hell out of there. If she made a break for it, she knew she could reach her back door in five seconds flat. Of course, the moment she set foot inside, her frigging neighbor would come hurtling down the alley and she'd have to wake up the next morning to do the whole thing over again.

No, she wasn't about to abandon her post because of some harmless—albeit disgusting—grass muncher. Not after all the bullshit she'd been through.

When she had moved from small town Missouri into the carriage house on the alley—the only place she could afford in rapidly gentrifying northwest Denver—she knew she'd have to put up with inconveniences like garbage trucks and the hammers, buzz saws, and boom boxes from near-constant construction. If the street on which she lived, lined with manicured lawns and brightly painted house fronts, was the pretty face of her block, the unkempt, litter-strewn alley was its unwiped ass crack.

So, the first time she was torn from sleep just after six o'clock by the roar and rumble of a passing vehicle, she assumed it was a fluke and drifted off again. But after two weeks of the same she bought a box fan, hoping the white noise would drown out the sound. No such luck, as the speeding machine actually shook the building like a miniature earthquake.

Then she bought vibration absorbing rubber pads to stick under the legs of her bedframe. Unfortunately, they did nothing. Furious at the routine interruption of her REM cycle, she found it harder and harder to get back to sleep. After all, other vehicles undoubtedly passed through in the morning without waking her, so what made this a-hole drive like the devil was after him?

After another few weeks of unwelcome wake up calls, she knew she had two choices: address the situation or move out. The next morning, she rose with the sun to peer sleepily from her bedroom window until a beige, ramshackle pickup truck whizzed by. Though the angle prevented her from seeing the driver, she recognized the rusty beater from the quadruplex on the corner. That night, she stuck a polite note under its windshield wiper asking the owner to please slow down or consider exiting via the adjacent street and left her name and address.

The next morning, she was ripped from a blissful flying dream by the truck's grumbling passage. Despite her outrage, she decided to be a good neighbor and give them another couple of weeks to knock it off. When two more weeks came and went without even the slightest reduction in speed or noise, she figured they must not have seen the note before it had fallen out from under the wiper and left an identical one.

Sleep-stealing business as usual from the mystery driver for yet another two weeks. Frazzled and exhausted, she left a third note, this one reminding the person they were breaking the fifteen miles per hour alley speed limit and if they didn't change their behavior, she'd have no choice but to report them to police.

Later that day she found the note wedged into her back door. On the other side someone had written in sloppy capital letters: "STOP PUTTING NOTES ON MY TRUCK! LIFE STARTS FOR MOST @ 6 A.M. ANY OTHER QUESTIONS YOU CAN COME TALK TO ME IN PERSON." It was signed, "Reg," and he had scrawled his address and apartment number three.

She was floored by how a simple request from one neighbor to another had turned into such an ordeal. It wasn't like she was asking him to serve her breakfast in bed. Still, if he wanted to talk face-to-face, it was a good sign he was open to reason.

Just after sunset, hopeful and a bit nervous, she walked

over to the quadruplex and knocked on apartment three, the squeaks, whistles, and chatter of a basketball game in the background, the stink of cat piss wafting out from under the door. When no one answered, she knocked again, to no response.

Confused, she hurried back to the carriage house for pen and paper and returned to the quadruplex. The basketball game had been shut off, replaced by an eerie silence from inside, and she knocked tentatively. Then louder. Nothing. Annoyed, she scribbled a quick note with her phone number saying she had stopped by, stuck it in the door, and walked home.

Twenty minutes later she got a text: "So what's wrong with my driving now?"

"I'm still just asking you to please slow down or take the other way out of the alley in the morning," she replied, following up with a smiley face despite her frustration.

"I'm not speeding!"

Seriously, who did this schmuck think he was? "But you are," she texted, pacing around her tiny kitchen. "I don't want to involve police, but I will if I have to."

"I've already contacted police and they told me I have enough evidence for a restraining order for harassment."

She forced a spiteful laugh at the absurdity of the perpetrator framing himself as the victim. "We both know that's not the case." Livid, her hands trembled as she typed. "I'm simply asking you to take your foot off the gas for three seconds."

"I've been driving down this alley for 19 years with no problems and I'm not about to change for some out of state busybody. Do not text my phone again."

Every muscle in her body taut, Alicia immediately called Denver Police Department's non-emergency number. The dispatcher connected her to Officer Bob Gibson who listened politely as she explained the situation, and he promised to pay her neighbor a visit. Satisfied things were finally under control, she felt the tension melt away from her shoulders.

When she was woken by the prick the next five days in a row, she merely smiled, knowing his days were numbered now the DPD was on the case. However, after another Monday of vehicular thunder, her confidence began to fade. And when Friday dawn rolled around with the same old bullshit, she called Officer Gibson. He apologized, saying how busy he'd been but assuring her he'd get to it that weekend.

If anything, the truck's sonic boom was louder that Monday morning and with a shriek of fury, she picked up the phone and dialed Gibson's number yet again.

"This is Alicia in the carriage house," she said through clenched teeth.

A barely audible sigh from the other end. "How can I help you?"

"You have any idea when you might be going over there?" She said as calmly as she could, her neck muscles straining to keep in her ire.

"I contacted the individual on Tuesday," he said.

"And?"

"They said they weren't speeding."

"But they are!" Alicia's voice shook. "Every day! For five months!"

"I'm afraid it's a he said, she said situation."

"Then send a fucking patrol car out here and catch him in the act!"

"Ma'am, we can't prioritize—"

"Then what good are you!" She hung up the phone.

For a full month she plotted and planned, concocting and discarding various schemes including letting the air out of his tires, scattering nails in his parking space, and pouring gallons of rubber cement in the middle of the alley. Of course, if anything out of the ordinary happened, she'd be the obvious—and only—suspect. Instead, she settled on driving to the hardware store and buying a two-foot high fluorescent yellow plastic boy that read "SLOW" across its torso, which she placed in her parking spot behind her Subaru at the edge of the alley.

The next morning, she was somehow unsurprised to find the little boy lying on its side, its body warped and mangled from what appeared to be a trampling. Fuming, she set it up again, this time jutting a foot or so out into the alley. The next morning it was gone.

At her wit's end, she was in the middle of researching which substances you could pour into gas tanks to keep vehicles from starting when she heard laughter from the alley. She ran over to the window and yanked up the blinds. Three houses away, a pair of landscapers in overalls sat on the tailgate of their flatbed eating sandwiches, their truck completely blocking the alley as if it were parked in their own private driveway.

She slid open the window, yelled "Fuck you!" and slammed it shut again. Cracking her knuckles, she called Denver 311 who connected her to the Right-of-Way Department, where she left a message for the inspector. An hour later, the inspector called back and explained how the landscapers had secured a permit to legally obstruct the alley—gaping, she knew she had her answer.

Right after hanging up, she logged on to Denver. gov and applied for a permit to block the alley for the following work week. That Friday, she received an email from the City saying her application had been accepted along with a $150 bill. She gladly paid via her credit card and triumphantly printed out the permit.

Sadly, the elk didn't care a lick for Alicia's permit and lumbered onward, a thin layer of snow glazing its rickety back.

"Hey!" she yelled, blowing a snot bubble from one nostril. "Look up, you idiot!"

The creature came to a halt. Lifting its head from the end of its long brontosaurus-like neck, it opened its mouth and let out a shrill squeaking whinny—almost like a whale song—that lasted several seconds. Her heart drubbing in her throat, she slowly backed away from the table as it lurched forward again, blocking any escape to her back door. She had put about ten feet between them when it waltzed up to the table and knocked it aside like the flimsy piece of plastic it was.

She hadn't seen it run but knew that even in its degraded condition it could easily chase her down, so she flung herself against a snowbank and attempted to climb to the top. Her toes lost purchase twice but, digging her bare fingers into the crunchy snow, she scrabbled up to safety.

Out of reach now, she gazed in fascination as the beast broke into a trot and, head down, rammed its antlers into the snowbank. Then backed up and did it again. Since Alicia posed no threat to the giant and it had no young to protect, it was clear the poor thing had gone mad with starvation.

Indeed, it kept slamming its head into the snowbank—four times, five times, six—until something shifted beneath her and everything went slow motion. With one final headbutt from the elk, the snow gave out from under her feet. She tumbled through the air in a sloppy cannonball, landed in the alley with a lightning strike on her right knee, and fell flat on her face on the ice.

Moaning in agony, one hundred percent certain she had broken her leg, she forced herself to a half-kneeling position on her good knee as the elk—its entire front half buried in the snowbank—struggled to back out, its testicles swaying underneath its scrawny rump. Loosing itself and shaking the snow from its head and antlers, it spun and snorted at Alicia, a thick black gum leaking from its rolling eyeballs. The stench of spoiled meat curdling her stomach, she dropped on her butt and tried to crabwalk backwards but only made it a few feet before the pulsing misery in her leg almost made her black out.

With another of its horrifying whinnies—a bugle, she remembered from some nature documentary— the monster reared up on its hind legs and whacked its enormous, split front hooves down on the ice, shattering it into shards. She held her breath as it took a step closer and repeated the act. Then another until it loomed over her, steam pouring from its flared nostrils like a demon. Out of options, she curled into the fetal position and pleaded to a God she didn't believe in.

From the far end of the alley, a familiar roar. Seconds later, a vehicle gunning up the gears and coming fast, tires crunching through the ice and snow. Lit up like a phantom in the beam of oncoming headlights, the elk turned to face its challenger.

A blaring horn shook Alicia enough out of her pain fog for her to roll awkwardly on her side and huddle against a neighbor's garage door, eyes shut tightly.

The growl of an accelerating engine and a sickening crunch.

She opened her eyes to find the elk flopping around on its side like a beached salmon, its back broken. Her neighbor's piece of shit pickup idled a few feet away, its front end dented and smashed to bits from the collision.

The driver side door popped open and a middle-aged Latina in a wool Broncos hat and fluorescent yellow vest reading "Traffic Control" stepped out, cradling a rifle. Without a word, she strolled up to the thrashing animal and cracked a round through its head, stilling it instantly.

Smiling, Reg turned to Alicia. "Guess that's what I get for speeding."

Alicia reclined across the back seat of her Subaru, the morning sun shining through the windshield, flurries floating down like sawdust from a faded blue sky. Her bad leg stretched out in front of her, she gauged her pain at a mere throbbing five—compared to the excruciating nine of twenty minutes before—thanks to Reg's Vicodin.

Sitting erect in the driver seat, Reg eased off I-70 onto York St., which Alicia barely recognized thanks to piles of snow heaped to either side of the roadway.

"Is it contagious?" Alicia's voice resonated pleasantly inside her skull.

"To elk, deer, and moose for damn sure." Reg's hands were at the proper ten and two position on the wheel. "But not to humans. Not yet, at least."

"How do you know so much about it?"

She shrugged. "I hunt. Been seeing these sick critters in the mountains for near on a decade. Some call them 'zombie deer,' but I think that's stupid." She shook her head. "Nah, it's exactly what it sounds like: Chronic Wasting Disease."

"And there's no cure?" Alicia mumbled the word "cure" under her breath a couple of times, enjoying the way her tongue pushed against her palate to make the percussive hard "c."

"Nah." Reg braked as they came to a gradual stop at a red light. "They're just hoping the herds will build up resistance. But it's only getting worse."

"And you're sure that's what this one had?"

"From how it looked, I don't know what else it could be. But the way it went after you—I've never seen that before."

"And the warts?"

"I'm no vet, but I do know the sad little buggers get all sorts of things wrong with them when their immunity craps out." Regina slowly accelerated to what couldn't have been a smidge over twenty-five miles per hour. Either she was toning things down to appease Alicia, or she really was a careful driver.

Moments later, they took a right and then a left, and the hospital rose before them like a high-rise mausoleum. And then Alicia was thrown against the front seat as they came to a skidding halt, the anti-lock brakes clicking.

Clutching at her throat, Reg turned around to peer at Alicia. "You okay?"

"Fine," Alicia snapped, scooching back on the seat. It was her fault for letting this maniac drive her—

Reg pointed at the windshield. Milling around on a patch of plowed lawn in front of the parking garage was a herd of no less than sixty scrawny mule deer grazing on the short grass. Alicia marveled at how each of their lean bodies resembled a map of the continental U.S., their rumps forming the western seaboard of California, Oregon, and Washington, their lanky front legs, Florida, and their goofy, big-eared heads, Maine.

Reg honked the horn. Every single one of them looked up and, in unison, began ambling towards them. Regina shifted into reverse, twisting her neck to glance out the back window, and then her body went limp. "Oh my God," she whispered.

Behind them another forty or so deer appeared, joining the other herd to completely surround them.

From inside of the parking garage, the largest, boniest

moose Alicia had ever seen—seven feet at the shoulder, its rack like a halo of bone—bolted out into the drive. Dropping its head like the blade on a snowplow, it broke into a full-on gallop, the deer herd parting to form an aisle as it headed straight for the Subaru.

Josh Schlossberg is the creator of Josh's Worst Nightmare (dedicated to biological horror fiction) and a founding member of Denver Horror Collective. His fiction has been published in Bards and Sages Quarterly, Campfire Tales, Demons, Devils and Denizens of Hell, Disturbed Digest, and The Rock N' Roll Horror Zine. You can find links to his work at JoshsWorstNightmare.com

THE DEAD SPOT
Angela Sylvaine

Since her eighth birthday, Clare dreamed of screams. The shrieking, laughing, breathless kind that came at the coaster's drop pulled from her throat as her stomach flipped and twisted.

The very first time she'd exited the Cyclone on wobbly legs, she'd smiled so big her face felt like it might crack right in half. A picture of that first ride, Clare's arms thrown high and her scarlet hair streaming behind her, sat framed in a place of honor next to her spelling bee ribbons, speech and debate society certificates, and soccer trophies.

Every day of her life, Clare's hours were scheduled and charted to allow nothing spontaneous, nothing exciting. Perfectly predictable. Perfectly stifling. Furthermore, she had no say in what was done with her time. Activities were planned and chosen for her based on specific criteria and goals. Even her friends were not her choice. They were the classmates and neighborhood children who had been selected and approved, deemed the right type.

Her mother insisted the opinions of a child were not

of importance.

There was one exception to this rule. On Clare's birthday, she was permitted an activity of her choice.

"Don't you want to do something else this year?" her mother would invariably ask, her hair pulled back in a severe bun and her clothes neatly pressed and tucked.

"No, thank you," Clare would answer.

And this year, her sixteenth, was no different. She would invite her perfectly acceptable friends to ride the rails of the coaster, to fly with her and be free. Not that they appreciated it, but that was their fault, not Clare's.

You can lead a horse to water, as her mother would say.

Freedom was Clare's obsession. In the dark of her room, out of the grasp of her mother's control, she planned, devising long mental lists of all the things she would one day do. Skydiving, base jumping, race car driving. Nothing was off-limits.

For now, she had one single day per year of freedom. And this year, her sixteenth, *was* different.

Her mother dropped her off at Lakeside Amusement Park, and something amazing happened. Something completely unexpected and unplanned. Clare saw Mia, simply standing amid the jostle of the crowd, staring straight up at the Cyclone, her face transfixed as if in worship.

With a confidence Clare had never previously displayed, she walked right up to Mia and introduced herself. They talked easily, laughed as if to long-held inside jokes, and met one another's eyes with an intensity that made Clare's chest ache.

Mia was like no one Clare had ever met. The human embodiment of a coaster, Mia made Clare feel reckless, free, and a little scared.

Her perfectly acceptable friends were forgotten.

Clare and Mia walked the crowded path through the park, not holding hands, but close enough that their knuckles brushed against one another every few steps. Darkness had fallen, and the park's rides lit up all around them. Speakers mounted on lampposts blasted pop hits, while the rides themselves played their own lilting soundtracks. Both girls wore shorts and tank tops, the uniform of a warm summer night.

Clare snuck a glance at Mia. Petite and lithe with striking white-blond hair worn in a pixie cut that accentuated her almost impossibly pale face, Mia was pretty enough, but that wasn't what fascinated Clare. Mia had a calm confidence, an otherness, a separateness, that made her seem untouchable.

They reached the Cyclone entrance, and Mia stopped and turned, pointed across the park. "The old Speedway is through there."

Clare tore her gaze from the girl and followed the direction of Mia's finger, but she couldn't see anything through the rides, spinning and flashing against the backdrop of surrounding trees.

"It's a big oval track surrounded by sections of bleachers. The kind with a sort of roof on them, to block the sun," Mia said.

Clare couldn't remember the track ever being open, and she'd been coming here for years. "Did you go there when you were little?" But that couldn't be, Clare was sure she'd heard the track had been closed for decades.

"I wish it was still open. Wouldn't you just love to sit in the front row?" Mia ran one hand down her arm, and her eyes took on a dreamy, far-off look. "Feel the wind and heat of the cars as they rush past, spitting little bits of gravel that pepper your bare skin."

Clare swallowed to wet her dry throat. "Why did it close?" she managed.

"There was an accident. A car spun out, crashed into the spectators." Mia grabbed Clare's hand, pulling her up the stairs to the coaster.

"Was anyone hurt?" Clare asked.

Mia didn't answer, must not have heard.

Clare glanced behind her, tried to see the track as they climbed higher, but it was no use.

There was a line for the Cyclone, but Mia tugged Clare past the waiting patrons and went right to the front where a young guy, probably close to her own age, directed those boarding the ride.

"It's my friend's birthday. So, we're going to cut the line and go first." Mia dropped Clare's hand and stared pointedly at the boy.

"No, it's okay." Red crept up Clare's face, and she focused on the wooden platform. If they got kicked out for breaking the rules, her mother would never let her come back.

"Of course, ladies, come on through," the boy said with a lopsided grin, opening the chain to allow them past.

Clare gaped at Mia. "How did you make him do that?"

Mia shrugged. "He wanted to. I just gave him an excuse."

They slid into the front car, Clare's favorite spot, and pressed the lap bar down tight. Many coaster enthusiasts like the back car, but not Clare. She liked the feeling of nothing but air and wide-open space in front of her.

When the car jumped forward, Clare couldn't suppress her giggle of anticipation.

Mia pressed close, and Clare was acutely aware of every spot where they touched. Her shoulder, her arm, her thigh, and the edge of her hand tingled from the charged contact of Mia's skin.

The click, click, click of the car lurching up the track

reverberated through Clare's bones. They approached the crest, the starlit night sky blanketing them from above, and the twinkling lights of the park scattered all around them.

The world stopped for a long moment as they hung at the top, waiting, anticipating.

Then they were pitched forward, down, rushing, racing.

Clare screamed, feeling out of control and free and so very happy. She glanced over to see Mia looking straight at her, seeing inside her, through her.

The coaster leveled out, and Clare gulped in a breath.

"Do you hear it?" Mia asked.

"What?"

"Close your eyes."

Clare did. The tug and pull of the Cyclone was even more intense in the total darkness, and she gripped the bar tight.

The ride slowed. Clare's heart thumped in her chest in time with the click, click, click of the coaster. Something brushed the shell of Clare's ear, and she gasped at the feel of Mia's lips. "Listen. You can still hear the race cars."

The chatter and laughter and shrieks of the amusement park faded into the background, falling away. The screech of tires and the roar of engines rose above the din. Clare's eyes snapped open.

"I hear them," she said, as they again approached the crest.

Mia pointed over the park, past the trees. "Do you see?"

Clare squinted, and there it was. Floodlights blazed, illuminating the oval track and sections of bleachers, waiting and ready for the racers and spectators. That couldn't be. The track was abandoned, wasn't it?

They were pitched forward again, and this time Clare

didn't scream, could hardly breathe. She felt lightheaded, dizzy, detached. Like she might float free from the constraint of the bar and straight up into the sky.

The car slowed as they rounded the final slow curve and hit the dead spot, where all the force from the ride dissipated in preparation for the return to the station.

Mia's face was suddenly just an inch away, her breath a soft caress. Clare closed the gap, pressing her lips to Mia's in a rushed kiss that ignited a slow-burning fire in her belly. She pulled back, tasting cotton candy.

They were back at the station, and someone pulled the bar up over their heads. Mia laughed and dragged Clare from the car, down the battered wooden stairs, back out to the midway.

Deliciously numb and warm, Clare let Mia lead her past the attractions, past the food stalls, through the throngs of people and off the paved path. They continued across the grass and into the dimly lit edges of the park, the sound of the crowds growing further away.

"Where are we going?" Clare asked, her voice husky, almost hoarse.

"You'll see."

Soon they reached the chain link fence that surrounded the park.

Mia dropped Clare's hand to grasp the fence, peeling back a section that had been cut to about halfway up, just enough to allow someone to slip through.

"Can we just go back to the park?" Clare whispered, worry cutting through the contented haze. "My mother–" She bit back the rest of her words, feeling small and much too young.

"I want to check out the old track." Mia's mouth pursed in a pout. "You don't have to come with if you don't want to." And with that, she turned and slipped through the fence and into the tall grass on the other side.

"Wait." Clare rushed forward, wedged herself through the gap. She hissed as a rough edge of the metal link caught on her arm and drew blood. "Mia? Are you there?"

The overgrown weeds swayed in the wind, whispering as they rubbed against one another, and somehow drowning out the laughter and celebration of the park behind her.

Clare caught a glimpse of blond hair ahead, a beacon in the night. She ran through the weeds, uncaring of the dry barbs scratching the bare skin of her legs. The rear of the track loomed closer, the back walls that enclosed each section of bleachers weathered and decaying.

Sweat beaded on Clare's forehead, her neck, her back. The breeze carried a trill of laughter.

"Mia," she said, catching a glimpse of movement in the gap between two sections of bleachers.

Clare found a trail through the overgrown bushes, a path pressed flat by the tromping of feet. She looked back to the safety and security of the park. She could go back, leave Mia behind.

No. Not today. Clare charged forward until she stood between the two sets of bleachers. Just ahead, another chain link fence rose the full height of the bleachers and extended in either direction, probably put in place to stop those in the stands from running onto the Speedway. There were no floodlights, just the illumination of the surrounding city lights. The track itself was cracked and overgrown with weeds. Several rusted cars still sat on the asphalt. Sadness clutched Clare's stomach as she walked along the fence, trailing her fingers along the barrier. She stopped short when she reached a section of the fence that had been torn and crushed inward toward the bleachers.

"I knew you'd come," Mia said from just behind Clare.

Clare jumped and pressed a hand to her chest. "I thought I'd lost you."

"Come on." Mia climbed the first few rows of bleachers to get around the fallen fence, then descended toward the gap that led to the track.

Clare scrambled after her, followed her out onto the cracked, weed-ridden asphalt, Mia's mere presence causing her breath to catch.

"I just love being under the lights. Feeling their glow, don't you?" Mia raised her face, eyes closed.

The lights flooded to life, and Clare gasped. She squinted up at the orbs lining the oval track, felt like she was staring into the sun.

Mia placed her hand on Clare's shoulder. "It's such a perfect night for the stock car races. We were lucky to even get tickets with this crowd."

The din of distant city traffic faded under the roar of the race crowd. Clare spun around, taking in the now repaired bleachers packed with hundreds of people. Their whoops and cheers filled the air. Clare's appetite perked at the smell of hot dogs and popcorn.

"I've never been to a race before," she said, beaming at Mia. Her mother would never have approved this, even on her birthday.

Mia grabbed Clare's hand and tugged her toward a car just a few feet away, a shiny silver coupe with the number sixteen painted on the hood and side doors. Clare stopped short, looking around her with a frown. "We should stay in the stands, shouldn't we?"

"We're competing in the race, silly." Mia opened the passenger side door and urged Clare inside.

Clare settled into the leather seat. The smell of dust and mold tickled her nose as the lights dimmed and the crowds quieted. Confusion clouded her mind. Why was she here?

Mia plopped down in the driver's seat and the flowery smell of her perfume, or maybe it was just the smell of her, cleared the fog from Clare's head. They were actually going to race and maybe even win! Clare would place the trophy on her shelf, and it would be taller and shinier than any of the others.

A gleaming skull keychain dangled from the ignition, and when Mia turned it, the engine growled to life, sending purring shudders through the metal frame of the car. When Mia stepped on the gas and revved the engine, Clare couldn't hold in her laughter. The raw power of the car filled her body with buzzing excitement. And to have Mia next to her, sharing this with her, was a feeling like none she'd ever experienced.

Mia threw the car into drive, and they shot forward on the track, squealing around the curve. Clare was thrown back against the seat, pinned by the inertia of the car, just like a coaster. The windows were open, and Clare thought for a moment that this was strange, but the thought fled as fast as it arrived. The hot summer air tugged at Clare's curls, and the scent of burnt rubber singed her nose.

Several sets of brake lights snaked in front of them, and blinding headlights pressed in on them from behind. The car lurched forward as Mia gave it more gas.

"Faster. More," Clare cried in delight and braced herself against the dash, her heart hammering in her chest. Next year, she'd ask, she'd insist on the Speedway for her birthday.

Cries from the spectators filled the air, rising in the night, and Clare couldn't stop smiling. They screeched around another corner, and Clare felt herself being flung into the air. Her stomach flipped and twisted as she flew, her body light as air, able to float right up into the stars. A laughing scream tore from her throat at the visceral freedom of the flight, at the feeling of being truly alive.

Clare didn't feel the sharp jab of the torn chain link fence or the rough edges of the bleacher steps as she landed in the stands, her arms and legs splayed out in impossible angles. Her hair fanned out around her head in a macabre scarlet halo, and though blood trickled from the corner of her mouth, a smile still split her face.

Mia crouched down beside Clare, brushed a stray curl from her forehead with a gentle touch. "I knew you'd stay."

There were no more bright lights, no more cheering crowds, no more racing cars. No more smell of popcorn or burnt rubber. There was only darkness and rot, rusted metal skeletons on the track, and the lingering sound of Clare's screams carried by the wind.

Angela Sylvaine still believes in monsters, both real and imagined, and always checks under the bed. Her work has appeared in multiple magazines and anthologies, including Dark Moon Digest, Disturbed Digest, and My American Nightmare. You can follow her on twitter @sylvaine_angela and you can find her online angelasylvaine.com.

THE GHOSTS OF CHEESMAN PARK

Grace Horton

A fresh box for each body/ adult coffins changed to child coffins/ they chopped them up so they would fit/ and I wonder/ what does the grave digger feel like while he's dying/ decayed flesh and bone stuck in dirt drenched with blood/ the bodies pulled from the restless ground half eaten/ and the city became restless/ haunted by the dead

Grace Horton is an EDM enthusiast who, like many other EDM enthusiasts, woke up in Colorado one day and decided to stay there. Her most popular topics are trauma, horror, and pineapples. She has an MFA in Writing from Naropa University and has been published in Bombay Gin and the 2017 SWP Guerilla Literary Magazine.

OLD GOLDEN ROAD
Jay Seate

Donald was locking his office door when the phone rang He looked at the instrument as if it was some alien creature. It was six o'clock and pitch-black outside. Although his bank was located on the corner of a busy intersection, traffic was nonexistent due to the frigid evening that wrapped itself around his world. From his doorway he could see the winter wonderland to be dealt with. The roads were icing over and he had a twelve-mile drive home. He didn't want to answer his office phone but he did.

"First National," he said hurriedly.

Whispering voices and scratching sounds.

The connection broke off with a soft click. The room suddenly seemed cavernous and foreboding, as an empty mortuary. He returned the phone to its cradle and turned everything off save for the lights that burned all night. The sidewalks were deserted. Outside, ice crystals swirled around him as he made haste from the bank's rear door to his Honda. The cold turned his breath into milky plumes.

He climbed into the car, the heat from inside the

building quickly seeping away. At least his Honda could be counted on to fire up even in the coldest weather. The ignition caught, but he let the engine warm for a moment before engaging the heat. He backed out of his spot and turned onto West Colfax. The lack of traffic made the signal lights heading west seem extravagant.

"Slow and easy. No rush," he told himself, for it was too soon in the storm to expect snow plows, especially on Old Golden Road.

Donald and his wife Marilyn had purchased a four-thousand square foot, two-story house, one of the early residences to go up along Old Golden Road. It nestled near the far edge of Golden close to the foothills of the Rocky Mountains. It needed some fixing up, but his family had outgrown one-half of a duplex in downtown Denver, and with the promotion to branch manager, it seemed the right time to take on new challenges. They reasoned their move would provide a more idyllic lifestyle, a place where his two daughters could breathe fresh air and his family could feel safer than in the city. A little Golden museum provided the opportunity to get a rudimentary history of the stretch from Denver to Lakewood to Golden.

Successfully navigating Colfax, he turned onto Old Golden Road. At the turn of the 20th century, it served as the main thoroughfare from Lakewood to Golden City, as it was first called. By the 1920s, a few stately homes had sprung up along unincorporated Golden, then known as Silver Town. Eventually, large stone pillars connected by shingled arches were built to serve as trolley stops. Although the trolley service was long gone, the monuments to elite country living still stood, imposing sentinels from a bygone era.

Donald soon discovered that small neighborhoods love their legends as much as their peach and pear preserves they put up in glass jars, so stories about this seven miles of road dotted with homes years past their glory and open spaces where horses and farm animals still grazed played well. He'd heard all the supernatural tales and—ghostly legends or not—their new house was a deal too good to pass up.

At this moment, however, his decision was not comforting. His car's heat wasn't putting out as it should. He grumbled and messed with the dials as he drove, mindful of ice. He was a good driver. No accidents, no citations, but rural winding roads could make anyone feel like a novice.

At a steady 30 MPH, he'd be home in close to fifteen minutes. He focused on the warm kitchen with Marilyn preparing a hot meal, and the girls either arguing or playing contentedly depending on how their day had gone. Had he made a mistake by relocating to a house with some renovations yet to be tackled? At least Marilyn had been a good sport even with unreliable gas and water pipes.

Being the only traveler on a perilous journey, his mind wandered from kith and kin to a universal legend of the unwanted passenger. Here's how it went: *A woman stops to get gas. After paying inside, a man yells something as she returns to her car. She quickly climbs in and drives away. Immediately, the man starts his engine and pursues her. He blinks his lights and honks repeatedly. On the radio, the woman hears about a maniac loose in the area. Her breath catches in her chest, certain that's who's pursuing her.*

The trailing car closes the distance between them. The pursuer tailgates her. She tries to outrun him, but can't. The road is slick and winding. Her car fishtails, but she can't slow down. The tires slide sideways. Panicking, she hits the brakes sending her into a spin. The rear of the car skids ahead of the front and off the side of the road into a ditch.

Shaken but uninjured, she sees the other car stopped on the road above. She jumps out and runs, her heart pounding beneath her breastbone. A house looms nearby. She rushes up the steps and frantically pounds the door until the homeowner opens up.

"A man's after me. He's trying to kill me," she cries, her body cold and her movements frenzied.

The motorist from the trailing car approaches the house as she cringes behind the homeowner. "Thank God you got out of the car, lady," her pursuer says. "When you went inside the station, a man climbed into your backseat. I did everything I could to warn you."

A small grin split Donald's face. Old Golden Road's whoppers also included a ghost boy by a bridge, Satan worshippers behind trees, and other sundry myths. He found these fanciful tales preferable to the prospect of a real event such as the backseat story, but either way, this dark road could tap into the dark side of one's imagination.

In spite of his care, one of his tires banged into a hidden pothole four miles into the journey, shunting the Honda into the oncoming lane. *No traffic, thank God.* He drove on, pondering the damage an icy slide could cause. Running off the road's soft shoulder and into a tree wouldn't be a good way to end a long, tedious day.

He turned on the radio. Nothing but static. He gripped the steering wheel a little tighter, his hands at ten and two, and strained to watch the road more carefully. Guiding the Honda dead center down the dividing line, the world on either side of the road seemed surreal, an icicle world from a fairy tale. The only reality was his vehicle and the part of the road caught in the headlight beams. The strange phone call. Was that the reason for his growing uneasiness? *Not far to go.*

Headlights appeared in the distance. He wasn't alone with Old Golden Road's potholes after all. The vehicle approached going much too fast for the conditions, its bright lights making his eyes squint. He slowed to 20 MPH and pulled as close to the outer edge of the shoulder as he dared.

Goosebumps raced over his flesh as the vehicle, a black sedan, blew by, the Honda shaking from its force. A miscalculation resulting in an accident could quickly turn him and his Honda into an unattractive burgundy waffle.

"Damned idiot," he groused, as he returned to a steady pace of 30. Better safe than sorry. The heater was still blowing cold and he shuddered.

Ten minutes from home at the most, provided the weather doesn't worsen. His spine tingled, but he held steady. "Only about five miles," he said aloud, his sense of urgency growing. He tried to focus on Marilyn and the kids and the warm kitchen where they would eat and talk and then drift off to their respective televisions and cell phones.

He was two-thirds of the way home when another pair of headlights appeared in his rearview. This vehicle approached rapidly as well. *What's with these local yokels?* Granted, they might understand the road and its weather conditions better than him, but whoever heard of the people around here being in a hurry? They sure weren't in a hurry when it came to paying their mortgages.

As the headlights approached, he had no choice but to inch onto the edge of the pavement again and give this crazy driver as much room as possible. The vehicle roared up to within a couple of car lengths, then it held its speed and trailed him. Donald slowed even more. If it hadn't been so cold, he would have lowered his window and waved for the vehicle to pass. But after a few moments, it sped from behind him and quickly swept up alongside the Honda.

Donald glanced over. It was a tank of a car. He could sense the heft of it beside him. Too big for the icy curves, he thought, and hoped it would pass quickly. The windows were dark, but he could see inside well enough to tell that the driver was a pasty-faced man older than himself, someone who should not be traveling at his rate of speed. The driver's head turned in his direction as if on a swivel, a sight as chilling as a kiss from a corpse. There was an antique look about the driver, like a figure out of a wax museum, no one he knew from town or from bank business.

As Donald stared, the vehicle gathered speed and inserted itself on the road in front of the Honda. Its headlights revealed the black sedan had no plates or distinguishing marks just like the vehicle that had passed him earlier. It looked a lot like a...he hesitated to even think about it. A Lincoln touring car, the kind presidents rode in, not the kind of vehicle you expected to run across at night.

The Honda's windshield took on a barrage of ice from the lead car's rear tires. The wipers fought the slivers for a few seconds before the car zoomed ahead, its taillights glowing like two red eyes until it disappeared into the darkness. He slowed down even more. Just another four miles to hearth and home. He tried to imagine the smells coming from their kitchen and the way Marilyn would smile at him when he trudged in from the garage.

No sooner had the taillights ahead winked out than the same car appeared once again to his left, like a black hulking ghost. His heart leaped into his throat. *It can't be* . The Lincoln recklessly swung into the lane in front of him missing the Honda by only a few inches and

splattering the same mess on the windshield. The

Honda's outside wheels hit the shoulder and he strained to hold the vehicle on course.

He's trying to kill me. Donald's sudden fear provoked a needle-sharp stinging in the base of the skull, a twisted knot coiled in the pit of his stomach. This joker was either into mindless aggression or had been made stupid by drink. Donald's heart pounded harder and faster as he suddenly remembered another legend about a phantom driver.

"Enough of this," he said loudly, craving a rational explanation. The driver was clearly nuts, traveling so fast at night on an icy road. But the paradox persisted. The same long, black car with the frightening driver. Philosophical questions about being singled out for ruin by a murderous crazy would have to wait. He just wanted to get home and off the road.

He slowly pulled onto the shoulder and stopped the car as the taillights ahead disappeared once more. The way his night was going, he couldn't keep from twisting around and looking into the well behind the front seat—a nutcase lying in wait would have been more acceptable than some mysterious road warrior with a death wish. He fished his cell phone from his jacket's breast pocket and called home. After the series of beeps, the phone rang and he heard the click registering a connection. There was no "Hello," just static, then voices whispering, the same sounds from his earlier phone call at the bank.

"Natalie? Jenny? If it's either one of you, please put your mother on."

An acute silence lasted for several heartbeats before the small screen went dark. He hadn't realized how truly frightened he was until he heard the sounds coming from his own house. *The girls weren't ones to screw around with the phone and why hadn't Marilyn answered?*

Fighting off panic, he put the Honda back in drive

and pulled off the shoulder, feeling a desperate need to get home. He was no longer concerned about the ice build-up or the other vehicle He was only worried about the safety of his family.

Just a couple of miles to go.

The car finally churned out a little heat, but he remained nearly as cold as the night air. A chill ran into the recesses of his mind and body. Fear had replaced the rationality of a man who spent his time managing numbers and balance sheets.

One last hurdle before reaching the driveway to his front porch—a narrow bridge over a shallow ravine known to be especially treacherous on evenings such as this. A speed limit sign warned drivers to slow to 25 MPH when crossing, even in good weather. He thought about using the cell phone to ring his house again, but wanted all his attention on navigating the last mile.

A hungry darkness lay on either side of the road. Everything had become unfamiliar, a mysterious shadowland. The headlamps lit peripheral fence posts and cast grotesque, shifting shadows along the route like creatures prowling the night. Occasional tree phantoms clawed out at him from both sides of the blacktop. In spite of the cold, a bead of sweat trickled from his temple down his jaw.

His penchant for numerical analyses pushed his accountant's mind into overdrive. Maybe it wasn't the black vehicle at all. Maybe it was the road itself— *Old Golden Road.* What an innocent moniker for this dangerous ribbon of pavement. Maybe an evil force ran under it like an aquifer he'd somehow tapped in to. Maybe the horrific legends gained purchase in the cold of night.

Was he hostage to a nightmare? The Lincoln passing him again—wasn't it like the nightmare about running but getting nowhere or a whispered secret known by everyone but you? He fought to keep his imagination from running amok. The black car was bad enough without images of unpleasant things leaping out in front of his Honda or swinging from a limb, and landing with a thump on its rooftop or the idea that the road itself was evil. Fear was one of the reasons they had left the city. Danger felt out of place and time on the road with the pleasant, melodic name. Until now. Yet here it was, fear clinging like cobwebs to a rational person—a banker for God's sake. The journey's events had planted the seed of a nervous breakdown.

Though the night closed in like a tunnel, the bridge was now in reach of the headlights, its railing on either side reminding Donald of two rows of teeth. "Almost there. Just like *Sleepy Hollow's* Ichabod Crane. Make it over the bridge to safety. I'll slow—"

On the far side of the bridge an ominous pair of headlights glowed. He held his breath, an awful, nauseous feeling sunk into his marrow. It wasn't imagination or paranoia, this was to be more than a game of chicken or insane recklessness. The Lincoln was there, waiting. And for whatever reason, the driver wanted to kill him.

His body was overtaken by a profound loneliness, one that froze him beyond the surrounding elements. Would he ever see his family again? What would they do without him? What would he do without *them*?

He started across the bridge, but by the time he'd driven a third of the way, the black vehicle started across at the other end and bore down on him at high speed. There was no turning back.

No chance to back up or let it pass. The image aroseof him and his Honda smashed like a pancake. But if he swerved to the right or left, he'd be into the ravine.

Onward the maniac came, right down the middle of

the road, racing straight for the Honda. Donald said a prayer, not for him, but for the forgiveness of his family for whatever transgressions he might be guilty of.

The Lincoln was doing sixty to his twenty, the momentum would carry the cars into a collision no matter what. Still, he had to do *something*. His life was reduced to the question of, should he drive off the bridge or keep going straight?

He had to get to his family. From some remote pocket in his mind, he remembered a saying he'd once heard. *If the devil comes a knockin', don't turn your back on him. Go toe to toe.* No time to hesitate.

The rational brain of a banker was now on holiday. This was his first reckless, even suicidal decision since, as a boy, he jumped into a rapidly moving stream to rescue his drowning puppy. Fate was in charge now.

He floored the accelerator. Adrenaline rushed through him like a blue flame as the two sets of headlights approached each other. A second before impact, he braced his arms, drew his final breath, and closed his eyes. In that split-second, he wondered if his life would flash before his eyes. Then he started to scream.

A horrific swoosh went past him—through him, like a jolt of electricity. He opened his eyes and hit the brakes. The Honda skidded and slid to a halt on the far side of the bridge. He relaxed his grip on the wheel. The car had apparently been no more than a phantom after all.

Fatigue replaced tension and he was no longer cold. *But why all of this otherworldly theatrics?* He felt on the edge of an alternate dimension, as if eyes on the other side were watching him. Exhaling a long, relieved sigh, he continued the final distance to his house, feeling the warmth of it even now.

The sky had cleared. Donald could see the stars wheeling in the outer darkness. As he turned the final bend on Old Golden Road, past a copse with its dark, bare trunks and limbs, he stared past a thicket of underbrush at a glowing light in the distance. Not the lingering rays of a departed sun, or the teasing palette of pastels signaling a reluctant dawn. It was something else: yellow-orange tongues of flame. Within twenty yards of the turnoff to his driveway he slammed the brakes and ground to a halt. Pushing himself against the driver's door, he couldn't get it to open.

A fire-truck, moving much too slowly, rolled down the road from the opposite direction and pulled into Donald's drive, blue and red lights flashing against the night. Smoke and crackling bursts of flames belched from every window and door of his house, reaching into the sky.

He was neither frightened nor even apprehensive. To the contrary, a quiet serenity overtook him. Why wasn't he out of his mind with grief, overcome by the suffocating weight of despair at the possibility of his family trapped inside an inferno and burning to death, their home becoming a funeral pyre? Echoes of dying screams should have assaulted him.

The answer, he felt sure, was coming in his direction. The long Lincoln trailed behind the fire-truck and a patrol car rolling up the drive to the burning house. Instead of turning with the other two vehicles, the transport rolled down the twenty yards of icy road toward the Honda. It passed him, but this time, it traveled slowly.

He could see inside the other car now. In the front passenger seat sat his wife, Marilyn, beside the lanky driver. In the back sat Natalie and Jenny, his daughters. For Donald, it hadn't been necessary to stare into the abyss and travel the stages of shock and denial. When the vehicle passed by, he understood everything.

He knew where the vehicle was going this time. It was

traveling to the icy bridge on Old Golden Road to pick up another passenger. The moon looked down with a vapid eye, its light producing a radiant glow to a spot near the bridge.

He could now see his burgundy Honda had careened off into the gully, its front end totally demolished. The engine block had been shoved through the firewall. The the truth hit his bloodstream like an injection.

The loneliness had lifted. There was just enough room for one more traveler next to his two daughters in the back seat. They wouldn't be on the treacherous road much longer. And he didn't have to worry about macabre voices on the phone, the bank, the wisdom of their move, or anything else real or imaginary. Sooner or later, the universe was about balance, like his spreadsheets.

Everything was settled now as he'd been given the opportunity to join his family to whatever destination they were headed, leaving one more story for the Old Golden Road.

Jay is a writer who stands on the side of the literary highway and thumbs down whatever genre that comes roaring by. His memoirs and essays report fact while his fiction incorporates fantasy, horror, or humor featuring the quirkiest of characters. He currently reposes in Golden, CO.
His website is www.troyseateauthor.webs.com

IF I SHALL WAKE
Desi D

The pain in my chest spiked. It had been progressively getting worse despite the fact I'd been taking those damn horse pills every single day. All the doctors agreed I needed a new heart, and soon. I should be taking it easy, avoiding stress while coming up with 1.4 million dollars for the transplant before my old pump gives out.

My fucking insurance determined this was a preexisting condition. Their CEOs behind the decision were lucky my focus had to be on earning money for my new heart. However, once I got my transplant, I planned on fitting each of those bastards with a body bag because of their preexisting condition of being assholes.

I only needed to complete this final job to afford my new ticker. I waited for my target, Joanna, outside of the Falling Rock Tap House on 19th and Blake Street. I had a clear view of her from my table on the patio. The buildings on each side of me blocked the breeze allowing the juicy burgers' scent to fill the air. My fries were crispy, just how I liked them. The place was packed for a Tuesday night, and still I was alone, invisible to those around me consumed with their drinks and conversations.

Denver, Colorado is an interesting town. When I landed at DIA, it looked empty like another small hick town. Then I reached downtown, where it transformed into a big city surrounded by a panoramic view of the mountains and blue skies. It wasn't overly crowded like L.A. or New York. There was a calming atmosphere I enjoyed.

Even now, I could almost see a star or two in the night sky. I might have to come back here after—a sharp pain constricted in my chest. I clenched my jaw until it passed. The thin air from being at mile high probably wasn't helping. The doctors had warned me not to overwork myself.

This job should've been easy, it should've been finished in Phoenix last week. I had followed Joanna for a couple of days attempting to learn her routine, but she didn't have one; she never did the same thing twice. She visited a few office buildings, took a couple of meetings at local restaurants or coffee shops.

Usually, this wouldn't have been a problem, and it wasn't surprising since she was a consultant who never seemed to sit still. My employer, Phantasm Ink Corporation, didn't specify what type of work she did or why they wanted her dead, and I didn't ask. I'd done a few jobs for them in the past. They paid well, and with my ticker threatening to give out, that was all I needed to know. Although I figured she'd seen or overheard something she shouldn't have and now was a loose end.

It wasn't difficult to slip a poison into her drink at a café in Phoenix. I just walked by dropping a small tablet into her cup when she looked away. She never even noticed me; I don't stand out. I am of average height and build, I keep my brown hair short, neat, unimpressive, I don't have any tattoos or wear anything that might get me noticed. This job should've been over then; however she didn't touch her nearly full coffee. It's possible she just bought it to be social.

From there I followed her to the humid sweathouse state of Texas. This time I placed the poison onto the door handle of her rental car. I don't understand how she managed to avoid it. I was sure I hadn't missed a spot. So, now here I was in Denver waiting for another opportunity.

I preferred to poison my victims, but I didn't use just any toxins, I made my own untraceable, fast acting, and painless blends. I may be a killer for hire, but I never made anyone suffer. I'd seen enough of that as a child.

Joanna stood at the bar less than twenty feet from me with a strained grip on her glass, as if it was going to try and escape while she spoke to the bartender. It wouldn't be easy to slip anything into her drink this time.

I could only see the side of her face, but she looked determined. Her long dark braid swung with each of her words. The bartender shook his head slowly, his thin graying ponytail brushed against the glass he had been drying for the last few minutes. The shiny bald spot on top of his head reflected the hanging lights. He was built like a boxer an expression of concern behind his thick black-framed glasses. From their body language, this was not just another meeting—they knew each other. Plus, he had been ignoring the other customers trying to get his attention, leaving their service to a scrawny bartender who didn't look happy about it.

He took a deep breath, setting the polished glass down, then pulled something from his pocket, sliding it to her like an illegal drug. However, I'd never seen drugs passed in a worn, dingy, ancient-looking cloth. Joanna closed her fist around the thing, and the bartender gently placed his hand over hers, leaning into her as he spoke.

She released her glass, shaking her head before pulling her hand free. She clenched the shaggy rag like it held the secret of life itself. A small light started to shimmer through her fingertips.

I rubbed my eyes; they had to be playing tricks on me. The pressure in my chest spiked, I looked down at my fries while I resisted the urge to grab my breast. The pain never lasted this long. I was too damn close to getting paid to stop now and I had already survived far worse. I would get my transplant before this worthless pump killed me.

I hadn't been born a killer, I was made into one—something I made my uncle regret. His farm is still known to this day as the Butcher's Farm. He didn't have conventional livestock. I survived when other kids didn't because I wasn't willing to accept my fate. I did what I had to, to survive.

For years, it was them or me. I always chose me, and that meant cooperating, being a killer. I was family so that was why I got the option to assist instead of being only a victim. I did my part and developed a talent for it. I never enjoyed the kills but when the opportunity arose, I took it, and my Aunt took a knife to the back. I was twelve.

This pump in my rib cage was just the most recent thing that wanted me dead. Well, screw it, too.

The pain receded.

"That looked painful," Joanna said, sitting down across from me. She took one of my fries. Strange, faintly glowing, blurry tattoos that might have been letters wrapped around her arms. They had to have been some of those new invisible ink tattoos that were becoming popular. "With your heart, it was smart to leave them unsalted."

Shit, she had taken advantage of my momentary distraction to approach me. I didn't let my surprise show;

I wouldn't give her the satisfaction of letting her know how off guard I had been.

Joanna chewed on her fry, waiting for my reply. I could see there would be no point in pretending I had no idea who she was, so I took a sip of water and waited for her to make a counteroffer for her life. There would be no other reason she hadn't called the cops.

She set the cloth before me. It had the slightest of a glow to it, a white light that gave the impression that my eyes were blurring, except it was the only thing out of focus.

The bartender she had been speaking to was gone. I angled myself to put my back up against the brick wall. Her friend wouldn't be sneaking up on me.

"OK, Shaun," Joanna said. "I'll go first. I'm here to offer you a job, come work for me."

I knew it. Still, she had used my name, so I was intrigued. None of my other marks had spotted me or figured out who I was. "How much money are you talking?"

"None," she said grinning.

Pain seized my chest then spread throughout my body. I tried to fight the darkness that swallowed my vision.

The world went black.

I awoke to blood-curdling screams as if from actors in a B-rated horror movie.

It took me a minute to remember where I had been. No one should've been able to get the drop on me unless I had been drugged. Shit, Joanna had made me, but when? I'd figure that out later.

The screaming was getting annoying.

I tried to open my eyes. My eyelids barely moved under a sticky substance I recognized as duct tape. It was not a sensation easily forgotten, no matter how hard I had tried. My uncle had loved the stuff. He had boxes full of it.

Joanna and those helping her would regret this. I tried to move my arms—nothing. I wasn't dead yet, so they wanted something. Probably the person who had hired me. They'd never get me to talk, and the stupid fucking movie didn't scare me. It was merely pissing me off.

The terrible odor of rotting flesh, antiseptic, and something far worse I couldn't describe filled my nostrils. I wanted to hurl.

On a positive note, at least my chest pains had stopped.

The screams grew louder, deeper, filled with all sorts of profanity, some of the words I didn't even know. I didn't want to consider they might be real, but the horrific smells that surrounded me insisted those sounds weren't from a movie.

I couldn't tell if the rising temperature was from the room or my growing panic. I pushed it down, reminding myself it wouldn't help, I had to keep calm so I could get out of there.

My fingers scratched something hard beneath me—a metal table by the scraping sounds. They had to be just like the tables my uncle had in the barn. Who was dead, I repeated to myself.

I couldn't move my wrists at all, just my fingers. My thumb touched the bare skin of my ass. Well, I hope Joanna was enjoying the view; this seemed a little extreme to get me naked.

I was starting to get a headache from this horrible movie my captors were playing, no pauses between the screams. The head games weren't going to work on me. I knew it had to be a movie. It had to be.

I tried to ignore the racket, but I couldn't help noticing

how they had gone from a high pitched girl's scream to deeper, huskier, raw hollers that could only come from a man. Movies never got that part right.

My heart pounded without chest pains to accompany it.

When I got out of there, I would take my time putting Joanna into the ground.

The metal slab beneath me got hotter, searing my exposed skin. My lips struggled against the tape as I screamed my rage.

Frantically, I scratched at the metal beneath my fingertips, trying to reach the tape. My arms, wrists, legs, ankles, neck, and stomach wouldn't budge. Sweat poured off of me.

Each scream from the other man was hoarser than the one before.

This could not be happening to me...

No.

No.

No!

This was not happening.

Fuck, this could not be happening, again. I had been in a crowd. This had to be a dream, a terrible, terrible nightmare. I should be able to control this, to wake up.

There was a bone-cracking sound followed by choking and gurgling noises.

Fuck!

Where the fuck was I?

What did they fucking want?

The screams from the man quieted down to whispers of pure terror intermixed with choking. He couldn't have been more than five or ten feet away.

Fuck!

Fuck!

Fuck!

I was panicking, not good.

I needed to calm the fuck down, get ahold of myself.

Panicking never helped. It didn't help me escape my sadistic uncle or his vicious wife. It wasn't going to help me now.

I'd gotten out of tighter spots. I'm a survivor!

Whoever did this would pay. They would make a mistake, then I'd escape. People who panicked died like the children my uncle had abducted.

Think, dammit. Think. There had to be something I could do to improve my situation.

I pushed my tongue through my lips, creating as much spit as I could. The tape was coming off. They had no idea who they were messing with. They'd find out soon enough.

The other smell that had been all around me registered in my mind: dried grains. The wheat and screams attached themselves to memories I had spent most of my life suppressing.

My aunt and uncle had been evil bastards with a private wheat farm in the middle of nowhere. That odor had filled the place along with the tears of children.

I wasn't going to surrender to the panic bubbling inside of me. They had made a mistake, and so would my current captors.

My uncle had gotten too eager about what he was going to do to a small freckled boy who wouldn't stop crying. My aunt took great pleasure in laying out the boy's misdeeds, which boiled down to not obeying. She had burned him, and he wouldn't stop crying.

Back then, they didn't doubt my obedience that had been forged from fear of what I had seen them do to the other children, from what they had already done to me.

I had kept my head then; I would keep it now.

My aunt and uncle had underestimated me. They'd

let down their guard, left my cage unlocked, a knife unattended, as my uncle dragged the freckled boy fighting and kicking away.

The kid knew, like the rest of us, that he wouldn't leave that room. He made so much noise my uncle didn't hear me stabbing my aunt, at first. Eventually, she was louder than that child had been.

I grabbed my uncle's keys and stole his truck before he finished checking on his dead wife. He chased me for almost a mile.

The smooth hot table beneath me, the duct tape restraining me- this was precisely how my uncle had strapped down bad little boys and girls while they waited for their final punishment. Their tears and moans still haunted my nightmares.

This scenario couldn't have been a coincidence. It was too similar. How had my captors known? I had changed my name, erased any connection I once had to them.

My rage tore at my throat through the tape in low, muffled groans. The more I struggled, the harder it became to breathe, but I didn't care.

The great state of Kentucky had fried my Uncle years ago. He was dead. I had survived.

The man next to me whimpered, no longer able to scream. I knew that sound. I pulled harder.

Someone laughed. A small delicate laugh. A little girl. Her small warm finger touched my bare chest below my collar, then lightly traced my breastbone. "Sssshhhh, don't waste your energy. It will be your turn soon."

I had always hated watching parents tickle their children. Their laughter annoyed me but until now, I had never found it frightening. I increased my efforts against my restraints, my heart thudding to break free from my chest.

The man's vocal cords were giving out. I could no

longer make out what he said. I didn't need to. He was begging to die.

Now that the man had stopped screaming, I could make out low moans all around me. There were others in this room. Metal scraped against metal.

I couldn't stop shaking.

The little girl sang, wiggling each of my toes, "One little piggy got cut off at the market. The second little piggy got smashed. The third little piggy melted away."

Adrenaline surged through me. I pulled, squirmed, tried to break free.

"I can't wait until it's your turn," she said, patting my leg. "The other man is no fun anymore. He's barely making any noises."

The poor screaming bastard next to me was still pleading for death. The deep voice of a man answered him, "You'll find no relief here." He sounded like my uncle.

The little girl laughed some more. I was shaking uncontrollably, my eyes filled with wet despair. This was not happening to me.

I had escaped. My uncle was dead. This had to be a nightmare, only a nightmare.

"Wake up! Wake up! It's time to wake up," I yelled through the tape.

Something the size of a small fist hit me in the balls. I saw flashes of light as pain shot up my body.

I was awake. There was wailing in the distance of horrific pain.

"It's your turn. I'll bet you'll be lots of fun," said the voice of a little giggling demon girl.

The sounds of a metal cart squeaked its way over to me. My heart froze. Bile rose from my stomach, filling my mouth, burning my nostrils. The tape was firm. I swallowed.

The dread of what was going to happen to me was maddening. Over the years, I've had nightmares where I was trapped in that barn again that felt so real I feared my escape had been nothing but a dream.

This was different; bound to a table, naked, blindfolded, waiting for a squeaky cart to reach me. Dammit, hadn't whoever they were heard of W-D 40?

I had gotten away only to end up right back here. I'd worked so hard to carve out a life for myself with the only skills I possessed so that I would no longer be a victim. And it was all for nothing. To end up on some other sicko's table, and now my defective heart no longer wanted to give out—just my luck.

I couldn't stop the uncontrollable laughter that took hold. My body shook, no longer stuck to the metal table—too much sweat.

The cart squeaked closer to me.

I was breathing too fast, my nose making a whistling sound. I felt like I was spinning. I wanted to pass out but there was too much adrenaline pumping through me.

I was about to break a promise to myself. I knew it was a stupid time to think of it, but I had promised myself I would never be this helpless again. Shit!

The squeaky wheels stopped next to me.

An icy chill ran down my spine. I recognized the sound of metal scraping against metal from an item being picked up.

The demon girl asked, "Where are we going to start?" She ran her finger down my bare chest again. "Can I get him started?"

There was a grunt of agreement. The girl tapped her little fingers against my stomach. I flinched every time she touched me, and she giggled with evident excitement.

"Goodie, he will be my first," she said. "Where should I start?" Her little fingers grabbed the end of the tape over my eyes then quickly pulled it off, along with some of my eyebrows and lashes. "I wouldn't want you to miss a thing."

The brightness blinded me at first; then everything slowly came into impossible focus. The room was small, and the walls were on fire. On fire!

The man standing over me was of average build with neatly combed short hair. The black fires of hate burned deep within his eyes. His complexion too pale, his smile like that of a clown, bleached skin caked with blood instead of makeup. The light nearest to him vanished, sucked into the massive, wing-shaped black holes spreading from his back. It hurt to look at them, as if they were trying to suck the light out of my eyes, too.

I peed, completely emptying the contents of my bladder. The demon girl took a slight step back, giggling.

She looked to be about eight years old with red curly pigtails and tiny little horns. She smiled at me, a bit of blood on her cheek like leftover frosting. Her eyes were blood-red, hollow, and consumed with animosity far darker than the word could describe.

I knew with an unholy certainty that this had to be Hell. There would be no mercy, no end, no escape from here.

That didn't stop me from begging.

The little girl grabbed my face forcing me to look at her. I tried to pull away, but she was stronger than me. My moans seemed to amuse her. She grabbed the edge of the tape over my mouth then ripped it away along with pieces of my lips. I shouted all the profanity I knew.

She placed her index finger over my mouth. "Shhh, it's not the time for that, yet."

For an instant, I saw my aunt shushing me as she tightened the straps around my wrists. My hatred for that woman momentarily surpassed my fear, and I tried to bite the demon girl's finger off. I missed.

Her blood-red eyes seemed to boil. She reached down, grabbed my nuts, and squeezed. "That was not very nice. I will teach you some manners by removing these first."

The shit flowed out of me, then.

Oh, God, this couldn't be it. Not this—what happened to the lake of fire? Throw me into that, but not this, not again.

I no longer tried to fight my panic, there was no point. I cried like a baby. I pleaded, begged. I couldn't stop myself. I knew there would be no rescue, no God coming to save me. No one helped me before, this time would be no different. I had to save myself.

I stopped my begging, to the demon girl's disappointment.

This wasn't fair, not after everything I had been through. But nothing about life had been fair, so it would be foolish to expect the afterlife to be any different. With effort, I focused on my anger, letting it take over; it was better than the terror.

I spit my defiance at the devil child. She raised her scalpel over my dick. I decided right then and there that not even Hell would succeed where my aunt and uncle had failed.

I pulled at all the tape that held me down. It loosened.

Lights flashed over my head, blocking out the burning ceiling. In the flickers, I saw the night sky, and my target, Joanna. With each burst of light, I rose from the table. My restraints dissolved, releasing me.

Joanna held that ancient cloth, whispering words I couldn't make out. A crowd of maybe a half-dozen people formed behind her, some cloaked in bright light.

The bloody man with the void-black wings grabbed me, pulling me back down. The demon girl squeezed my testicles harder as she pushed me down. Thankfully, she had dropped the scalpel. I saw spots from the pain between my legs. I clenched my jaw shut; they would get no more screams out of me.

Joanna's voice rose, though I still couldn't make out any of her words. The neon white tattoos along her arms glowed. They were more distinguishable to him now, written in a language he'd never seen before.

The demon girl released a high-pitched scream, "No, he's mine! He doesn't get a second chance! He's already made his choice! He's mine! He's mine! Give him back, he's mine!"

The pain stopped; everything went out of focus.

A moment later, Joanna held me on her lap. "Welcome back to the land of the living," she said.

My ribs and balls still burned from where those creatures had grabbed me. Everything hurt, pain pulsated through my chest.

The people cloaked in light seemed to fade from existence as the gawking crowd came into focus behind Joanna. Sirens blared in the distance.

"Easy now," Joanna said. "If you die again, I don't think I can bring you back."

My weak heart had given out. So how was I back? And why was my target helping me?

"I wouldn't recommend killing me," Joanna said in a low voice. "My power is what's keeping you alive. You should take me up on my job offer."

"Fuck you."

"I could always send you back," she said, lifting the cloth.

The drumming pain in my chest beat in unison with the thrumming flare -ups of my still burning nuts. The sirens faded, replaced with the distant echoes of wailing that surrounded me.

Go back to that demon child, or bide my time working

for Joanna until I could figure a way out of this mess. It wasn't even a close call. I nodded my agreement.

She placed the cloth against my neck. The strain on my heart receded. Shit, this sucked.

Desi D is a writer of contemporary fiction, fantasy, space opera, and non-fiction. She has a B.A. in creative writing and an M.F.A. in Writing Popular Fiction from Seton Hill University. She has always had an overactive imagination and stories to tell. For her, writing was inevitable. It was the only way to satisfy the voices inside her head. Every character wants their story told, and she will write as many of them as she can. When Desi D is not writing, she is dreaming of faraway places and the people who live there. She lives in the beautiful state of Colorado where she was born and raised. Nothing in her life is simple, not even her pets. She has two cats and one dog who is allergic to cats.

THE BLUE LADY
Sean Murphy

There was nothing I liked more than my four-year-old son, Connor, coming into our room in the morning, sleepily crawling into bed and cuddling. Except the time he said it was because "The Blue Lady" from the closet wouldn't leave his room.

"What lady?" I asked, half asleep.

"The Blue Lady, she comes in the window and stands in my closet," he said from between me and his mom, Shellie.

It wasn't the words he used that made the hairs on my neck stand up, it was the casualness and confidence with which he said them. At that point, I was fully awake and more than interested in the story.

"Start again, kiddo," I said, playfully ruffling his hair.

"She flies in my window and stops in front of my closet. I don't say anything. But she always turns and stares at me. Her hair looks like the wind is blowing, but my window is shut," he said in that sweet, little kid falsetto. "She's wearing a blue cowboy dress. She's come the last few nights." His voice registered no shock. After all, he was four and didn't know this wasn't normal.

By then, Shellie was also awake and listening. We both sat, stunned, as the little person in the middle of the king-sized bed told us "The Blue Lady" had no teeth and no eyes.

"How do you know she doesn't?" I asked, not really wanting to know the answer.

He thought for a minute, as if looking for the right way to say it. "She smiles at me, I don't see teeth, only a really long tongue, pointy like a snake's. She doesn't blink and when I look at her, I don't see the color part of her eyes, just the part that's always white." He motioned to his own eyes to illustrate what he meant. "Except hers are all black."

He fell silent for a minute while he searched for the TV remote, his favorite Toon Disney show was on. My pulse pounded in my chest and thundered in my ears as I tried to come up with an explanation as to what in the holy hell just happened. I glanced at Shellie—she felt it too: the sinking feeling this was not made up but happened just minutes ago. My morning cup of coffee wouldn't be needed.

As my perfect little child watched TV and dropped Pop Tart crumbs on my side of the bed, I wondered how this story had come to him. It had to be a story: Nothing like that exists, certainly not in Littleton, Colorado. Had he watched something scary on TV? Had I watched something scary on TV and he saw it? Was it just a nightmare? My mind pinballed through various scenarios and possible explanations as to how whatever this was could have gotten to our little one.

My first parenting instinct was to check his room for anything abnormal. I moved cautiously, slowing as I got closer to the door. I entered and was met by the blue and red walls I had painted, cars driving along the baseboards, planes flying on the wallpaper border above me. I checked the window; closed like he had said, the window lock still clasped.

Throwing the closet door open, I found nothing. Clothes on hangers, small tennis shoes, and toys on the floor. I looked around as if this was my first visit to his room, inspecting every corner. Something had gotten to Connor; I wanted to know what.

I backed out of his room, careful not to take my eyes off the space. The selfish part of me hoped it would blow over by lunch. It had to be a dream, a terrible dream, but still something that would fade as the day went on. My second selfish thought was not to mention it, out of sight out of mind.

The day went on as most Sundays go, laundry, grocery store, and then to my in-laws for family dinner. When we entered their house, both our ghost-seeing four-year old and his two and half year-old brother, Ryan, went directly to the cookie jar and then to my father-in-law Richard's den to watch their favorite Disney movie. Richard happily went with them as Shellie and I took up our positions around the kitchen island and started to recount the week's events. By the time we got to Wednesday, Richard returned from the den with a questioning look.

"What's with the look?" Shellie asked.

"Both boys are asleep," he said with a worried tone.

"Neither napped today, it'll be a long night getting them to bed." Shellie rolled her eyes at the thought of the fight coming later.

"It's not like both to doze off. The little one sure, but not both. Are they getting sick or something?" Richard asked, a touch of worry in his voice.

After a quick glance to me, Shellie fast-forwarded her weekly tale to that morning and told them about the encounter with The Blue Lady. When she finished there was an awkward silence as the grandparents seemed to mentally go through any and all possibilities of how this could've happened to their oldest grandson.

Kathy, my recovering Catholic mother-in-law, seemed to have an idea but didn't say it out loud. However, my pragmatic and grounded father-in-law did speak. "I believe him."

We all looked at him, dumbstruck.

"You believe him? That he saw a ghost?" Kathy said.

"Yeah, why would he lie? And anyway, that's a pretty wild story for a kid his age to make up."

Kathy scoffed loudly at the notion, but the worry in her eyes said otherwise. She walked out of the kitchen and into the dining room long enough to mutter something and cross herself before returning.

The rest of the night went as usual; we had dinner and talked. As the boys were saying goodnight to their grandparents, Richard looked down at our oldest. "Don't be scared. If that lady comes back, tell her to leave."

My son gazed up at his grandpa and nodded. Then, without a word, headed out the door toward the car. We all shared a quizzical glance and followed the kids out to the car.

As bedtime approached, we were a little worried the whole ordeal would be an excuse for Connor to come into our room. So, Shellie and I decided I'd stay in his room with him until he fell asleep.

When he got under the covers, I read a short story to him. Then we talked about what would happen at school the next day, and after a few minutes he drifted off. I went to the rocking chair in the corner of his room, which hadn't been used since he was a baby. I sat and waited for a while.

The routine went on for the rest of the week. Friday

came and I was working late, and the nighttime duty fell to Shellie. By the time I got home she was on the couch, wine in hand, rom-com on the TV.

"How was it tonight?" I asked

"Fine, he went right to sleep." She moved over, and I joined her in watching Hugh Grant and not really pregnant Julia Roberts sit on a park bench.

That night around two in the morning I was roused out of sleep by a little hand tapping my cheek. I got one eye opened in time to see Connor climbing into bed with Shellie and me. He crawled over me to his spot between us and fell asleep. I went back to sleep as well, telling myself I would revisit this in the morning after coffee.

That next morning Shellie and I were ready to ask why we had a visitor, when he offered up the reason.

"The Blue Lady came back," he said in between mouthfuls of Trix.

"Oh? What happened?" Shellie asked as innocently as she could, though I could see her tension. Something was messing with her first born and it wasn't funny anymore. If The Blue Lady wasn't already dead, she soon would be.

"Same thing, she always comes in the window and stops by my closet."

"Always? How often is this?" Shellie asked for us both.

"All week," he said, as if it was normal as a sunrise.

"Really? Your dad and I have been in your room this week and we didn't see her."

He put the spoon down and looked to each of us in turn. "She knew. She waited for you to leave."

Goose bumps everywhere, I stopped mid-sip and stared at my son as if he had just dropped an F-bomb at Christmas dinner. "H-how," I stammered.

"She told me. I asked her to leave, like grandpa said. I said, 'Get out, leave me alone' but she smiled and said 'No, never.'"

"Without teeth?" I asked. "You told us she didn't have teeth, just a long tongue. It's hard to talk like that." I was trying to reason it more for myself than to prove him wrong. It's terrifying to think of something you can't stop—let alone see—invading your personal space.

Connor just shrugged and said, "She whispers. Sounds kinda like a snake 'cause of her tongue." Then went back to his Trix.

"Dad," he said, not looking up from the bowl.

"Yeah?"

"She said she doesn't like you. Or Mom, either." He looked up, fear touching the angelic little face.

We stayed with him at night after that, both for his peace of mind and ours. Things finally got back to normal later that week, and after a while we stopped talking about The Blue Lady.

The calm lasted seven or eight days. When it started again, it was different than last time.

Connor described a whooshing sound upon her entering, and he could hear her breathing and her skirt rustling. She seemed to be getting more real, almost solid. He was upset, to say the least, and I didn't help the situation. I was convinced this was a figment, a stress-related dream, something explainable and benign. My wife was not so quick to jump on board the logic train. She felt he was seeing something, but what it was, she had no idea; her mother's intuition worked overtime.

As I was leaving for work the next day well before the sun was up, I entered the family room on the way to the garage. A head shot up over the back of the couch and I practically jumped out of my skin.

"Why are you on the couch?" I asked, trying to not

sound as startled as I was.

Connor didn't say anything, just sat there looking scared, sad, and tired all at the same time. The silence grew and then we both said together, "The Blue Lady."

"How?" I asked.

"The same. I see her come in, I can hear her dress moving. When she came in tonight, she knocked my lamp over on my bed table, and she smiled and hissed. When she went into the closet, I ran down here."

I sighed. I had no idea what was causing this, what had brought this back. Could it be stress from school? Friend issues? Both? I carried him upstairs and put him on my side of the bed and went to work.

The following weekend, Shellie and I had plans to go out with friends. But a cold had traveled around Shellie's office and found its way to her, and she decided a bed and humidifier were better company. I took both boys and we went to our friends', which fit into both our plans; Shellie would get a night to rest and not be around screaming kids, and the kids got away from the cold.

We got home around 10 p.m. that Saturday night to find all the lights on. I opened the garage from the car and noticed that even the garage lights were on, the door to the house ajar. I parked in the driveway and, as quietly as I could, made my way inside. The place didn't appear to have been robbed or vandalized. The TV in the family room was on and turned up louder than normal. I skulked through the bright lights of the kitchen to the stairs leading to the second floor.

"Shellie?" I called from the bottom of the stairs

"Is Mommy OK?" Ryan asked. Connor stood in the doorway between the house and garage, hesitant to enter.

"Yes, she's fine. I'll go check." Upstairs, Shellie met me at the bedroom door with a five- pound dumbbell in her hand raised and ready to crack a skull, a look of utter terror on her face. After a tense moment, shaking from fear, she lowered the weight, her eyes watery.

"Why didn't you answer me when I called down before? You scared the hell out of me!" She almost yelled, her voice cracking.

"We just got home, I saw the lights on everywhere and I came up to check on you. I didn't hear you say anything."

"No! NO! You came in like forty minutes ago and I yelled down to you. You didn't answer. I heard the door close and thought you had gone back outside. I yelled again and heard a crash like something falling in the garage. I came downstairs and the dog started barking and then whimpered and ran upstairs. I got freaked out grabbed the weight and went back upstairs too."

One of the boys called for our dog Bailey. Bailey was not a big dog, far from it, but she wasn't a whimpering, whining dog either. She came out from underneath a stack of clothes in our walk-in closet, sniffed the air, cried again, and went back in.

Shellie looked at me with wide eyes. "Someone was here! In the house! OH GOD! What if—" She made for the stairs, yelling for the boys.

I went to the bedroom and grabbed the first thing I could find, a baseball bat by my nightstand. I passed Shellie and the boys in the upstairs hallway and proceeded to head down to look around.

The first floor was small: the living room, a small dining room and kitchen. I made the rounds of each room, bat ready. My hands shook and my breathing was rapid. I found nothing.

I made my way out of the kitchen and down to the basement. Nothing again.

Still shaking, I left the basement and went back

upstairs. Then, I remembered Shellie's remark about the garage noise; the boys and I had come through the garage to get in the house. When I had opened the garage door from the car, the lights had been on. I was terrified of the idea that I had walked by an intruder with my children.

I went back out and looked again; no one was there. The house was clear and there was nothing out of place, both our front door and patio doors were locked, and the pet door was down. I gave the all-clear, and the boys made their way to the family room and turned the TV back on. My wife stayed upstairs.

The next day Shellie and I talked about what had happened. She retold the story of hearing people in the house, of the dog hiding. She was still shaken.

"There's nothing out of place, nothing was touched or moved." I shrugged. "Even the basement was OK—the door was closed so it squeaked when I opened it."

"When I went upstairs after getting the weight, the door was open," she said.

I was a little taken aback by this. "When I checked around, the door was closed, and the lights were off. I figured you went down to get a book or something. Those were the only lights off in the whole house."

Shellie's face lost some of its color. "It was open when I went upstairs, and the light was on. The boys had been playing down there before you left and left it on. That's where Bailey was looking before she ran upstairs." Shellie pointed to the top stair of the basement stairwell.

"She was looking downstairs?"

Even more color drained from Shellie's face. "I came down because of the noise. I was scared and turned on all the lights, except the basement lights, which were already on. Bailey was standing at the top of the stairs looking down when her head snapped up. She growled and started barking, then whimpered, and ran upstairs like someone had hit her. That's when I grabbed the weight and went back up, too."

I was taking it all in and was trying to come to a reasonable conclusion when Connor spoke from behind us.

"The Blue Lady doesn't like dogs." Then he turned and walked off.

I've always loved Halloween and all the ghostly, ghastly things that come with it. I've found tarot cards to be cool to look at but nothing more and Ouija boards toys made for sleepovers. Yet, here I was, slowly becoming a believer.

Meanwhile, Shellie was more than convinced The Blue Lady was real.

As I was getting ready for work one morning, I was surprised by Bailey in the hall. Growling from the top of our second-floor stairs she was in full-on fight mode, teeth bared, hackles up. I called to her but got no response. Seeing nothing but our dark living room below us, I walked around the dog and headed downstairs.

As I got to the bottom of the stairs and turned to go into the kitchen, a blue streak flew past me, up the stairs, and over a yelping Bailey.

Terrified, I froze at the sight of an older woman with no eyes, just empty holes. Her dress was ripped and torn; her smiling mouth toothless with a serpent tongue. The hallway grew darker, as if the little bit of light in hall was trying to get away from her.

Then the woman floated backwards through Connor's closed bedroom door. Seconds later, the door flew open and my oldest son bolted out in the hall.

"You saw her?" he asked.

I nodded, unable to catch my breath.

Ryan opened his door and stuck a sleepy head into

the hall. "Mommy?"

Shellie had joined us from our room. "It's OK, Ryan," she said. "What happened?" she whispered to me.

I swallowed. "I saw her."

"Who?" Shellie asked, eyes wide with fear. "You saw… The Blue--"

"Yeah." I cut her off, hearing the name gave her more substance. I was still shaking.

"It went past me and up the stairs."

"Is Bailey OK?" Ryan peeped.

Shellie held the dog and looked her over briefly. "She seems to be."

Ryan nodded, still half asleep, and went back into his room.

"I told you," Connor said. "She doesn't like dogs." He gave me a look, not an I-told-you-so look, more of a now-you-know look.

"Whatever it was, went through his door," I said to Shellie, motioning to Connor's room.

"Who," Shellie said. "I don't think it's a what, anymore."

As if on cue, a cold breeze drifted by my neck, giving me goose bumps. Shellie screamed, grabbed my arm, and pulled me into the bedroom.

"Ow, what the fu--" I managed.

"It's behind you!" She yelled and pushed past me, grabbing Connor who stood motionless in his doorway, his face gone a pale, sickly white. The Blue Lady had gone past him—or through him—and come back into the hall.

As Shellie got to him there was a loud screech, like nails on a chalkboard. I grabbed my ears and cringed. Shellie hugged Connor tight, as if he had just been pulled from a sinking ship.

"NO, NEVER!" a voice screamed.

Ryan opened his bedroom door as The Blue Lady vanished back down the stairs. He stared, unblinking.

Shellie's soft sobs came from behind me.

Since our introduction, The Blue Lady has made a few more appearances over the years. Doors slammed shut, windows opened. Once she threw Connor's iPhone into his wall, leaving a hole in the drywall.

We've come home to find candles lit in the kitchen. A wet moldy smell comes and goes and seems to follow you from room to room. If any of us are home alone, there seems to be a more concerted effort on her part. Shrieks can be heard; I've heard sobbing coming from the second-floor bathroom.

As for Connor—now twelve--if you ask him about The Blue Lady, he'll shrug it off, say it was a little kid thing, a dream or something.

There are times when Shellie and I will go out with friends, have dinner and drinks, and get home late. Upon entering the house, we find all the lights on and all the doors open, Connor downstairs asleep on the family room couch.

Ryan, as usual, will be asleep in his room. But Bailey will be standing alert in the upstairs hallway in front of Connor's open bedroom door.

Sean Murphy Lives in Littleton with his wife, Shellie and their two sons Connor and Ryan and three dogs. When not working as a nurse, Sean enjoys reading and writing. Sean is currently a student at Metro. State, seeking a Bachelor's Degree in English.

MOUNTAIN LOVERS
Bobby Crew

Liam slammed on the brakes as he veered the Subaru off to the side of the mountain road.

"Jesus, what the hell is wrong with you?" I demanded.

He stared ahead in raging silence at the trees illuminated by the headlights, his chest rising and falling with every huff and puff I hated when he got like this, almost as much as I enjoyed pushing him there.

We'd left downtown Denver less than an hour ago, and in that short time, I had managed to turn our romantic Rocky Mountain drive into a complete disaster with just a few choice words and a couple of simple commands. He hated when I told him what to do, but he so often needed to be told what to do.

He flung open his car door and jumped out, stomping around to my side of the car.

"Here we go," I muttered.

He yanked open the passenger side door so hard I thought he might rip it off. The big ape was strong enough. "Do you want to fucking drive, then?" He yelled.

"I'm really sorry," I said, doing my best to make my

voice soft and calming. I crossed my arms protectively over my chest. "I didn't mean to piss you off."

"You always mean to piss me off. It's what you do!"

I had to admit, he was right. I loved the way the vein on the right side of his head slithered around under his skin when he was pissed. Something about his rage, the energy he released, the shift in his pheromones when he was heated, never ceased to rekindle my own fire. It's the strangest feeling, being terrified and so very aroused at the same time. I never grew tired of that feeling.

I narrowed my eyes at him but made no attempt to move from my seat. "You know I can't drive."

A beam of light shone in the rearview mirror as another car slowly made the winding turn around the side of the mountain. We were just outside of Boulder, not the most remote location, so complete discretion was key.

"Just get back in the fucking car," I growled.

His dark eyes widened at my tone. He hesitated, gripping the top of the open door so tightly his arms were shaking, but then obeyed like a good ape. He slammed the car door closed and moved back around to the driver's side. He waved politely with a fake smile as the other car slowly pulled up beside us on the narrow road.

"Are you OK?" a male voice called from the car.

"Oh, just having a lover's quarrel," Liam said, brushing a hand nervously through his thick greasy hair. "But everything will be fine."

The man looked through the window at me and squinted his eyes as if he was straining to see me inside the Subaru. He gave a hesitant nod to Liam. I rolled my eyes and turned away from the man and looked out at the night sky.

As the other car hurried up the road, Liam climbed back into the Subaru.

"Should we follow them, or turn back around?" he asked, appearing to have calmed down a bit. His voice still lacked any enthusiasm or endearment. He hadn't forgiven me yet.

"Lover's quarrel," I cackled. "Am I still your lover?"

"Always and forever. That was the deal." He looked at me, straight-faced. I loved his eyes; his irises were so dark they were like two little black holes I could climb into and curl up in forever.

Forever described our relationship perfectly. The decades blended together like swirls of multi-colored paint. No matter how shitty things got, no matter how violently we fought, I was always his, he was always mine, and we always made it work. That's love, *real* authentic love. And that was also our binding eternal agreement.

"Was he handsome?" I asked, referring to the driver of the other car. "I didn't get a good enough look."

"You always prefer the men, don't you?" This time he smiled. "His girlfriend was a real looker."

I leaned over, laid my head on his shoulder, and closed my eyes. "Follow them," I whispered in his ear. I didn't know if he could feel my head there on his shoulder. In all these years, I never asked.

How many times had he killed me?

The first time was still the most vivid, the most brutal, and the most unexpected, of course. It was the first time I really understood Liam in his entirety. I had always felt so safe with my giant, protected, and that was important in those times, especially for us and our so called *unnatural* love.

He took his time breaking my bones and ripping them from my body. He didn't just snap, he'd gone completely mad. I'd seem him kill before, but not like that. The first death was by far the worst, but not because of the pain. It was because out of all the times he had killed me, the first time was probably the only time I didn't deserve it.

We found the couple as they were getting out of their car. They'd found a patch of grass that worked as a parking lot and were putting on their hiking packs. They looked over at our headlights.

He was right, the girl was quite beautiful, a natural beauty. She had very dark skin, a soft angelic face, with light brown eyes, and her black hair was combed out in a curly fro.

The man was average looking, still attractive, but I'm sure it was his personality that sealed the deal. He was thin, with long dirty blond hair tied back in a bun. He put a hat on and attached a headlamp to it.

"You're right," I said. "I much prefer the girl this time."

Liam continued driving up the road, careful not to drive too slowly so that the two of them wouldn't suspect we were interested in them.

I always loved hiking at night. With all the recent transplants to Colorado, it was almost impossible to hike a trail without seeing people every two steps. But at night these trails were virtually deserted. You pretty much had the whole mountain to yourself. The mountains were important to us; they were necessary for our way of life. It always had to be done on a mountain top. To this day, the gods take all their ancient symbolism very seriously. That's why Colorado was the perfect place to call home.

Liam drove on for another mile or so before finding a place wide enough to park. "Will this do?"

"Looks deserted enough to me." I looked ahead and behind for any source of light. "Plenty of space between us and those hikers. Is there a trail here?"

"No, we aren't going to use any trails."

"Perfect."

He climbed out of the car, and I waited patiently for him to come around to open my door like a real gentleman. "Right this way, monsieur." He was suddenly cheerful.

"We should hurry," I stated. "If anyone drives by, I'd prefer they didn't see us."

"You're the one lagging," he said as I stood up from the car. "Besides, don't you love to watch?" he teased.

I almost beamed. "You know I love it when you put on a show." I wanted to kiss him, to be clutched to him, but it would have to wait. I watched as he popped the trunk and pulled out the long, heavy rolled-up rug.

"Need any help?" I offered politely, even though heavy lifting was the very last thing I wanted to do. Don't get me wrong, I can do quite a lot in spectral form. Hell, I'm probably even stronger in some ways, but it was beyond exhausting. It takes lifetimes of practice to be able to launch people or furniture across the room, and they make it look so easy on television.

"No need, I've got it," he groaned as he hoisted the heavy roll over his shoulder. He truly was the strongest man I'd ever met.

"Then I'll be the light that leads you into the night." I motioned for him to follow me into the trees and up the mountain.

Despite the heavy load, the ape matched me stride for stride, stopping only once to switch the load to the other shoulder. He reminded me of the ancient king Sisyphus, pushing the boulder up the mountain, only this boulder wouldn't come tumbling back down. I did my best to help him avoid low branches and step over roots and rocks.

"This should do nicely." I stopped in a small clearing. "Right here will be the perfect place." The ground was soft and flat, perfect for digging.

He half dropped, half unrolled the rug, and the half-naked body fell out onto the pine needle-covered dirt.

I stared at the body, or what was left of it. The side of

its head was caved in, the jaw hung to the side, and both arms were bent and broken. Some of the fingers were missing from the hands. "You really did a number on me this time," I said, sitting on top of a fallen tree. "I was just getting used to that body."

I had loved that body. It was the closest we had ever found to my true form, my first form. I'd hardly got to live inside it for a month before Liam completely succumbed to his inner carnal beast.

How many bodies had we littered across the Rocky Mountains?

There was nothing quite like it, Liam's rage. It was so terrifying but that threshold—

that unknown line between feeling you're safe, or wondering if you're about to be torn apart—

that's what never ceases to get me off. It was always a gamble; was I going to get a violent orgasm, or was I going to die? I never grew tired of that feeling.

Liam unraveled the rest of the rug revealing a shovel and began to dig.

I watched and waited as he made a shallow grave and then gently placed my old body into it. He brushed back my corpse's matted hair to get one last look into my cold dead eyes.

He buried me and covered the loose dirt with pine needles before resting on his knees and staring at the grave in silence.

He didn't move for several minutes. He was saying a silent prayer to the gods for me, while asking them to accept this new offering of death. They always accepted it.

"I wish you would have let me enjoy it a little longer," I whispered. "It felt like being home."

He didn't respond with words, but I saw a tiny trail of wetness escape his left eye.

"Don't fret, my love." I knelt beside him and leaned my head on his shoulder again.

I guess it really didn't matter how many times he had killed me. That was the deal, after all. As twisted as we were, the gods were so much worse. Their contracts were binding, and their torture was as eternal as it was repetitive. "We'll manage. We always do."

He nodded and looked up at the starry night from atop the mountain. He always seemed at his most vulnerable after burying me, as if he still felt some remorse for that first time he killed me. He still blamed himself.

It *was* his fault that we were damned. One moment of doubt was all it took for his jealousy to spoil his mind. I had never been unfaithful to him—even back then when our love affair could have gotten us both killed I remained completely his. He doubted me, and so he murdered me. Shortly after, he realized I had been telling the truth. His guilt was so overwhelming he found a way of impressing the gods and convinced them to bring me back, and to bind our souls together for eternity.

I wanted to kiss him, to let him lay his head in my lap while I played with his hair, and climb into those cavernous eyes, to comfort him. My big ape, I never did tell him I forgave him. I don't think I ever will.

"Now, bring me the flesh of that girl," I demanded, my tone growing harsh. "Her body will do quite nicely." The truth was, in my spectral form was the only time I have ever been strong enough to hurt Liam. In death, I was more powerful than I had ever been in life.

"Whatever you desire, my love," he said tenderly. He was always sweetest after I died.

Tracking those hikers would be simple enough, and since there were two of them, Liam was bound to put on quite the show. I could just hear the rhythm of bones snapping in my head like music. Mr. Man Bun was bound to squeal and howl and beg, and I'd watch from his lover's eyes. I did always love to watch, and that look someone gives you before they die, that last glimmer of hope before total helplessness as they think that their lover will at least try to help them, only to see me smile. I never grew tired of that feeling, either.

"Lead the way," he said.

We stood up, and he gathered the rug and shovel, before following me through the night.

Bobby Crew has been writing horror since elementary school. Due to his twisted imagination, his parents thought they were raising a serial killer, but thankfully he chose to keep the killing on paper only. He grew up in Denver, Colorado, and is the creator of The Horror Crew Productions, a brand new indie publishing press that focuses primarily on LGBTQ horror.

LEFT BEHIND
P.L. McMillan

The tires of my sedan hum on the road as it ribbons onward into the heavy night. Riverdale Road is sparse in the way of streetlights and fellow travelers. It's a lonely stretch. A few houses have been built on the west side, while shadowed fields on the east give credit to the eerie legends I'd read about it.

Roads like these are the bread and butter of America's ghostly roadmap. I smile a bit to myself. I should make sure to remember that and add it to my scrapbook. I glance over at my boyfriend, Alan, who is entranced at whatever it is he has pulled up on his phone. He's not the ghost chaser type, but he loves me enough to come along on my adventures.

"You can pull up anywhere around here, Claire," Zora says from the backseat.

"What about the gates?" I ask.

Zora's boyfriend, Ross, chuckles a bit, causing the familiar, bright flicker of anxiety to nip at me.

"Did I say something wrong?"

"Well, the 'Gates of Hell' don't actually exist anymore,"

Zora says. "This place has pretty much all changed since that guy killed his wife. I mean, there was no reason to keep them up after the guy burned his own house to the ground. The gates were just these little rusty things from what I hear, nothing to write home about."

"Really," she goes on. "It seems like supernatural activity happens anywhere along the length of the road, so this should be good enough. Look, there's a mile marker right there. Maybe we'll see one of those bloody handprints that are supposed to appear on all the road signs."

To my left, distant house lights twinkle, a vague reminder of civilization. I activate my turning signal, despite there being no one else on the road, and pull onto the dirt. I turn off the car, and the four of us sit there in the shadowed interior of my sedan.

I feel a momentary flutter in my belly, wishing I'd come here with only Alan. We'd just moved here for Alan's work. I was working odd jobs and, being introverted myself, Alan kept saying we needed to get out more, make friends. So here I was. Trying to make friends.

I take a deep breath and open my door. After a moment, the other three passengers do the same, and the four of us step out into the night. Summer's warm touch is still present in the small breeze that sends the field grass whispering. Alan yawns and stretches his arms.

"Want me to grab the bag?" he asks and starts to the back of the car without waiting for my answer.

I take a second to gaze out at the field where, supposedly, a man went mad and murdered his wife and children. The familiar thrill of fear rolls down my body and I savor it. Getting the creeps from a ghost story is preferable to the daily anxieties I feel in my life.

"Everyone got their flashlight?" Ross asks.

I don't know either of them very well and that puts me on edge. Alan met Zora through work and had mentioned to her that I loved urban legends and haunted houses. She had told him about the cursed stretch of road near Thornton, called Riverdale. Next thing I knew, we were going on double dates. Zora was all right, carefree, if a bit arrogant, but Ross was not the type of guy I usually make friends with. Still, Alan wanted me to try. Try and make friends.

"Well, let's go and bust some ghosts." Alan has pulled out the little backpack I'd brought and tosses me the camera.

The plastic equipment smarts as it hits my hands; it's my clunky polaroid camera that I'd gotten at a second-hand shop. One of my favorite things to do is try and capture things on film. People will always claim it's fake if it's digital, so I only ever take Polaroids. Plus, it makes for good scrapbook material.

I can't help but smile, and Alan gives me a wink. I toss him the car keys, which he catches easily.

"Keep that in the backpack, OK? I wouldn't want to lose it and have us trapped out here for the ghosties!" I laugh.

I lead the way off the dirt of the breakdown lane and into the thick grass. To keep my hands free, I have a headlamp on. A wooden fence guards this side of the field and runs parallel along the road for as far as I can see. I climb over, placing my hands gingerly to avoid splinters.

"Zora, you said you've been here before, right?" I say, feeling responsible to make sure everyone is having fun and feeling entertained because this is my hobby and they are only here because they were asked to come.

"Yeah, but I didn't see anything. Not a single devious jogger, bloody-handed boy, or lady in white either. Really, Claire, I don't know why you find all this dumb shit so fun," she says with a small laugh.

"I heard that the lady everyone sees at the side of the road is the ghost of the man's wife, looking for her children, or maybe her husband for revenge!" Ross says, punctuating the last word with a theatrical cackle.

"I feel like if the city bothered to add more streetlights along the road, then no one would be *seeing* these ghoulies anymore," Alan says. "People watch too many horror movies."

"We should have come on a full moon," Ross says. "Then maybe we could have seen a werewolf too."

I tell myself it doesn't matter that they think I'm silly for wanting to believe in this kind of stuff.

Ahead of me, the field stretches on and disappears into a dark void. The moon is covered in thick clouds, so the only true light is from the flashlights, which sweep in savage beams over the grass and weeds. I have walked farther ahead from the others, trying to find that same delicious shiver, that same sense of foreboding I had before, but the others are laughing and talking too loudly. Any sense of atmosphere has been smashed to bits.

"You know," Zora says. "Maybe we'll see that old madman after all. From the version I heard, his wife was blonde. Maybe he'll think you're his wife come home and come out for a nice, big kiss!"

She jumps at me, hands curled up in claws. I scream and hate myself for falling for such a childish trick.

"That's not funny, OK?"

"No, honestly! Look!" Zora is laughing as she shoves her phone towards my face.

Curiosity was always my greatest weakness—just call me Pandora—so I take the phone. She has a browser open to some ghost story site. The header of this particular post reads "FAMILY HAUNTS RIVERDALE ROAD." Underneath that is an image, which seems to be a poor photocopy of an actual hardcopy photo. In it, a family stands in a line in front of a partially completed house. The solemn, stiff-backed father—supposedly the one who went insane—is on the right. Next to him are two bored-looking children holding hands. On the very left is the mother, a kind looking thing with a small smile and a blonde braid that hangs over one shoulder.

"See, she could be your twin!" Zora exclaims, grabbing her phone back.

"Just because we're both blonde—"

A short cry and a curse interrupts me.

"Ross?" Zora runs to where a flashlight rocks back and forth on the ground.

"Well, there's a ditch here." Ross appears, almost out of nowhere. "The grass completely hides it."

Standing in the ditch, the grass comes up to Ross's chest, meaning the ditch must be pretty deep. Zora helps her boyfriend out.

Turning away, I try and mask my impatience. I strain to see in the darkness, but there's nothing to find. Wherever the house had been, there's no sign of it now.

The air is quiet and smells sweetly of the grass being crushed underfoot. Overhead, where the clouds have thinned a bit, I can see the faint pinpricks of stars. I bring my camera up to my face and take a photo.

The photo develops in my hands. I examine it with my light and see nothing unusual, just headlamp-highlighted grass fading away into black. No spirit orbs or ghostly apparitions.

"Did you hear that?"

I jump again. Alan stands next to me, looking off to the right.

"Hear what?" I say.

"I don't know, I thought I heard—I don't know, laughing?"

"That's not funny, Alan," I say, but feel that tightening of my nerves.

"Are we going or what?" Zora walks up to us.

"I just wish the house was still here, even just the remains of one." My shoulders slump. "It's kind of hard to get into the spirit when it's just an empty field." I take another picture in a different direction.

"I don't know what you want me to say, babe. It is what it is," Zora says with a casual confidence I envy.

"Whoa." Ross pulls the picture from my hand. "There's the house!"

We crowd around. There, in the photo, is a shaky azure outline of a large plantation-style mansion. Just like the one in the picture along with the blog post Zora showed me. I look up. There is no house in the field, nothing but the endless expanse of night.

"Should we—should we go over there?" Alan asks me.

"Yes." I begin making my way through the grass.

"Probably just a flaw in the film," Zora says from behind me. "I don't see anything when I take a picture on my phone."

"Do they know why that guy killed his wife?" Alan asks.

"No one knows. I heard he went crazy as soon as the house was built and that was that. They never even caught or convicted him," Zora replies.

I take another photo, pausing to let the others catch up. I hadn't realized I had been practically jogging. The film develops and shows the house closer, the outline of the building still smeared and ethereal. In front of me, I can almost make out a faint shimmer. The temperature has dropped, but the wind has picked up. Faintly, I catch the whiff of smoke under the sweetness of the grass.

"You know what, Claire," Zora's voice shakes. "I don't

think this is a good idea anymore."

Something crunches under my feet, and when I look, I find gravel between the stalks of grass: the remains of an old driveway. I take another picture. In the faint blue, eldritch outlines, I can make out a wavering front porch with staggering pillars holding up the roof. The mansion is two stories with three windows along the second floor, two larger windows framing the smeared front door.

"Oh my God, just look at it." I hold the photo out for the others to see.

"Claire, I think we should go back." Alan has retreated a few steps.

I'm shivering. A chill from the late hour, or something else entirely?

"It reeks of smoke," Ross says.

"It's the house, the one that burned down. Don't the blue impressions above the roof look like flames?" I turn to them with photo in hand, only to lose my smile.

They've all backed up, putting at least five feet between us. Zora grips her elbows with white knuckles, her shoulders hunched as if warding off a chill. Ross has his hands shoved deep in the pockets of his jeans, his foot tapping frantically in the grass. Alan is half turned away, looking ready to run at any moment.

"This is honestly so freaky," Ross says.

"Please, please, please, can we just go?" Zora chimes in, her bottom lip out in an unattractive pout.

I open my mouth and close it again. I've finally found something worth finding. My chest is the site of two warring states: frustration and anxiety. I want to stay and explore this phenomenon and yet, I know I'll agree to leave.

"Just one more picture." I feel almost out of breath, the rush of fear mixed with adrenaline.

They don't say anything, but they also don't start

back, so I turn to take my last shot. I have no reference points, and the horizon is completely dark. All I can do is center the remains of the driveway at the bottom and in the middle of my viewfinder.

I snap the shot.

The camera whirs and vibrates in my hands as it processes my picture, finally spitting out the Polaroid. I hang the camera around my neck from its strap and hold the photo in the palm of my hand, watching it. I know I'm stalling to stay a little longer, the atmosphere practically electric. The picture melts into the film like quicksilver. Ice jolts through me, starting at my fingertips, up my arms, and straight to my heart.

The house is almost perfectly centered, looking as insubstantial as it has in the other photos. Only now there is an addition: a man. He stands in front of the porch as if having just left the house for a walk. He's a tall, slender figure cut in rough blue strokes. His face is distorted, his eyes mere smears of black.

"It's him, the husband!" I yell. "I have a real-life picture of a ghost!"

"Claire!" Alan is at my side, hands fisted at the bottom of my shirt. "Claire!" He tries to pull me away.

I look up.

"Oh my God, he's coming through," I whisper breathlessly.

He starts as a faint silver shimmer, which swirls and coalesces into a ball of blue St. Elmo's Fire. Glowing tendrils stretch out in delicate filaments like veins. The reek of smoke billows around me, only now I can smell a thicker stench: cooking flesh. The whipping night winds bring thin screams from the house.

Alan pulls me around, his hand crushing my wrist.

I stuff the photo into my pocket and glance over my shoulder. The azure filaments thicken into hazy limbs.

There he is.

The camera painfully pounds against my chest as I run.

"Eliza!" The voice from beyond is thunder, causing even the ground beneath my feet to tremble. Savage heat floods over us. I'm sweating from the heat, from running, from fear. I look back again. I have to; I can't resist.

"I won't let you leave me! You *belong* to me!" The man is a swirling storm of brilliant violets, indigos, and aquamarines surrounded by a sparking red halo. Behind him, the field is gone, the hint of horizon and clouds gone, only a flat, hungry void.

"ELIZA!"

I pull up the camera and snap a shot, biting the edge of the photo as it slides out

"Which way is the car?" Zora is screaming; she hasn't stopped screaming since the ghost manifested.

"This way! I'm sure it's this way!" In the lead, Ross is struck first.

A flare of turquoise erupts in front of him, enveloping his entire left side. He lets out a short squeal and falls to the grass. Carried by her own momentum, Zora trips over him as the spout of eldritch flame twists into shape and becomes the ghost. He ignores Ross and Zora, who lay prone on the ground in front of him, instead focusing on me.

He raises a hand whose edges swirl up in hungry licks of otherworldly flame. My jaw aches, I'm still clenching the edge of the photograph between my teeth. I pull it out, slide it into my pocket, and find Alan's hand. The ghost's aura explodes out in a supernova above him, sparking up into the night sky, setting it on fire.

"Him? *HIM?* That's the man you've been seeing behind my back? Eliza!?"

"Oh hell, Claire, he thinks you're his wife!" Alan

shakes my hand from his and takes a step away from me.

"Alan?"

"Don't you look at him! Don't you dare, Eliza! You're *mine!* You're *my* wife!" The ghost doesn't step towards me so much as glide. As his translucent legs slide through the grass, the plants wither and blacken. Zora is back on her feet and pulls a dazed Ross after her. He's clutching his left arm, which hangs limply at his side.

"I'm taking you home, and you will never leave me, you'll never leave me again."

"Alan?"

But Alan's already running, skirting around the ghost, and sprinting past Zora and Ross. The ghost's head twists as he follows Alan's escape, so I take the moment to run, banking around his right side. As I pass, his head jerks and those gaping holes where his eyes should be point right at me, and the iciest blast of hatred rakes my exposed skin like broken glass. The camera is flying left, right, left, choking me with its strap, so I pull it off and fling it to the ground.

Behind me, the ghost howls. The field spreads out endlessly in front of me. I scan for the road, for the lights of houses on the opposite side of the road, for the car. There's only darkness. I glance back, and he's gone.

Pale periwinkle buzzes across my face. He's apparated in front of me, arms straight forward and hands curled in claws. I dodge beneath him, frostbite digging into my cheeks and across my scalp, and pull a hard right.

"Don't you dare turn your back on me, you bitch!" The ghost's scream is piercing and makes my heart skip a beat.

My eyeballs ache from the strain of keeping them wide and unblinking, staring straight forward into the darkness, waiting to see if the specter will appear in front of me like he did before. A spark of light against metal as the beam of my headlamp sweeps over something. I don't react fast enough and run straight into a fence. The air is punched out of me as I fold against the top metal rail and a bright, sharp pain lances through my arms as barbed wire rakes my skin.

I'm the one screaming now, and I fall onto my back, curling up against the pain as blood runs hot over my hands and onto the grass.

There's no time.

There's no time.

I roll onto my hands and knees and launch off again, following the fence. I spare a glance back and there he is, in pursuit.

"I'm not your wife!" I scream. "Alan! Alan, where are you?"

There, up ahead, a break in the fence. I have a stitch in my side, a clamp that tightens and tightens into my ribs as I gasp for breath. My arms have curled up against my chest, a reaction to the pain, and ribbons of flesh from my mangled forearms slap against my belly as I run.

I twist to the right, my feet sliding on trampled grass, and am through the gates. Ahead, I can finally see the road, the light of the houses opposite. Where's the car? Where is everyone else?

"Alan!?"

I pitch forward. I feel a sharp snap and a flicker of black. Regaining my footing, I charge through the grass.

I look back. I have to look back.

There he is, at the gates, legs spread wide and hands raised above his head as he howls. His scream catches me in a wave of pure, icy rage, stealing my breath from me.

I turn away. The road is so close, and headlights are coming my way. I stumble onto the breakdown lane and skid to a stop, so I don't end up in front of the speeding car. I wave my arms above my head, the headlights blinding me. There's no way they can't see me.

"Help me! Help me, please!"

I flinch back as the car blasts past, not even slowing.

"NO!"

I turn to follow it and recognize it. That's my car. Alan had the keys. They left me. They left me here.

"ALAN!"

He doesn't even slow the car. He had to have seen me, I'm right here!

Behind me, I hear a soft sob, a shuddering breath. I turn, my heart thundering. Half a block away is a woman in a long white dress. I open my mouth to call to her, to warn her, when I notice a second woman, also clothed in a white dress. Both have long blond hair. Like mine.

I turn again in the direction that Alan took as he fled, leaving me behind.

One, two, three more women stand on the same side of the road as me, all in white dresses with long, unbound blonde hair. They look after the receding taillights of my old sedan. I can hear some of them weeping, others lower hands they had raised in a silent plea for help. We are all here, waiting for help.

I look down. I'm in a white dress. The wounds in my arms are gone, my flesh whole and pale. I feel nothing, not even a numbness. Nothing but a heavy sense of sorrow. Of loss.

I turn and look back the way I came. The ghost is gone, so I start back to the gates between which I had passed. I don't even reach them before I find it.

My body.

It's lying in the same ditch Ross fell into earlier. The tall grass that's hidden this culvert is crushed beneath my body. I'm face down, back severely arched, legs akimbo, arms pinned beneath my chest. The back of my head presses against my left shoulder, the angle of my neck acute. Unnatural. It doesn't even look like I had time to react as I fell. It must have happened so suddenly.

I sink to my knees, feel nothing when I should feel the harsh scrape of grass. I reach down into the ditch and touch my own cheek and my fingers sink in, effortlessly.

I'm tired. So tired. And sad.

Alan left me behind. My supposed friends left me behind. Would they come back? Were they going for help? Who would tell my mom what happened?

I stand and turn to go back to the road when something catches my eye. I bend over. It's a picture from my Polaroid, which must have fallen from my pocket as I fell.

It shows the house, in all its blue pearlescent glory. Coming from the front porch with a snarl on his face is the man who chased me across the field. Off to the right, I can see several ghostly women in long dresses, the same women I saw at the edge of the road. His victims, the ones he chased before me.

I look up over the shadowed field, and the house is there, only now it's solid. Its windows blaze with light, and a silhouette moves back and forth across one of the upstairs windows. I can feel its pull, like the dangerous call of a siren's song. Those blazing lights promise safety and warmth, even though danger lives within its walls.

I see a shadowy figure sitting on the porch swing. A match flares and he lights his pipe as he sits, waiting.

I turn my back to the house. There is still some night left, and maybe, just maybe, another car will come and maybe, just maybe, I can flag it down. Maybe I can get someone's attention and draw them to where I lie, and they can take me away from here.

P.L. McMillan has published short stories in Sanitarium Fundead, Neat, and Gehenna & Hinnom. Her website is plmcmillan.com.

DEEP VEINS
Travis Heermann

1861 - Colorado Territory

The candlelight flickered as Frank hammered the drill into the milky vein of quartz. Emmet held the drill granite-steady on his right shoulder, twisting it a quarter turn after each of Frank's blows. Frank's gaze fastened on the mushroomed steel butt of the drill as he swung the sixteen-pound sledge, driving the point deeper, deeper, until it would reach sufficient depth to fill the cavity with black powder and blast away.

Emmet's face was a mask of concentration—a missed swing could cause severe injury for both of them. The cramped shaft did not allow enough freedom of movement to hold oneself well clear.

Then a blow drove the drill deep, out of Emmet's hands.

"We punched through," Emmet said.

"Looks like," Frank said.

Emmet worked his leather-gloved fingers around the drill shaft and tried to prize it out of the hole, allowing

Frank a moment's respite to set down the hammer. His shoulders and back were a mass of aching knots, as always by this time of day. He tipped back his canvas hat, careful not to disturb the flame of the small oil lamp resting upon the leather brim and wiped the sweat from his brow. The heat of the lamp warmed his head uncomfortably, but no one partial to a life of soft splendor decided to scratch the Yellow out of the earth.

Emmet yanked the drill out of the hole, and a blast of tainted air followed, a strange fetid stench. He clamped a glove over his face. The invisible miasma swirled around Frank, the power of it punching him in the nostrils, getting thicker rather than abating, until his breast seized tight. Emmet hooked an arm under Frank's and pulled him away.

"Let's go! Come on!" Emmet cried. Frank finally got his feet under him, and they ran together.

Emanations of deadly gases from the bowels of the earth were a well-known hazard to hard-rock miners, and the Grubbs boys didn't have a canary to serve as a warning. The tunnel stretched toward the waning daylight. Their feet splashed in the constant trickles of water on the floor.

For the full two hundred feet to the surface—first a hundred a feet of dense, solid granite, and then the last hundred feet of slide, as the loose surface boulders and earth was called—the stench hounded them like the putrescence of a hundred open graves, but mixed with some earthy, metallic tang. They ran hunched over to make sure they didn't bash their heads into a low-hanging knob of granite or ceiling beam.

They burst into their camp, gagging and coughing. Fading light the color of the metal they sought filtered over the forested peaks of the valley. A warm breeze swept away the lingering stench, fluttering the roof of their tent, and whispering through the leaves of a nearby aspen grove. The mountainside lay as quiet as Eden.

Far below their claim lay the silver thread of Clear Creek, meandering through boulders and forest. Fifty yards to the left lay the burbling stream they used to sluice the gold flake from pulverized quartz. Twenty yards to the right, Sniffles the burro watched them placidly from his long tether.

"You all right, Frank?" Emmet coughed.

Frank nodded.

Emmet was the younger of the two brothers, but shorter and sturdier, built like a buffalo rather than a gawky mule deer. Frank even had the ears to match, sticking out of his head like a stagecoach with the doors open.

Frank said, "We'll give it a mite to let it air out." He took a deep breath to help clear the ache out of his lungs.

Meanwhile Emmet poured some of this morning's coffee into a mug, swished it around, and swallowed. "I can still taste it."

Frank reached for the cup and Emmet handed it over.

The coffee was cold and bitter, like Frank's soul would be if they didn't manage to find more than dregs soon. After five months of digging, they'd found only enough gold to whet their appetites, only enough to pay for the most basic supplies. A couple of outfits had landed good results from placer mines down in the valley, but the Grubb brothers had staked their claim far enough from the Georgetown camp to discourage claim jumpers.

Emmet must have seen the thoughts on Frank's face. "Don't worry. We'll hit soon. The color was too good to leave us disappointed for long."

"Unless that assayer was a crook," Frank said. He hadn't liked the look in that man's eye.

"Why would he lie to us?"

"Take our money. Keep us guessing until the bigger fish swallow us whole."

A promising chunk of quartz back in March had netted them fifty dollars in gold flake and prompted them to pour their full energy into this spot, this claim, this pinhole in the earth. But the gold had dried up. All these weeks of back-breaking work, feeling like they were looking for water in the desert, had taken a toll on his spirit.

"You reckon she'll wait for me?" Frank said.

"Good Christ, Frank," Emmet said with an exasperated sigh.

Frank knew it was a well-worn topic of conversation, but he needed some hope to cling to.

Emmet said, "We're going back to Georgetown so filthy rich she'll smell us coming all the way from the Clear Creek fork. Maybe that void we just hit will open up into the mother lode."

"You think so?"

"I know it. I feel it in my bones."

Frank nodded, the reassurances assuaging the ache of overtaxed muscles and over-yearning heart. Mollie Hogan's smile sparkled in his memory like a vein of pure silver, a forest of red hair and speckling of freckles across a dainty nose like the red earth of the Kansas Territory, or Colorado Territory, or whatever they were calling it nowadays.

His plug-ugly countenance had never brought the young ladies beating a path to his door. Until Mollie had given him the kind of smile that opened doors in him and lured him out to speak to her, and she found him agreeable enough to spend an afternoon picnicking at Mount Prospect Hill Cemetery. Her hand was calloused and strong when he took it and told her he was going to marry her, that he was going to make her a rich woman.

She had laughed, a fine musical sound without disdain in it, and told him it was a pleasant sentiment. She would come with him to Georgetown. Doubtless there was a living to be made as a laundress and cook among the unwashed miners. But she couldn't marry every man who made a similar claim in a time when gold fever was drawing hundreds, thousands of men from the east. A woman with a pleasing face and healthy figure heard more than her share of such declarations of love.

"I'll wait for you in Georgetown. You come back with something, Frank Grubbs. I believe in you."

The longing to kiss her that day now paled in comparison to his regret that he hadn't had the guts to do it, nor on the ride into the mountains. How many times had he dreamed of stealing a kiss?

"Let's go blast that hole and see what's on the other side," Emmet said, drawing Frank out of his habitual train of thoughts.

The blast opened a two-foot hole into a black nothingness.

Frank peered into the hole while Emmet went to retrieve lanterns from their tent. The light from his oil lamp on his hat met nothing but blackness. The thickness of the wall, about two feet, prevented peering deeply into the beyond. It would take some clearing away. The hour was growing late, and his muscles were taxed, but he took up his pickaxe and set about expanding the opening. The quartz gave way to his steel, and when Emmet returned, they made quick progress, until the point where one of them could slip through the hole.

An uncommon excitement kicked Frank's heart into a higher speed as he slid headfirst through the opening, lantern extended on one arm, the rock digging into ribs and forearms as he wormed forward. The brighter light of the lantern revealed a cavern of extensive dimensions, and their opening was situated about fifteen feet above the floor. Pale, stone fangs from ceiling and floor caught the yellow-orange glow. The air was moist, and dripping water echoed through the space.

Frank withdrew and said, "We need the rope. I'm going in to take a quick gander."

"Are you sure? It's getting late and we're both tired."

"We surely ain't found any gold today. This is too curious to go to sleep on."

Emmet went back for rope, and they secured it to a hook driven into a fissure. He wanted to follow Frank inside, but Frank stopped him. "One of us needs to stay here and haul me up. The hole is too high to reach from below. If our hook works loose, we're dead men."

Emmet's head bobbed in acknowledgment, so Frank went feet-first through the hole this time, and Emmet lowered him down.

When his feet touched the floor and he backed away from the wall, he surveyed the chamber. The walls sparkled with crystalline stars reflecting his lantern light, or the eyes of a thousand night creatures watching him from the shadows.

Above, Emmet whistled with awe. "Sure is pretty."

The stench from before forced Frank to breathe through his shirt, unpleasant but bearable.

The cavern narrowed and squeezed down some hundred feet from the hole, forcing him to bend at the waist, rough stone scraping across his back. One of the walls gleamed like pristine quartz, shades of milky white and pink, darkening to streaks of amethyst. He was no expert on precious stones, but he might find some buyers for big chunks of amethyst. He started to call back to

Emmet what he had found, until he spotted a gleaming yellow thread between layers of quartz and granite. His heart stopped. He moved closer.

Emmet's voice was faint. "What is it?"

It was too good to be true. Frank didn't want his initial thrill to be proven unfounded. It could be fool's gold.

As he reached out to touch the yellow trace, he knew there could be no question.

"Gold!" he called to Emmet.

"Gold?"

"Gold!" In the lantern light it seemed the vein of gold pulsed with the life of the earth. Laughter of joy bubbled out of him. "We found it! We found it!"

Tomorrow they would haul the equipment down here and start digging in earnest. His skin went as taut as a drumhead as he imagined the sensations of Mollie Hogan in his arms.

Emmet gave a hoot of joy.

The vein continued down into the darkness, drawing his attention into the deeper places, but this was enough for tonight. With renewed purpose and vigor, he turned back up toward their opening.

The change in perspective, however, revealed a branch in the cavern he had missed. A surge of curiosity gave him confidence he could follow this passage for a short distance without becoming lost, so he did.

A general incline of perhaps fifty yards proved easy walking. What brought him up short was not Emmet's distant hollering, but some things scattered over the floor that were not rocks.

Bones.

They formed an array, splintered and scattered, perhaps twenty feet across. In the exact center stood a strange shape, a sort of domed helmet with an upright fin down the center and a swooping brim, badly rusted.

He stepped gingerly around ribs and long bones to reach the helmet where it lay at the center. He picked it up by the fin, and something clattered out and rolled against his foot.

A human skull.

Heart surging into his throat, he cried out and dropped the helmet, which banged to the stone with an echoing clang.

In the distance, Emmet hollered something Frank's couldn't catch.

Nearby lay a steel breastplate in a similar state of decay, leather straps and buckles eaten away by time.

About twenty feet farther up the passage, he spotted another helmet. Then another a bit farther on.

The more he looked around, however, the more he realized that the bones—the human ribs, the arm and leg bones—had been carefully arranged, the way a child might arrange sticks into a pattern on the ground. He could not fathom the image, but there was no mistake.

His former elation drained away, replaced by cold, leaden dread.

"This looks like an old Spanish helmet," Emmet said. "Saw one in a picture book once." He turned the rusted helmet over and over.

Frank shivered at the memory of the way the skull sounded and felt when it hit his foot, hollow and dry.

"This must mean there's another entrance around here that we haven't found," Emmet said.

Frank shook his head and pointed down the mountain slope to the north, in the direction of the Georgetown camp. "I think it used to be over there, but whatever opening was there is gone. It was a solid cave-in."

They chewed quietly on hardtack and pemmican, ruminating, until darkness and chill descended and drove them into the warmer confines of their tent, where they soon bedded down for the night.

Frank's sleep was fitful as golden veins danced with bones in his fading imagination.

When he awoke, bright, silvery moonlight played through the tent flap. Sniffles let loose with a tremendous *heehaww* that sat Frank straight up on his cot. It was not like Sniffles to raise a ruckus at this time of night. Frank groped in the dark for the shotgun and hurried outside barefoot, wearing only his union suit.

The full moon cast silver dust over the mountainside, illuminating all in stark black and gray.

A deep, coarse sniffing sound near their crates of foodstuffs turned his bowels to water, and he turned slowly around expecting the shape of a bear rummaging through their supplies. Something was indeed hunched over one of the crates, sniffing.

He cocked both barrels of the shotgun. It was loaded with slugs for just this purpose; a load of buckshot would only put a bear in a pucker.

The click of the hammers brought the creature upright, but it wasn't a bear. It stood tall and thin like a man. An Injun in their camp counting coup? A tommyknocker venturing out of its earthen home? "Hey, now, what are you doing there?" Frank said.

The figure's head turned to regard him, but kept swiveling like an owl's, cranking around an impossible degree to observe him, and its eyes gleamed like those of a night creature caught in the light. And there was something about the face that sent warm piss down the leg of his union suit.

Slope-shouldered, forward slumped and impossibly gaunt, with an unkempt shock of greasy hair atop a pointed head. Its legs bent backwards like a dog's.

Frank cried out Emmet's name, spasms in his fingers

squeezing both triggers. The double explosion jerked the shotgun muzzle high, and orange sparks and thick smoke exploded into the night.

The thing dropped to all fours, snatched something on the ground with long, clawed fingers, and charged toward the mine entrance, dragging a substantial burden as if it weighed nothing.

"Emmet!" Frank cried again. "Get out here!"

The black mouth of the mine entrance swallowed the creature and its burden.

Emmet didn't come out of the tent.

"Emmet!"

Frank had once seen a chimpanzee in a zoo run on all fours like that. Circling to the tent flap, he opened it, and the moonlight revealed Emmet's empty cot.

His sleep-addled mind registered the two limp, flopping arms disappearing into blackness.

He ran to the mine entrance. "Emmet!"

In the distance, the sounds of something dragging over the planks covering the shaft floor diminished.

His hands trembled so badly he could barely hold the match to the lantern wick. He jumped into his trousers and boots, and reloaded their father's shotgun, hands spilling more powder onto the ground than down the barrels. As he fumbled, images of those lantern eyes and a protuberant snout flashed in his mind's eye. He set the tin onto the head of the powder barrel and jammed wadding and slug into each barrel.

Emmet would know what to do, he always had—but he was gone. Frank was the elder, but Emmet possessed the hardier temperament. How could Frank return to Baltimore and tell their mother he'd let Emmet get eaten by some strange beast? As an added precaution for light, he lit the wick and thrust his mining hat onto his head, then stuffed his pockets with candles.

With a deep shuddering breath, lantern in one hand, shotgun tucked under the other armpit, he hurried into the shaft.

Of course, it looked no different in the dead of night, but something about the hour still sent cold spiders crawling up his neck.

"Emmet! I'm coming!" he shouted into the black.

That thing had moved with a speed that further unnerved him. How could he ever catch it?

As he ran, the bobbing lantern cast a dizzying array of shifting shadows on the rough-hewn stone walls and wooden supports, a feeble globe of blessed illumination with him at the center.

A dark, wet smear appeared on the floor planks.

"Emmet!" he cried.

He reached the opening into the cavern, finding more blood smeared on the rough stone. He slung the shotgun over his back. The rope and hook seemed secure, but he was forced to douse the lantern and hook it to his belt to keep both hands free to lower himself inside. With rope in hand, he stuffed himself feet-first through the opening, half-expecting some rubbery black claw to seize him by the ankle and drag him into the earth's bowels like Emmet.

As he set his feet on the cavern floor, the blackness pressed in around him like cold water, as if the air itself was thickening. His heartbeat was the only thing he could hear as he re-lit the lantern.

Calling Emmet's name, he set off into the deeper blackness, hanging the lantern from his shotgun barrel to keep the gun at the ready.

Deeper he went than before, through caverns and passages that narrowed and expanded, twisted and turned, following blood smears, dreading the moment when he might encounter something larger than a smear.

An hour must have passed by the time the blood smears petered out. How deep he had come he had no notion. A mile? Two? He had moved expeditiously, hoping to catch the creature and yet fearing the moment of confrontation.

How much oil remained in his lantern? In his hat lamp? He doused the hat lamp, chiding himself for not realizing that he might need both to get himself out of here. With the candles, he had at least a day's worth of light, but if it all ran out, he would be left with only a handful of matches and nothing else to burn. He turned the wick down to its lowest level to conserve fuel, leaving him only a tiny guttering flame by which to see.

Another hour passed. Each step deeper made him yearn for another spot of his brother's blood to lead him on. He couldn't turn back. Not now. Not even if he found a whole nest of those things.

But he was growing weary. He quenched his thirst from a trickle of wetness on a cavern wall. It tasted awful, chalky, but it wet his tongue.

The edge of his circle of light had grown so nebulous, his eyes so bleary, that he almost walked straight into the yawning abyss that opened before him.

His feet teetered on the edge, arms windmilling as he fought for balance. In the lantern's flailing arcs, the flame went out, plunging him into profound blackness. He fell back on the floor, lantern clattering beside him, gasping for breath. He was not a praying man, but he now thanked the Almighty with everything he had.

He lay there for a moment, regathering his wits, his vision blacker than if his eyes were closed. After a time, he became aware of a sickly, greenish-blue glow casting shadows on the ceiling, emanating from the abyss.

Rolling onto his belly, he inched forward, feeling for

the precipice. He peered over the edge into a cavern vast beyond comprehension, painted with light on walls and structures. Towers and buttresses, catwalks and spires, minarets and pylons, all limned in swaths of blue-green algae. Odd angles induced a dizziness he could not blink away.

From the depths came peculiar meeping, mewling whispers. Black specks moved across the blue-green tapestries like ants.

Distant whispers echoed up to him, but the voices were so guttural he couldn't be sure they were speaking words at all.

"...what is it..."

"...a long time since we have..."

"...juicy..."

Snatches of other languages interspersed what he heard, Spanish, some heathen Chinese and Injun tongues, all intermixed with that peeping, meeping, mewling.

"...fresh meat on the foot out there..."

"...too fresh..."

"...no more eating worms and algae..."

"...too long below..."

A sudden sniffing sound like he had heard in camp, but right on top of him, yanked a gasp out of him. He scrambled away from the lip of the abyss. One flailing hand brushed something cold and rubbery. The other arm brushed the lantern, sending it clattering over the edge and into the void. Time stretched into eternity before the lantern struck anything, impossibly distant. Cold breath brushed the stench of fetor and blood across his cheek.

His hand closed over the shotgun. In the faint glow, a nebulous, low-slung shape shifted its stance, regarding him. With a ragged, rasping cry, he raised the shotgun, cocking both hammers. The muzzle flash blinded him again with no reckoning of whether he'd hit it. The cavern's confines redoubled the report, blasting a faint, muffled whine into his ears and masking all other sound. The acrid stench of powder smoke filled his nose, along with something pungent and sickly, the stench of the grave.

He flung himself away from the void, back up the passage, relying on his memory to take him as far as it could from the lip of that awful abyss.

Stopping to listen for pursuit, he fumbled out a match to light his hat lamp.

The mewling, meeping chorus grew louder, lending frantic speed to his heels.

Running in the opposite direction altered his perspective so profoundly he would have been lost immediately if not for Emmet's blood trail.

For at least a mile he ran, up, up, around, ducking and climbing and squeezing, each breath like a strip of lung being raked out.

At the top of a vaulted galley, curtained by sheets of wavy, nacreous stone, he paused to look back. Well outside the feeble sphere of his hat lamp's glow, lantern-like eyes hovered in the blackness, some standing high, some slinking low, regarding him as he regarded them.

Given the alacrity with which the first creature had dragged his brother away, they could have long since brought him down like wolves on a wounded elk.

But these wolves were playing with him, curious about him, thoughtful, calculating.

He ran on, praying for his hat lamp to stay alive. For at least two more miles he ran and stumbled and gasped and wept, up and up, round and round.

Behind came that damnable noise, like the sound of demonic infants speaking their own language.

What sounded like Emmet's voice reached out to him

from behind, washing like a shipwreck from the tide of infernal noise, calling Frank's name. "Stop...wait...want to see..." The sound of it made him pause.

But it couldn't be Emmet. Emmet was dead, and they were picking their teeth with his bones.

And other voices. "...fear makes it tender, it does..."

"...juicier..."

"...dash out its brains..."

"...hang it to ripen..."

"...slurp out its veins..."

On and on, he ran, praying for deliverance. Surely, he had stumbled on a portal to Hell.

The creatures had been trapped in the earth for untold centuries, millennia. Ever since the Spaniards found them and collapsed the entrance to this underworld.

What would these monsters do if they got loose? They would find plenty of unsuspecting prey in the Georgetown camp and among the lone prospectors dotting the mountainsides.

They would find beautiful, sweet, kind Mollie, sleeping in her tent, helpless in the black of night.

That was when he knew what he had to do.

The rope still hung where he had left it. In the endless flight, moments of doubt had plagued him. The sight of it sent fresh vigor coursing through him and he hit the rope like a climbing monkey.

As he climbed, the presences behind him closed in.

The muzzle of the shotgun slung across his shoulders caught against the hole's rim. He struggled to draw it in. Lantern eyes gleamed with the light of his hat lamp, closing in.

Finally, with a shrill curse, he shrugged the shotgun off and let it fall, then jammed himself through the opening, tearing furrows in his skin. He gasped for the fresh air of the upper world and flung himself upward.

Primal instinct urged him to flee into the night and not look back. But the creatures would find him. Even if he reached Georgetown, no one would believe him. Out here, there was no law, no cavalry.

He burst into the moonlight, giving Sniffles a start. The burro regarded him with sleepy indifference as he seized the rim of the barrel of powder they used for blasting. No strength remained in his arms save that of desperation. The half-full barrel centered under the slide, where the shaft was most unstable, should be sufficient to collapse the shaft.

He shoved the barrel over and rolled it into the tunnel, his muscles like limp steaks.

He met them sixty feet inside. They slunk along the floor, clung like bats to the roof beams, their claws scratching the rock and their eyes like dying lanterns.

"...it has the powder..."

"...like the others..."

"...seize it..."

"...gouge its flesh..."

"...*cometelo*..."

"...*yao ta*..."

"...twist its neck..."

"...chew it..."

"...*masticalo*..."

"...*dapo gutou*..."

"...*tekeli-li...tekeli-li*..."

"...wait, the powder!"

Twisted, once-human faces took shape in the guttering light. Hungry, slavering, splintered yellow teeth in elongated snouts, noses shrunk to slits, pointed ears sticking from mops of greasy black hair, skin bruise-black and rubbery, long arms, long fingers tipped with black talons.

They poised less than twenty feet from him. He had no fuse.

He righted the barrel, glanced over his shoulder for one last look at the moonlight, and thought of Mollie's lips as he struck the match.

Freelance writer, novelist, award-winning screenwriter, editor, poker player, poet, biker, roustabout, Travis Heermann is the author of The Hammer Falls, The Ronin Trilogy, and co-author of the horror-western Death Wind. His short fiction appears in anthologies and magazines such as Apex Magazine, Alembical, the Fiction River anthology series, and Cemetery Dance's Shivers VII, and others. He lives in Aurora, Colorado, where he enjoys cycling, collecting martial arts styles and belts, torturing young minds with otherworldly ideas, and monsters of every flavor, especially those with a soft, creamy center.

THAT TIME MAGGIE GHOSTED ME

Jeamus Wilkes

I was about to delete the YesKnow dating app on my phone when I saw its icon had a little red dot with the number eight resting on it. Eight YKInbox messages. As in eight more than what I had when I checked two weeks ago on a drunk Friday night. I flushed a little bit. Pulse rising, I checked myself.

She hasn't messaged you or said boo in three weeks, man. Leave it alone. You always get caught up in this shit only to be crushed because you ruin it with over-communicating. Don't—

I tapped the YesKnow app's icon. The YKInbox's eight messages had five from magistra83. Maggie.

Fifteen years my junior and six inches taller than me, Maggie was "intrigued" by my profile, interested in exchanging messages with me, and made the first move on YesKnow. I took a lot of shit from my sister Rossi the Realtor in regard to Maggie's age, and I had my own misgivings about it. These misgivings revolved around how it seemed the general public, especially females, react to "old" men dating "young" women. This reaction involves an apoplectic eye roll and an exclamation falling somewhere between the sarcastic "of course," and the blunt "disgusting."

I got over this exaggerated-in-my-mind obstacle after an initial flurry of exchanged messages over four days with Maggie. This flurry revealed her to be intelligent, funny, and the best of challenges where we didn't see eye to eye. We graduated to using YesKnow's glitchy YKVideoChat. That's when I became smitten. Or at least infatuated. We then chatted for half an hour or more every night for weeks, either by video or texting.

She loved Talking Heads but hated KISS. Huge points on the first, and I decided to not subtract points on the second. Maggie's smile was wide, and her shoulder-length chestnut hair was prone to going wild with very little laughter. She liked my smirk, was tickled that I played xylophone in high school marching band, and thought my earring was "badass." We both liked the horror genre quite a bit, including its wide and varied offerings in film, books, TV, and such. King was her favorite mainstream horror novelist, and some guy I never heard of named Ryman Northmark was her favorite indie horror tale-spinner. She hated people making tall-person comments or jokes, especially ones directed at her. She checked, double-checked, and checked yet again with me that if we ever met, I would be OK being seen with a woman half a foot taller than me.

Her parents lived somewhere near Cape Cod, which explained the Bah-stuhn layer in her speech—especially when she got excited about something—and said my voice was "metropolitan and thigh-shivering deep." She moved to Colorado to go to school on a scholarship, ended up staying, and currently lived close to downtown Denver. She loved haunting coffee shops, comedy clubs, delis, poetry slams, used clothing stores, improv, and open-mic nights.

She dug that I was an artist, half-dug that my day job was in shipping-and-receiving logistics and appeared genuinely interested in my artwork. She even gave what seemed to be glowing and sincere compliments of my pen-and-ink pieces. The jigsaw puzzles, true crime books, and criminal justice reference volumes that populated the bookcase behind me—in the limited view my webcam provided—told her I had "sweet smarts," and when I repeated her but said "street smarts," she corrected me back to "sweet smarts." Maggie often had cello music playing in the background, texted intelligently with minimal abbreviations, and had an undergraduate degree in social work. Her day job was a mystery, but I was fine with her withholding any info she wanted to until she felt safe to share it. I'd learned my lesson in that regard when I was regrettably pushy on details from other YesKnow parties.

So, I didn't push at all for her to give up a Facebook profile, phone number, or email address, and we let things ride in the safety of YesKnow's communication platforms. We exchanged dating and relationship horror stories and had sort of an unspoken agreement that she'd let me know when we should do the meet-for-coffee thing.

She seemed not only not bothered by, but relishing our age difference: me, being fifty and her, thirty-five. One night in a YKVideoChat session, I made what I thought was a harmless crack about being a "daddy" to her because of my age. Her response was sober.

"That's bordering on being an insulting thing to say, Paul."

My tail was between my legs.

She continued, "We haven't been friends that long, and, well...but...surely you think more of me than that."

I think she saw in my stuttering apology and wilted look that I regretted the daddy comment, and she shifted gears in a manner that made my blood run its warmest since we began communicating. She moved a short strand of hair away from her face and smiled at me while looking directly at the camera eye, her eyes appearing to meet mine. "I'm not a girl, Paul. I'm a woman who wants to meet you. I think we should—possibly—hen—sto—for—ye—"

The video chat glitched and broke up Maggie's voice at first, then fractured her image into pixelated scrambles and digital distortion.

"Fuck!" I responded. "It's breaking up again, Maggie. I'll YKChat you."

But she messaged my phone first.

> **magistra83:** The timing on this video thing is for shit.
>
> **xpauliex:** I know. Christ, how many times has this happened?
>
> **magistra83:** Too many. I was trying to tell you I'm down for meeting somewhere this Thursday or Friday night if you want. If your schedule allows. Something low key.

I probably overdid my fist pump as I nearly dropped my phone.

> **xpauliex:** That sounds awesome. I'd love to see you.
>
> **magistra83:** Cool. There's a booksto...

The rippling ellipsis that represents the other party still in process of messaging had shown for a short bit, then went away. "Booksto" was the last word I'd gotten from her for weeks.

When I did hear from her again, the circumstances were significantly different. Until that time, the passage of days was mind-bending and dark.

Firstly, the interrupted communication was an odd thing. You normally have to press a "send" button on any chat or messaging programs, and I wondered why only a partial sentence got transmitted. She was talking about meeting in one moment, and then...nothing. I kept replying or trying to re-initiate conversation with things like "???" or "Hey, did I lose you?" and the desperate, "Was there something I said that was offensive?" And several times when I texted my phone number or email to provide a method of communication outside of YesKnow.

Nothing. No responses in my YKInbox, other than the irritating "hey cutie" and "I'm sooooo lonely" phishing and spam messages and YesKnow's tedious upgrade marketing emails, but that was it. No Maggie.

My sister Rossi was matter-of-fact about it. I lived in a studio apartment in Northglenn, so she met me for breakfast nearby on one Saturday morning I was pining for Maggie. Rossi the Realtor stirred her coffee while we sat in Gunther Toody's, my breakfast turning colder by the second, the muted sound of cars going too fast down 104th in the background. Rossi's plate was clean, save for a few crumb-speckled syrup remainders. My pancakes had one or two bites out of them, the sagging leftovers pitiful and shoved to the side on the plate. However, I did continue to drain my coffee.

"Don't take it personal, P," Rossi said. "Maybe there was an ex-partner she wasn't quite over whose reappearance may have landed right in the middle of her messaging you. Or a family emergency. Or some kinda trigger that may have clammed her up. Or illness. Or some skeleton might have started falling out of her closet that she didn't want you to see. Or a million other things. Or just one thing."

"Yeah," I nodded. "Whatever. I've run through shit like that in my head so many times, I can't count. It's the lack of information that makes it hard, sis. No goodbye. No fuck you. No 'hey I'm no longer interested.'"

"It doesn't fucking feel good, I know." She leaned back. "I've been ghosted, and more than once. I'm sorry, Paul. It seemed like you really liked this woman."

I shook my head. "I'm half-a-century old. When am I going to be able to shrug this shit off?"

Rossi put my hand in hers. "Don't apologize for connection, Paul. Shit, some people don't know a good thing when it's right fucking in front of them. Or even right beside them."

However oddly phrased, I appreciated Rossi's sentiment. But it did absolute zero in helping fill the hole that appeared in missing just the simple communication and conversation I'd been sharing with Maggie. I realized that somewhere in those weeks of messaging and video chats that I'd fallen for her. I should know better, with an ex-wife and trail of multiple-failed relationships, but... yes. Fallen.

And now, everything sucked. Forced conversations with coworkers left a garbage taste in my mouth. Chinese food with more thrown out leftovers than what made it into my digestive system. I surfed Denver area animal shelter sites, considering a pet to fill the loneliness hole, and finally settling into being really fucking old and giving up on garbage people and garbage TV and garbage communication and social media garbage and the fucking trough of sites and apps like YesKnow and garbage garbage garbage and more garbage and trying to fill more holes or maybe even just one hole with just a little more palatable garbage.

A few days after meeting with my sister, I was at home and very near flopping into bed with exhaustion when a second wind gripped me like a drug addict scavenging the surroundings for a fix. I grabbed my phone and tried one more YKInbox message and YKChat text. Hours later, nothing. Again, no response.

Two more weeks went by, and on an overcast Monday while I was at lunch at work, I was about to delete the YesKnow app on my phone—even the sight of its icon was maddening--when I saw I had eight YKInbox messages. Five were from magistra83. Maggie. My heart raced.

I had to renew my subscription to YesKnow before I could access my inbox. The few seconds it took to use Google Pay seemed like forever, and then, finally, YKInbox popped up.

DATE	SENDER	SUBJECT
10/5	magistra83	theTimingonthisvideo-thingisforshittooMany-iwastryi...
10/5	magistra83	thetiMingonthisvideo-thingisforshittoomany-Wastryi...
10/6	YesKnow Support	Take your photos up a notch with YKPhotoPhix!
10/7	YesKnow Support	Your safety and privacy is priority one at YesKnow
10/8	magistra83	theTimingonthisvideo-thingisforshittooMany-iwastryi...
10/8	magistra83	thetiMingonth7isvideo7hi-gisfo3rshittoo4many5W...

| 10/8 | magistra83 | hjklWf7lHhekjhjkhk73kjg-hkjdlhlk4grehiQv5xnc-burhkf... |
| 10/8 | YesKnow Support | Renew YesKnow now and |

stay in the game!

I was excited, gut-punched, and confused. The subject lines were gibberish, and the queue of Maggie's emails were punctuated by YesKnow's standard marketing . Shit, why didn't she just try to use my email or call? I tapped her first email, and the confusion deepened. I called in sick to work as my concentration on anything outside of Maggie was for absolute shit. For the next few hours I just examined what landed in my inbox:

```
theTimingonthisvideothingisforshittooMany
iwastryithetImingonthisvideothingisforshi
ttooManyiwastrylthetimingonthIsviDeothing
isforshittoomanyiwastryithetimingonthiSviD
eothIngisforshIttoomanyiwastryiThetimingon
thisvideothingisforshittooManyiwastryithet
imIngonthisvIdeothingisforshittooManyiLast
ryitheImingonthisvideothingisforshittooMan
yiwaStryithetimingonThiKLKLKLKLKLKL
KLKLKLKLKLKLKLKLKLKLKLKLKLKLKLKL
LKKLKKLKKKLLLKLKLL
```

I recognized the repeated lines of text as fragments copied from her last messaging session with me: "the timing on this video thing is for shit too many I was tryi-" repeated over and over, with no spaces, and scattered capitals throughout, and the odd repeating "KL." Her second email looked similar, but the pattern of capitals was slightly different. Her third email looked identical to the first. Her fourth email was similar to the first and third, but had a repeating pattern of numbers—7,7,3,4, and 5—scattered throughout:

```
thetiMingonth7isvideot7hingisfo3rshittoo4ma
ny5WthetiMingonth7isvideot7hingisfo3rshitto
o4many5WthetiMingonth7isvideot7hingisfo3rsh
ittoo4many5WthetiMingonth7isvideot7hingisfo
3rshittoo4many5WthetiMingonth7isvideot7hing
isfo3rshittoo4many5WthetiMingonth7isvideot7
hingisfo3rshittoo4many5WthetiMingonth7isvid
eot7hingisfo3rshittoo4many5WthetiMingonth7i
svideot7hingisfo3rshittoo4many5WthetiMingon
th7isvideot7hingisfo3rshittoo4many5W
```

As far as surface appearance, the fifth email was most disturbing, as it was an incomprehensible paragraph of gibberish. If Maggie was more abstract or indifferent in her behavior toward me, I might have chalked all this up to some woman fucking with my head. But she wasn't either of those things. Granted, our world was limited by the half-assed platforms available to us via YesKnow, but I knew enough to know something was wrong.

"I can't believe you trashed a work day because of this," Rossi had said over the phone. I'd sent Rossi screenshots of the emails. "She's messing with you and frankly it's pissing me off, Paul. She's knows you're invested and for whatever sick reason she's getting off on it." I hung up on Rossi and ignored her, "Did you fucking hang up on me?" text. I set up my laptop computer on my dining area table, parking my phone and a beat-up legal pad next to it.

As pissed off as I was at Rossi's dismissal, I couldn't help but return to the odd phrase she used in trying to comfort me during our conversation at Gunther Toody's. Shit, some people don't know a good thing when it's right fucking in front of them or even right beside them.

In the interior meltdown I was having over all of this, Rossi's word kept hanging on me as I tried to unpack the mysterious emails. I started by writing the capital letters in the first email message in order: T, M, I, M, I, I, D, S, D, I, I, T, M, I, I, M, L, M, S, and then the repeated KLKLKLKL. I pathetically tried to translate it to Roman numerals, but that made no sense. Fuck. I closed my eyes and Rossi's words came through my thoughts again.

Shit, some people don't know a good thing when it's right fucking in front of them or even right beside them.

Right in front of them. Right beside them. In front of me. Beside me.

I imagined a good thing in front of me. A good person. I imagined Maggie sitting across from me at my tiny dining table. Then sitting beside me. The thought was both beautiful and heartbreaking. Her smile and her gestures and her facial contortions and her laughter and her mock outrage and her caramel eyes and her chestnut hair and her long fingers and her Pink Floyd T-shirts and her digging my inkwash illustration of a Zephyr Zodiac and her use of big words and her calling me on my crap and her not giving a squirty shit that my Criminal Justice undergrad and Creative Writing grad degrees went unused on my day job and her likes and her gunmetal nail polish and her dislikes and her interest in me and her interest in improving the world and her desire for a dog someday and her desire for maybe a home and her cravings for phở and her wanting to meet at the booksto—

Right in front of them. Right beside them. In front of you. Beside you. In front of me. Beside me.

"Fuck!" I yelled. I opened my eyes and threw up my

hands and moved away from the computer and notepad.

I pulled on a hoodie, put my phone in my back pocket, put on some tennis shoes, and left my apartment to walk around Croke Reservoir. The trail was a little muddy from the previous night's rain, but I didn't give a shit, and muddied up my shoes good and proper. Others were using Croke's bike and jogging trails, but I barely noticed them. Getting out of my apartment and walking at a decent clip helped me calm down somewhat. I had my phone with me but I didn't look at it once.

After two trips around the reservoir, fatigue landed on me like a heavy blanket. I'd been spending weeks sleeping like crap and eating like a rat. As obsessed as I had become with Maggie, my twin sized bed, pillows, and comforter called to me with the promise of sweet rest. I landed on them after near-stumbling into my apartment and barely closing and locking the door. Yes, rest. The sweet dark of sleep.

Sweet sleep. Sweet smarts.

My dreams were only a replay of my conversations with Maggie, save for one difference: In those moments of glitchy, interrupted-signal communication, split-second images came through that my waking mind couldn't recall. The quiet mental frustration in trying to remember exacerbated as I plugged away like a zombie at my job in the following days, the oh-so-exciting world of entering data relevant to international shipping and the logistics involved.

Occasionally, my mind thought it remembered those brief flashes; unsettling images of which I could only recall their morbid emotional resonance and none of their visual specifics, whether abstract or detailed. When I woke up from my nap, my mind slipped into neutral. It had done this before, out of self-defense.

"Either Maggie's fucking with you, or someone using her YesKnow account is seriously fucking with you."

I almost replied, "Tell me something I don't know, Rossi," but I didn't. I think my uneaten pile of food and my eyes following the activity outside Gunther Toody's window—a blackbird snacking on a prairie dog's 104th Avenue-flattened remains—already told my sister a sizeable portion of everything going on inside me.

In my peripheral vision, Rossi sipped her coffee. "Tell me what I can do, Paulie. You look like hell and I'm afraid this whole hating-your-job-on-cruise-control while you die inside is making you die outside. You're acting worse than you did after that monster Nomi had used and abused you—"

"What in the actual fuck does any of this have to do with Nomiki Hoyborg?" I was kind of jolted by my own emotional flare when my eyes met my sister's.

"Ah, you see? There's Paul. It just took the pleasant memory of that screeching Greco-Nordic hairbag Nomi to wake him up!"

After my divorce was official in November of 2014, Nomi was the worst possible choice I could have made. A rebound, and a rebound so hard that it led many to believe she was the demise of my twenty-five-year marriage to Rowan. And I could explain to people from now until the end of fucking time that Rowan and I always had a weak marriage, but people would nod with the "Yeah-yeah, whatever, you asshole" look in their eyes, somehow associating Nomi as the homewrecker and me as the dumb cuck that went after her.

They were right about the latter—I was the dumb cuck in that whole two years' worth of verbal and physical abuse train I endured from Nomiki Hoyborg. But most everyone who knew me and bothered to comment on it came across that I was deserving of it. Especially those who knew me and sort of liked me but knew and loved my ex, Rowan. More than one person inquired as to why I was "slumming it" with Nomi. How do you explain to someone you were simply trying to make it work with a woman you were initially burning with lust for, but now ducking literal and metaphorical punches from? So, after two years of wild sex and her slapping me around with her mouth and hands, I'd gotten enough of Nomi and left her, the restraining order a gift to myself.

Other overall good byproducts included the mass removal of fake friends, a moderate removal of front row critics, and the singular removal of my head from my ass. All of it was the purest of hell to go through, but heavenly in its rearview mirror outcome. At the mention of Nomi's name, those two years and their few months of aftermath had compressed themselves into a bullet of memory that my sister had just fired squarely into the center of my brain.

"Ah, you see? He's there. There's Paul. It just took the pleasant memory of that screeching Greco-Nordic hairbag Nomi to wake him up!"

And through the bullet of memory my eyes never left my sisters'. "You're right," I said. "I can't let anyone tear me up like that again."

I plunged myself back into my day job while polishing my résumé at night. I deleted the YesKnow app from my phone. I journaled and had a reckoning with myself, recounting my mistakes, my bad decisions, my wicked decisions, and the desire to continue to learn from them, rectify them, and move forward. My laps around Croke Reservoir increased.

And then, on my way to work one winter morning, I saw the digital billboard. I was stopped near 104th and I-25, ready to enter the freeway southbound. On the billboard was an advertisement for YesKnow, and among the young models' faces that flashed on the billboard, I saw Maggie's for just an instant.

The car behind me honked. After flipping it off in response, I whipped into an Applebee's parking lot, got out of my car, and saw the YesKnow advertisement cycle through the stream of multiple ads on the billboard. The cold air bit at my face, but my attention was riveted. The next time the ad cycled through, it wasn't Maggie's face, but the hair was the same. I sat there and watched through several cycles. It wasn't her. I was satisfied--albeit rattling--that my mind had simply pasted her face onto someone with similar features.

"Fuck," I muttered, getting back into my car. As I got on the freeway, springing up from the Best Buy parking lot was an even clearer view of the billboard, and it landed on my eyes for another show. The YesKnow advertisement scrolled by again, and it was Maggie.

Fucking hell, it was Maggie, this time a choppy animation showing her throw her head back in the exact manner I'd seen her do with that Maggie laugh and toothy open smile. Her hair landed in a messy arrangement as the advertisement finished and moved on to some goddamn car dealership. I nearly caused the car behind mine to rear end me as I slowed and came to a stop on the shoulder of the freeway. I got out of the car, oblivious to the honking parade as I walked around to the front of my car and started staring at the billboard again. No Maggie.

She only appears when I'm not looking for her. Fuck.

Eventually I got back into my car and eased into the daily tragedy known as Denver traffic. I was an hour late to work and provided no excuse for my supervisor, who'd reached the end of her patience and wrote me up. It had been leading up to this for some time, with my erratic behavior punctuated by regularly visible fatigue. After sitting through the write up like a dipshit waiting in a dentist's office, I got back into my workday and finished it out. My mind's eye saw Maggie throw her head back again and again.

When I got home that night, I poured myself a juice-glass full of ice and whiskey. I retrieved from my closet the legal pad I'd used in trying to decipher her emails. I fired up my laptop and logged into YesKnow. My account was still there and the number of emails had remained the same. That was a bit curious, but I'd only wanted to look at those enigmatic ones, anyhow. I wanted to turn the first email over again in my head, reviewing all my notes on the capital letters. T, M, I, M, I, I, D, S, D, I, I, T, M, I, I, M, L, M, S, and then the repeated KLKLKLKL…

My sister's voice was so clear in my thoughts, she may as well have been sitting right next to me, saying them again: *Shit, some people don't know a good thing when it's right fucking in front of them or even right beside them.*

Right in front of them. Right beside them.

I went back to the original email and looked at the letters right beside the capital letters. My eyes naturally moved to the right, so I began to scribble the letter just to the right of the capital letters. The result made the hair on my arms stand stiff and cold:

IAMATSEVENTHANDAAMATH

Immediately my brain began to separate the words, and so I put a slash between them:

I /AM/AT/SEVENTH/AND/AAMATH

My breathing began to speed up, my head feeling my

pulse on every agonizing beat. But what was AAMATH? Then my eyes moved to the bottom of the email, the repeated KLKLKLKLKLKLKL, and after a few minutes of staring at the odd "AAMATH," I wrote the entire message in the only way it could be interpreted:

I am at Seventh and Kalamath

In those moments of not being entirely sure who Maggie was, Rossi's words still came crashing through: Right in front of them. Right beside them.

Immediately I went into Google Maps. The street view of West 7th Avenue and Kalamath Street showed an intersection I'd probably been through a few times during my residence in the Denver metroplex, but paid no attention to because of its unremarkableness like most intersections leading to downtown: older residences being gradually overwhelmed by businesses and developers buying them up and flipping, converting, or bulldozing them.

That section of Kalamath was one way, southbound. On the northwest corner was a Phillips 66 gas station/convenience store. The northeast corner had the square two-story Open Media/KGNU station headquarters. The northwest corner had an avocado-painted cinder block eyesore housing Reitler and Rolfowich, Attorneys at Law. At the southwest corner sat three small and similarly designed brick houses, snugged up tightly against each other. They all looked older, but newly flipped. The Google Maps picture was from November 2018, so it was fairly recent. For a ridiculous moment I imagined Maggie living in one of those houses and simply wrapping up directions to her residence inside riddles and obscure clues.

But I knew in my heart this wasn't the case. And that's when fear began to genuinely grip me. My house grew colder, and my mind replaying everything about Maggie and her cryptic messages began to torment me. And Rossi's words. Right in front of them. Right beside them.

Maggie's view of my bookcase from my webcam angle revealed the bulk of my criminal justice studies, puzzles, and cryptography books. The letters to the right of the capitals were the actual letters she used to send a message. Another bookcase to the right of the webcam, just outside its view, was filled with horror novels I'd collected over the years, most of them ghost stories.

magistra83. My head began to pound. I Googled "Maggie, 1983, Denver, missing, death." Scrolling a few links down the results, one of them led to an archived Rocky Mountain News article that opened up hell's mouth—into which I was sticking my head.

Margaret "Maggie" Sherie Traynor, 35, an Englewood, Colorado resident, had gone missing from a Cheesman Park music festival on July 30, 1983. The picture of a scanned newsprint Olan Mills-style portrait photo showed an attractive woman with heavy metal hair held up by Aqua Net. Concentrating on her face and reimagining the 1983 makeup, it was unmistakably Maggie.

Fuck.

I backed away from my laptop after closing it and left every light on behind me as I went to my bedroom, locked the door, took off my shoes, crawled into my bed, and tried to catch my breath. The only other time in my life I felt like this were those few weeks when Nomi was stalking me and threatening to murder me and every member of my family. At the time I'd had a few bruises and stitched up cuts to compound that fear. One particular nasty cut was when she came across the top of my right hand's carpal and metacarpal area with some giant Rambo-looking hunting knife. I still had the rosy scar outlined in bright almost-white mottled flesh to remind me of the months it took to fully recover from the pain. I looked at the scar while I was lying there in bed, and surprised myself at the next emotion that came flooding in.

Anger.

I briefly rubbed the scar and then threw the covers off of me, got up, put my shoes on, took some aspirin with tepid tap water, and grabbed my phone. I typed in "seventh and kalamath, denver" on Google maps, and pressed the DIRECTIONS icon. The last thing I grabbed on my way out the door was my heavy hoodie. It was cold, and it was only going to get colder.

I parked at the Phillips 66, as there was no street parking in any direction on 7th or Kalamath for several blocks. On my way there I ran Maggie's communication with me up until this moment through my mind. At first, I wondered why she had beat around the bush and hadn't just come out and told me she was a…a ghost.

Thinking that through a little longer, I could see how immediate disclosure would have been disastrous on all fronts. She knew the weeks of introduction were necessary before her cryptic messages would start showing up. It had to be a mystery, in some ways, for it to prime my horror-aesthetic pump in my emo brain. But it still didn't answer everything about all this weird and scary shit. Why me? Why through a dating app? Did she run away, or was she killed?

Standing at the corner in the bitter cold for several minutes, I finally said aloud, "What do you want me to see?" The stoplights directed impatient lanes of twilit traffic for several minutes before I closed my eyes and yelled, "Maggie!"

I dropped my head and opened my eyes, staring at the sidewalk. I pulled out my phone. Would she have more messages for me, now that I was here? The zero-new-messages YKInbox said no. When I looked up, a person was standing just behind a four-foot FOR SALE sign in front of the small house on the southeast corner. They were facing me and wore some kind of long coat. A breeze kicked up a few strands of shoulder-length hair.

Maggie.

I yelled out her name again, and she motioned with her right hand for me to come to her. I put my phone in my back pocket. I crossed Kalamath, dodging the honking cars and the yelling drivers here and there, and when I reached the northeast corner, I looked into the front yard again. This time Maggie stood inside the house, looking out one of the front windows. No coat but a U2 t-shirt I saw her wearing more than once during our video chats.

I crossed 7th and a white Beetle nearly ran me over. I mouthed "sorry" to the driver who threw his hands up at me. I crossed the rest of the way to the sidewalk in front of the house, the metal house number illuminated under a now-lit porchlight. Maggie was no longer in the window.

Not seeing a doorbell, I knocked on the front door, then behind the screen saw a digital deadbolt like my sister Rossi had on hers. They could be opened either by key or electronic password on an alphanumeric keypad. Real estate companies liked them because they didn't have to do the old school combination key box thing on empty houses. After several knocks and no answer, I looked at the keypad again, and remembered the repeating pattern of numbers in one of Maggie's cryptic emails. 7, 7, 3, 4, 5. I pressed the numbers and the enter button, and a long beep sounded as a red X illuminated above the keypad. No go.

Right in front of them. Right beside them.

I keyed in a different set of numbers, this time the numbers that would be just to the right of 77345: 8,8,4,5,6, and then the enter button. The lock whirred, and with a final click of the deadbolt's disengagement a green check mark appeared on the keypad. I opened the door and a blast of even colder air hit me. Although it was quickly turning dark outside, the porchlight and ambient light of the neighborhood could not penetrate the pitch blackness just inside the door, even when I opened it fully.

"Come inside, Paul," Maggie's whispered, crystal clear even through the street sounds. It chilled me, not in the context of it being a dead woman's voice, but that it was a real voice; one not clouded by digital representation through a computer or phone speaker. I hesitated. I really could not see a fucking thing beyond the threshold of the doorway.

"What's wrong?" she said.

"I'm goddamned scared," I said. "What is all of this, Maggie? I-"

"Come in Paul and close the door behind you. Come be with me for just a little while." No whispers this time. Just the normal tone of voice of the woman I'd fallen in love with, coming from behind a cloak of time, death, and impenetrable darkness. So, of course, I entered .

If the cold outside was biting, the cold inside 948 West 7th Avenue was snapping and chomping. I felt for my sweat-jacket's hood and pulled it over my head. I couldn't see my hands, or anything. I reached for my phone in my back pocket.

"Your phone's flashlight won't work in here," said Maggie. Her voice sounded not far away, maybe three feet, if that.

"You can see me, but I can't see you?"

"I've had a lot of time to learn how to see in this kind of darkness. And my eyes are something quite different these days."

I exhaled and shivered. "Maggie, it's…so…cold."

"I'm sorry," she said. "I'm tied to this house. Bound to it. I was able to communicate with you through great effort, but at a great cost and it made me ill for a while."

"Spirits can get...sick?" I said.

"Yes. We can. I don't want to put your body through much more, Paul, so I need you to give me your hands. Hold them out."

I slowly bent my elbows and raised my hands and felt Maggie's warm hands take them.

"Being partially corporeal is a hard trick, but I can do it. And I have to do it so I can talk to your mind. Talking to your mind is so much easier than talking to your ears."

She let go of one of my hands and I felt her palm and fingers against my cheek. That's when my head felt odd and warm for a few moments, and then suddenly my mind exploded with memories, images, sounds, and olfactory intrusions at a furious rate.

One moment I was standing in the crowd at Red Rocks Amphitheater, watching U2 perform and seeing Maggie in the crowd, with Heather Locklear-feathered hair. She turned to me and said, "This is where he first saw me." Then the crowd slowly morphed into a looser gathering, and we were now in Cheesman Park, and a band I didn't know was on stage, and then I was looking at a faceless man following Maggie to her car.

The crowd trickled away and the intersection of 7th and Kalamath sprouted up through the ground, houses shooting up alongside trees and buildings falling into place like lego pieces, the streets rolling out like butcher paper, and this intersection was quite different, the stoplights cruder, and the television antennas and giant satellite dishes popping up everywhere. 948 West 7th Ave had different colors on its woodwork and the bricks were unpainted. In front was a jade green van, its back doors open and a faceless man hauling music equipment crates out of it. I knew Maggie was in one of them, yet she was also standing in that same spot where a FOR SALE sign would be planted decades later, and she was motioning for me to come inside and follow the faceless man.

I was in 948's basement without much memory of how I got there, as Maggie's fingers against my face were now pressing the fast forward button on my brain. I was trembling when I saw a shallow grave in the basement and Maggie lying in it nude, stabbed and beaten, a torn and bloody U2 shirt tossed aside with other trash.

The final scene in this psycho-spiritual film reel of vignettes was a vision of Maggie, vengeful spirit with hard-learned powers of temporary corporeality. She manifested herself as a bloody, raging member of the undead to seek revenge against the faceless man, and revenge is exactly what she delivered. Without a sense of location, it was in some back alley that Maggie had come to the faceless man and made him piss his pants just before she ripped him apart, starting with his eyes. She screamed and then in this final scene she turned to me, bloody face and whitened eyes suddenly contorting into sadness.

"He's tied me to this fucking house, Paul, and I cannot be here anymore." We were in the basement again, this time the grave covered up and cemented over. "I want to be bound to you, and I am begging you to let me do so. It will take some time, and it will not make your life easy. But I cannot be in this fallow ground anymore. Moving my bones won't do anything. It's the ground that's anchored my spirit. I can't go very far from here and I've driven people into madness and suicide by trying to latch onto them to free me from this place. But I know you won't do those things."

Rage and fear and sadness welled up within me, and this overwhelming sense that she wanted to show me more, but for now this short communique was all I could get. I'd have to do some digging on my own, but later . I fell to my knees in darkness, and briefly felt the embrace of Maggie before it was gone in the bitter cold dark of 948's entryway.

After calling out for her several times, there was no answer. I felt my way back to the front door and left the house, engaging the lock. It was full on dark outside, but it seemed like daytime compared to the dark inside 948. On the sidewalk I turned towards the front window, the curtain settling as if someone had just been there a moment earlier.

I took out my phone and called Rossi.

She answered, "Hello, baby brother."

"Rossi the Realtor, I need your help."

"What's up?" she said.

I closed my eyes and imagined Maggie's head falling back in laughter. "I want to buy a house. I already have it picked out."

"Holy shit," she said. "Um. Okay, where is it?"

"Right in front of me."

Jeamus Wilkes is a horror fiction and nonfiction writer via his online platform of jeamus.com. He also hosts the Jeamus After Midnight podcast. Jeamus currently resides in Golden, Colorado with his family and an inordinate amount of small yellow dogs.

LAST WORDS: CANNIBAL KINGS AND QUEENS
Larry Berry

Let be the finale of seem.
The only emperor is the emperor of ice cream.
- Stevens

There are few things more treasured by the human heart than acts of divination. From reading tea leaves to the entrails of sacrificed animals, a thousand generations have sought to see the future in the improbable. While this was often a reach toward anticipating good fortune such as a long-sought marriage, just as often the act of foretelling revealed a need to sense the tread of approaching evil.

The writers in this anthology are all men and women who came to a place where the one necessary thing in their lives was seeking out this dark stranger and drawing its face using the printed page as a canvas. Quantum physics tells us that when they embarked on this act of origination, they created a timeline and strange events that did not exist before. Which asks the question: Which appeared first, the knife or the desire to use it?

Evil exists in Colorado, a current of existential force

outside of time.

In the Anasazi ruins in Hovenweep and Chaco Canyon there are charnel pits where the skeletal remains show bone polish from severed body parts being cooked and stirred for prolonged periods, the bone ends rubbing against the surface of the pot. These lost cities are empty of anything but dust, for the Anasazi empire disappeared into a last long darkness that cannot be explained by drought or famine. Some nameless entity sought them out and lured the race into red shadows. What we see and hear in Mesa Verde is the echo of their last insanity.

Evil leaves emptiness, desolation, and a shadow-land in its wake. It doesn't matter what your beliefs are. The evil that exists in Colorado believes in you.

Let us put finger bones in an ivory cup inscribed with incantations from the *Book Of The Dead* and offer them to a few of the writers who gave us such a wonderful collection. The question we ask is to tell us about the evil they saw before the story was ever written.

Stephen Graham Jones contributed one of the most powerful stories in this anthology because he's a writer who has chosen to pursue darkness—and the evil that lives within it—as the motive force in his fiction. The author of nineteen novels, few Colorado talents have written as well in defense of the nightmares that penetrate the barrier of sleep and become a kind of contagion.

In talking to him about the nature of evil and how he came to write this unique tale, Stephen commented: *"Some of my favorite horror is built on the inside of a thing not matching the outside. I think this has to be why evil clowns are scary—the wrapper and the contents are at odds with each other. That's what I wanted with this story, anyway.*

"Something that, at first glance, is innocuous, just

another cyclist in Colorado, you can hardly not see one every twenty yards on the road. But that's just on the outside. On the inside, I kind of doubt this thing is even human. It doesn't seem to be driven by human concerns, anyway. It's not hungry, it's not mad, it's not doing this for revenge. It's just pedaling through, is maybe trying to figure how this world works.

"What violence it gets going, it's not even personal, which makes that violence, to me at least, hurt more, since it's not directed, it's just casual, it didn't even really have to happen. And now this thing'll just get back on its bike, keep going, never think about this afternoon again."

As I write this, the day is passing, a span of hours normal in the blandest sense, and yet, night is on the approach, traveling fast from the east, and the nocturnal creatures are waiting for the rise of darkness. As writers and as readers of dark speculative fiction we, too, anticipate the night world and the moveable feast of a good horror story. In truth, when we experience terror, a kind of night is with us in which there is comfort.

Angela Sylvaine perceives evil in a terrifying way, her stories equally special in their originality. On the subject of literary malevolence, Angela comments: *"To me, the scariest monsters are those that you don't see coming, those that disguise themselves as a friend. They tempt and manipulate by embodying our deepest and most secret desires. This is the evil I love to explore in my stories, because it's seductive and cruel and infectious, like a virus.*

"In "The Dead Spot," Mia embodies this captivating evil, drawing Clare away from the family amusement park filled with joy and laughter, and toward the abandoned speedway full of rot and neglect. Clare wants to believe the lie, wants to finally give in to her heart's desire, and so goes with reckless abandon into death's embrace. Smiling and

screaming."

Both writers conjure an evil able to change its shape, manifest itself as illusion, and convincingly hide what it most desires. In this incarnation, that which walks with us may become the very entity we most fear.

Gary Robbe writes subtle, insidious horror stories, and one of his best tales is showcased in this collection. For Gary, evil can be conjured in this way: *"My biggest fears seem to center around loss. Loss of self. Loss of what we love. Loss of control. The loss of everything that was and will be. Nothing, to me, is more terrifying than being in a situation where we have no control, within and without ourselves.*

"The idea for "Scrape" came from the thought that just because a house was torn down, it doesn't necessarily mean that it's still not there. And what if a family moves into a new house built on that very spot, only to find that they are forever trapped in the original house, a claustrophobic world that defies all explanation, a world where there is no escape, even with death and madness. On the outside a new typical Denver townhouse complete with rooftop deck, and a family growing over the years and living normal lives. But in the same place, in a different universe, the same family trapped forever in the old house, no control over what they experience, no control over the brief glimpses into their parallel selves who are able to move in the outside world. Pure madness. Pure loss."

Gary's words slip inside the psyche and build a nest of bones. As an author, he seems to write from a place few of us suspect.

With him on a road into a lightless horizon is Carter Wilson, who conjures tales on a road trip into the darkest circuits of the heart.

Carter offers this comment on the devil behind the

story he wrote in collaboration with literary artist Joshua Viola, which is as sly as both their fictional worlds: *"The way I look at evil is it being extremely ambiguous. That is to say, I'm much more interested in a perpetrator of violence/menace being wholly convinced that what they are doing is right and just. Villains who are evil for the sake of being evil are boring to me. We are all capable of doing horrible things, though very few of us would do so just for kicks. Two opposing forces, each honestly convinced in the righteousness of their path, and neither considering evil as an existential trait, can make for delicious storytelling."*

The last word on evil goes to Colorado Springs author Carina Bissett whose writing, like a prism, is composed of countless colors. Carina's story in *Terror at 5280'*, as befits a poet, is a virtuoso performance: *"It seems as though everywhere you look, there are billboards and articles claiming that great joy and happiness can be found in a communion with Nature. However, I happen to be a classical literature nerd, and I fall more in line with Washington Irving and Nathaniel Hawthorne: There are things in the woods that will fuck you up, and I want nothing to do with Nature's wild places and the denizens that live there.*

"Give me a five-star hotel with everything shiny and clean over a rustic, possibly haunted, mountain lodge any day. I personally can't conceive a more dreadful experience than being trapped in an isolated hotel in the middle of winter. Perhaps this is why there's an underlying unease that permeates my story.

"There might have been an earlier version of myself who wanted a floor-length fur coat, but that was back when I didn't really think about the fact that those furs came from living animals. The waste of life for sheer vanity is something that haunts me to this day. Nature isn't

inherently evil, but it has the power to destroy with the ruthlessness of total devastation, which is why it wouldn't surprise me if someday I discover that I, too, have a debt to repay."

While Stephen, Angela, Gary, Carter, and Carina gave us an additional black teardrop to go with their stories, all the writers in this anthology began by contemplating darkness capable of reaching out and manipulating our fates. In a sense, they read the patterns in the wind and built us a nightmare that exists in a possible future. Like a postman who always knocks twice, is this something to fear? Does each story's second coming lie ahead at the crown of some final hill or is it running hard even now, in fast pursuit?

With Cannibal Kings and Queens, we can only anticipate the sorceries they weave.

Lawrence Berry is a professional writer specializing in horror and dark fantasy, with a preference for the short form. Current work can be found on his Amazon and Goodreads Author Pages: https://www.goodreads.com/lawrenceberry and amazon.com/author/lberry

DENVER HORROR COLLECTIVE

Darkening Denver's doors

D e n v e r H o r r o r . c o m

The mission of Denver Horror Collective is to facilitate, celebrate, and inspire horror writers and artists throughout the greater Denver metroplex and Colorado's Front Range Rocky Mountain communities.

To be kept abreast of the Mile High City's burgeoning literary horror scene go to denverhorror.com and subscribe to our free monthly e-newsletter The Epitaph.

And if you're a horror writer or artist based in or around Denver (or beyond) and would like to get involved with the group, email us at submissions@denverhorror.com

Darkest Wishes,
Denver Horror Collective

www.ingramcontent.com/pod-product-compliance
Lightning Source LLC
Chambersburg PA
CBHW020922110726
47900CB00001B/255

* 9 7 8 1 7 3 4 1 9 1 7 0 7 *